A PLACE BEWITCHED
AND OTHER STORIES

A PLACE
BEWITCHED
AND OTHER STORIES

Nikolai Gogol

Translated from the Russian by
Constance Garnett

Selected, with a Preface by
Natasha Randall

riverrun

Constance Garnett's translation of Gogol's works were first published by Chatto & Windus between 1922 and 1926.

This edition published in 2018 by

riverrun

An imprint of

Quercus Editions Ltd
Carmelite House
50 Victoria Embankment
London EC4Y 0DZ

An Hachette UK company

The authorized representative in the EEA is Hachette Ireland,
8 Castlecourt Centre, Dublin 15, D15 XTP3, Ireland (email: info@hbgi.ie)

This selection and preface © 2018 by Natasha Randall
Natasha Randall asserts her moral right in the copyright of the preface.

A CIP catalogue record for this book is available
from the British Library

PB ISBN 978 1 78747 548 9
EBOOK ISBN 978 1 78747 549 6

10 9 8

Typeset in Monotype Fournier by CC Book Production
Printed and bound in Great Britain by Clays Ltd, Elcograf S.p.A.

Contents

Contents

Preface

THINGS GO ASTRAY IN the vivid worlds of Gogol's stories. A nose is found in a loaf of bread, a wounded soldier vanishes into notoriety, a non-existent wife is cut from dream-fabric, and there are 'next chapters' that never appear. And these negations, these ontological collapses, shift and energise the landscapes in his fictions. Sometimes, it is the devil at work, but, as the narrator of 'The Nose' asks us: 'are there not inconsequences everywhere?' This collection pulls together a variety of inconsequences from across Gogol's oeuvre but they are all the literature of evanescence. People are spontaneously transported, as in 'A Place Bewitched', or they are not as they seem, as in 'Nevsky Prospect'. Buildings warp at the edges of avenues – and these are as strange and unreal as theatre sets, and yet as convincing as live performance. Gogol gives us 'inconsequences' – rare and improbable events, delivered with stray, minuscule details. In them, we witness a catalytic reaction: the graphic and the strange at once. This is why his stories continue to fascinate us.

Nikolai Gogol was born in 1809 in the small Ukrainian town of Sorochintsy, the third of twelve children born to the small landowner Vasily Gogol and his young wife, Maria Ivanovna. He was a nervous and sickly child, by all accounts, with poor vision and a skin disorder. As a short school-boy with an outsized nose, he shuffled mutely through school, taunted by his peers as 'the mysterious dwarf'. In tandem with this miserable childhood experience, his talents were germinating: he read books, and above all, he developed the witty and acerbic capacity for observation that would emerge in his literary work.

Just nine years after Gogol's death in 1852, Constance Garnett was born in Brighton, England, and following a childhood of illness, she went to Cambridge University and worked as a librarian. After marrying Edward Garnett and having a child, she started learning Russian at the age of thirty and had begun translating Russian novels within a couple of years. Over the ensuing forty years, she would translate over seventy volumes of Russian literature, including Gogol's short stories, which she tackled in her latter years, from 1921.

Consider the challenges of translating Gogol – he who is poised at the fulcrum of early realism and the absurd. He writes that fish 'run around' while flies, wasps and bees gang together. In his stories, grasshoppers scream, and fragrant grasses thrust themselves at you through carriage doors, flicking you pleasantly on the hands and face. These details form charged landscapes too – sometimes to arouse in us contempt, sometimes sympathy. He delivers to us the oppressed and the abused, and he mocks the vulgar manifestations of the middle classes. His tales are inflected with shame, and soaked in the deeds of the devil and other 'unclean spirits'.

Critics of Garnett are hasty and myopic in their appreciation of her translations. Garnett was particularly attentive to idiom; she was an Edwardian lady striving for a slightly earlier English: 'It would show grotesque insensibility to produce a translation of Gogol . . . written at the same time as *Pickwick*, in the language of today's newspapers. I am particularly proud of having translated *Dead Souls* into English of the period in which it was written.' This is not to say that her language in Gogol was Dickensian – usually not – but there is one instance of translation in this collection that is both Pickwickian but utterly Gogolian where she translates '*yabedniki*' (here used to describe official persons) as 'pettifogging attorneys'. Such renderings are excellent strokes of language, of which there are so many in these pages.

We would do well to appreciate that Gogol's language is littered with dialect that is virtually untranslatable into English. Gogol himself was irked by the Ukrainian turns of phrase that were replaced in his Russian publications: 'There is chasm of such phrases and expressions, which we, the Little Russians, think will be understandable for Russians if we translate them word for word, but which sometimes destroy half of the meaning of the original . . . Remember that your translation for the Russians, loses all the Little Russian revolutions and constructions.'

'A Place Bewitched', the title story of this collection, contains both the Russian and Ukrainian words for 'watermelon' – and Garnett, stuck between three languages, is forced to give them the same word in English. Likewise, many of the characters speak ungrammatically – how could she render that without seeming to have made her own mistakes? The translator, no matter her time, cannot easily be ungrammatical, and dialects never travel well.

Meanwhile, a rare instance in these pages of prudish restraint is truly Gogolian in its canine contortions: an old man is shouting at his friends that they should dance with him, and he calls them '*sobach'i deti*' which literally means 'the children of dogs'. Garnett has it as 'puppies' – which is indeed demure – but other translators have it as 'sons of bitches', which is excessively vitriolic. As an example of the adjustments made to this new edition of Gogol's stories, this phrase has been changed to read 'sons of dogs', to capture the pejorative moderation of the expression. But otherwise I found Garnett's translation to be no more prudish than the original Russian.

I have made adjustments here and there, sometimes to include small dropped fragments and occasionally to correct a misappropriated gesture. Garnett, like Gogol, is sometimes prone to displacement. At one point, in 'The Carriage', Garnett simply omits a particularly confusing sentence: a description of a soldier who was 'lathering' the village oaf. The confusion is understandable: first, the term Gogol uses to pinpoint the location of this altercation describes the place of public punishment in a village square, for which I eventually found the word 'ravenstone' in English. And further, the 'lathering' is given in confusing imagery, coming soon after a reference to moustaches, but which, I realised in editing this text, ought to convey that the officer was delivering blows to the man. The story 'A Place Bewitched' has another such moment. Garnett and many other translators have written that the old man of the story, when he danced on his pumpkin patch, was stopped halfway through his dance, frozen by invisible forces – but in fact, the correct translation should tell us that the old man is stopped in his tracks halfway across the pumpkin patch. Halfway through the patch, not the dance: it is a sort of Gogolian mishap of translation, which matters only because the story describes a bewitched place, and not a bewitched dance. But these moments were rare, and witnessing the balletic linguistics of Garnett's translation at close quarters was awe-inspiring, for she is a meticulous chaperone to Gogol's bewitched places.

Natasha Randall

A Place Bewitched

and Other Stories

A Place Bewitched

A TRUE STORY TOLD BY THE SACRISTAN

UPON MY WORD, I am sick of telling stories! Why, what would you expect? It really is tiresome; one goes on telling stories and there is no getting out of it! Oh, very well, I will tell you a story then; only, mind, it is for the last time. Well, we were talking about a man's being able to get the better, as the saying is, of the Unclean Spirit. To be sure, if you come to that, all sorts of things do happen in this world . . . Better not say so, though: if the devil wants to bamboozle you he will, upon my soul he will . . . Here you see my father had the four of us; I was only a silly child then, I wasn't more than eleven, no, not eleven. I remember as though it were today when I was running on all fours and set to barking like a dog, my dad shouted at me, shaking his head: 'Ay, Foma, Foma, you are almost old enough to be married and you are as foolish as a young mule.'

My grandfather was still living then and fairly – may his hiccough be easier in the other world – strong on his legs. At times he would take a fancy ... But how am I to tell a story like this? Here one of you has been for the last hour raking an ember for his pipe out of the stove and the other has run behind the cupboard for something. It's too much ...!
It would be all very well if you didn't want to hear me, but you kept worrying me for a story ... If you want to listen, then listen!

Just at the beginning of spring Dad went with the waggons to the Crimea to sell tobacco; but I don't remember whether he loaded two or three waggons; tobacco fetched a good price in those days. He took my three-year-old brother with him to train him betimes as a dealer. Grandfather, Mother and I and a brother and another brother were left at home. Grandfather had sown a patch of ground by the roadway and went to stay at the shanty there; he took us with him, too, to scare the sparrows and the magpies off the patch. I can't say it came amiss to us: sometimes we'd eat so many cucumbers, melons, turnips, onions and peas that upon my word, you would have thought there were cocks crowing in our stomachs. Well, to be sure, it was profitable too: travellers jogged along the road, everyone wanted to treat himself to a melon, and, besides that, from the neighbouring farms they would often bring us fowls, turkeys, eggs, to exchange for our vegetables. We did very well.

But what pleased Grandfather more than anything was that some fifty dealers would pass with their waggonloads every day. They are people, you know, who have seen life: if one of them sets off on a tale, you would do well to prick up your ears. To Grandfather it was like dumplings to a hungry man. Sometimes there would be a meeting with old acquaintances – everyone knew Grandfather – and you know yourself how it is when old folks get together: it is this and that, and so then and so then, and so this happened and that happened . . . Well, they just run on. They remember things that happened, God knows when.

One evening – why, it seems as though it might have happened today – the sun had begun to set. Grandfather was walking about his patch taking off the leaves with which he covered the watermelons in the day to save their being scorched by the sun.

'Look, Ostap,' I said to my brother, 'yonder come some waggoners!'

'Where are the waggoners?' said Grandfather, as he put

a mark on the big melon that the lads mightn't eat it by accident.

There were, as a fact, six waggons trailing along the road; a waggoner, whose moustache had gone grey, was walking ahead of them. He was still – what shall I say? – ten paces off, when he stopped.

'Good day, Maxim, so it has pleased God we should meet here.'

Grandfather screwed up his eyes. 'Ah, good day, good day! Where do you come from? And Bolyatchka here, too! Good day, good day, brother! What the devil! Why, they are all here: Krutotryshtchenko too! And Petcherytsya! And Kovelyok and Stetsko! Good day! Ha, ha, ho, ho . . . !' And they fell to kissing each other.

They took the oxen out of the shafts and let them graze on the grass; they left the waggons on the road and all sat down in a circle in front of the shanty and lit their pipes. Though they had no thoughts for their pipes; what with telling stories and chattering, I don't believe they smoked a pipe apiece.

After supper Grandfather began regaling his visitors with melons. So, taking a melon each, they trimmed it neatly with a knife (they were all old hands, had been about a good bit and knew how to eat in company – I dare say they would have been ready to sit down even at a gentleman's table);

4

after cleaning the melon well, everyone made a hole with his finger in it, drank the juice, began cutting it up into pieces and putting them into his mouth.

'Why are you standing there gaping, lads?' said my grandfather. 'Dance, you sons of dogs! Where's your pipe, Ostap? Now then, the Cossack dance! Foma, arms akimbo! Come, that's it, hey, hop!'

I was a brisk lad in those days. Cursed old age! Now I can't step out like that; instead of cutting capers, my legs can only trip and stumble. For a long time Grandad watched us as he sat with the dealers. I noticed that his legs wouldn't keep still, it was as though something were tugging at them.

'Look, Foma,' said Ostap, 'if the old bugger isn't going to dance.'

What do you think, he had hardly uttered the words when the old man could resist it no longer! He longed, you know, to show off before the dealers.

'I say, you devil's spawn, is that the way to dance? This is the way to dance!' he said, getting up on to his feet, stretching out his arms and tapping with his heels.

Well, there is no denying he did dance; he couldn't have danced better if it had been with the Hetman's wife. We stood aside and the old bugger went twirling his legs all over the flat place beside the cucumber beds. But as soon as he had got halfway across and wanted to do his best and cut some capers with his legs in a whirl – his feet wouldn't rise from the ground, whatever he did! 'What a plague!' He moved backwards and forwards again, got to the middle of the dance – it wouldn't go! Whatever he did – he couldn't do it and he didn't do it! His legs stood still as though made of wood. 'Look you, the place is bedevilled, look you, it is a visitation of Satan! The Herod, the enemy of mankind has a hand in it!' Well, he couldn't disgrace himself before the dealers like that, could he? He made a fresh start and began cutting tiny trifling capers, a joy to see; up to the middle – then, no! It wouldn't be danced, and that is all about it!

'Ah, you rascally Satan! I hope you may choke with a rotten melon, that you may perish when you are little, son of a dog. See what shame he has brought me to in my old age . . . !' And indeed someone did laugh behind his back.

He looked round; no melon patch, no dealers, nothing; behind, in front, on both sides was a flat field. 'Ay! Sss! . . . Well, I never!' He began screwing up his eyes – the place doesn't seem quite unfamiliar: on one side a copse, behind the copse some sort of post sticking up which can be seen far away against the sky. Dash it all! But that's the dovecote in the priest's garden! On the other side, too, there is something greyish; he looked closer: it was the district clerk's threshing

6

barn. So this was where the Unclean Power had dragged him! Going round in a ring, he hit upon a little path. There was no moon: instead of it, a white blur glimmered through a dark cloud.

'There will be a high wind tomorrow,' thought Grandad. All at once there was the gleam of a light on a little grave to one side of the path. 'Well, I never!' Grandad stood still, put his arms akimbo and stared at it. The light went out; far away and a little further yet, another twinkled. 'A treasure!' cried Grandad. 'I'll bet anything if it's not a treasure!' And he was just about to spit on his hands and begin digging when he remembered that he had no spade nor shovel with him. 'Oh what a pity! Well – who knows? – maybe I've only to lift the turf and there it lies, the precious dear! Well, there's nothing for it, I'll mark the place anyway so as not to forget it afterwards.'

So pulling along a good-sized branch that must have been broken off by a high wind, he laid it on the little grave where the light gleamed and went along the path. The young oak copse grew thinner; he caught a glimpse of a fence. 'There, didn't I say that it was the priest's garden?' thought Grandad. 'Here's his fence; now it is not three-quarters of a mile to the melon patch.'

It was pretty late, though, when he came home, and he

wouldn't have any dumplings. Waking my brother Ostap, he only asked him whether it was long since the dealers had gone, and then rolled himself up in his sheepskin. And when Ostap was beginning to ask him: 'And what did the devils do with you today, Grandad?' 'Don't ask,' he said, wrapping himself up tighter than ever, 'don't ask, Ostap, or your hair will turn grey!'

And he began snoring so that the sparrows who had been flocking together to the melon patch rose up into the air in a fright. But how was it he could sleep? There's no denying, he was a sly beast. God give him the kingdom of Heaven, he could always get out of any scrape; sometimes he would pitch such a yarn that you would have to bite your lips.

Next day as soon as ever it began to get light Grandad put on his smock, fastened his belt, took a spade and shovel under his arm, put on his cap, drank a mug of kvass, wiped his lips with his shirt and went straight to the priest's kitchen garden. He passed both the hedges and the low oak copse and there was a path winding out between the trees and coming out into the open country; it seemed like the same. He came out of the copse and the place seemed exactly the same as yesterday: yonder he saw the dovecote sticking out, but he could not see the threshing barn. 'No, this isn't the place, it must be a little further; it seems I must turn a little towards

8

the threshing barn!' He turned back a little and began going along another path – then he could see the barn but not the dovecote. Again he turned, and a little nearer to the dovecote the barn was hidden. As though to spite him it began drizzling with rain. He ran again towards the barn – the dovecote vanished; towards the dovecote – the barn vanished.

'You damned Satan, may you never live to see your children!' he cried. And the rain came down in bucketfuls.

So taking off his new boots and wrapping them in a handkerchief, that they might not be warped by the rain, he ran off at a trot like some gentleman's saddle-horse. He crept into the shanty, drenched through, covered himself with his sheepskin and set to grumbling between his teeth, and reviling the devil with words such as I had never heard in my life. I must own I should really have blushed if it had happened in broad daylight.

Next day I woke up and looked; Grandad was walking about the melon patch as though nothing had happened, covering the watermelons with burdock leaves. At dinner the old chap got talking again and began scaring my young brother, saying he would swap him for a fowl instead of a melon; and after dinner he made a pipe out of a bit of wood and began playing on it; and to amuse us gave us a melon which was twisted in three coils like a snake; he called it a

9

Turkish one. I don't see such melons anywhere nowadays; it is true he got the seed from somewhere far away. In the evening, after supper, Grandad went with the spade to dig a new bed for late pumpkins. He began passing that bewitched place and he couldn't resist saying, 'Cursed place!' He went into the middle of it, to the spot where he could not finish the dance the day before, and in his anger struck it a blow with his spade. In a flash – that same field was all around him again: on one side he saw the dovecote standing up, and on the other – the threshing barn. 'Well, it's a good thing I bethought me to bring my spade. And yonder's the path, and there stands the little grave! And there's the branch lying on it, and yonder, see yonder, is a little light! If only I have made no mistake!'

He ran up stealthily, holding the spade in the air as though he were going to hit a hog that had poked its nose into a melon patch, and stopped before the grave. The light went out. On the grave lay a stone overgrown with weeds. 'I must lift up that stone,' thought Grandad, and tried to dig round it on all sides. The damned stone was huge! But planting his feet on the ground he shoved it off the grave. 'Goo!' It rolled down the slope. 'That's the right road for you! Now things will go more briskly!'

At this point Grandad stopped, took out his horn,

sprinkled a little snuff in his hand, and was about to raise it to his nose when all at once, 'Tchee-hee,' something sneezed above his head so that the trees shook and all Grandad's face was spattered. 'You might at least turn aside when you want to sneeze,' said Grandad, wiping his eyes. He looked round – there was no one there. 'No, it seems the devil doesn't like the snuff,' he went on, putting back the horn in his bosom and picking up his spade. 'He's a fool! Neither his grandfather nor his father ever had a pinch of snuff like that!' He began digging, the ground was soft, the spade simply went down into it. Then something clanked. Putting aside the earth he saw a cauldron.

'Ah, you precious dear, here you are!' cried Grandad, thrusting the spade under it.

'Ah, you precious dear, here you are!' piped a bird's beak, pecking the cauldron.

Grandad looked round and dropped the spade.

'Ah, you precious dear, here you are!' bleated a sheep's head from the top of the trees.

'Ah, you precious dear, here you are!' roared a bear, poking its snout out from behind a tree. A shudder ran down Grandad's back.

'Why, one is afraid to say a word here!' he muttered to himself.

'One is afraid to say a word here!' piped the bird's beak.

'Afraid to say a word here!' bleated the sheep's head.

'To say a word here!' roared the bear.

'Hm!' said Grandad, and he felt terrified.

'Hm!' piped the beak.

'Hm!' bleated the sheep.

'Hm!' roared the bear.

Grandad turned round in a fright. Mercy on us, what a night! No stars nor moon; pits all round him, a bottomless precipice at his feet and a crag hanging over his head and looking every minute as though it would break off and come down on him. And Grandad fancied that a horrible face peeped out from behind it. 'Oo! Oo!' A nose like a blacksmith's bellows. You could pour a bucket of water into each nostril! Lips like two hogs! Red eyes seemed to start out above and a tongue was thrust out too, and jeering. 'The devil take you!' said Grandad, flinging down the cauldron. 'Damn you and your treasure! What a loathsome snout!' And he was just going to cut and run, but he looked round and stopped, seeing that everything was as before. 'It's only the Unclean Power trying to frighten me!'

He set to work at the cauldron again. No, it was too heavy! What was he to do? He couldn't leave it now! So, exerting himself to his utmost, he clutched at it. 'Come, heave-ho!

Again, again!' And he dragged it out. 'Ough, now for a pinch of snuff!'

He took out his horn. Before shaking any out though, he took a good look round to be sure there was no one there. He fancied there was no one; but then it seemed to him that the trunk of the tree was gasping and blowing, ears made their appearance, there were red eyes, puffing nostrils, a wrinkled nose and it seemed on the point of sneezing. 'No, I won't have a pinch of snuff!' thought Grandad, putting away the horn. 'Satan will be spitting in my eyes again!' He made haste to snatch up the cauldron and set off running as fast as his legs could carry him; only he felt something behind him scratching on his legs with twigs . . . 'Aïe, aïe, aïe!' was all that Grandad could cry as he ran his utmost; and it was not till he reached the priest's kitchen garden that he took breath a little.

'Where can Grandad be gone?' we wondered, waiting three hours for him. Mother had come from the farm long before and brought a pot of hot dumplings. Still no sign of Grandad! Again we had supper without him. After supper mother washed the pot and was looking where to throw the dishwater because there were melon beds all round, when she sees coming straight towards her a barrel! It was rather dark. She felt sure one of the lads was hiding behind it in mischief and shoving it towards her. 'That's just right, I'll throw the water at him,' she said, and flung the hot dish-water out.

'Aïe!' shouted a bass voice. Only fancy, Grandad! Well, who would have known him! Upon my word we thought it was a barrel coming up! I must own, though it was rather a sin, we really thought it funny when Grandad's grey head was all drenched in the dishwater and decked with melon peelings.

'I say, you devil of a woman!' said Grandad, wiping his head with the skirt of his smock. 'What a hot bath she has given me, as though I were a pig before Christmas! Well, lads, now you will have something for bread-rings! You'll go about dressed in gold tunics, you sons of dogs! Look what I have brought you!' said Grandad, and opened the cauldron.

What do you suppose there was in it? Come, think well, and make a guess? Eh? Gold? Well now, it wasn't gold – it was dirt, filth, I am ashamed to say what it was. Grandad spat, dropped the cauldron and washed his hands after it.

And from that time forward Grandad made us two swear never to trust the devil. 'Don't you believe it!' he would often say to us. 'Whatever the foe of our Lord Christ says, he is always lying, the son of a dog! There isn't a ha'p'orth of truth in him!'

And if ever the old man heard that things were not right in some place: 'Come, lads, let's make the sign of the cross!

That's it! That's it! Properly!' and he would begin tracing crosses in the air. And that accursed place where he couldn't dance he fenced in and bade us fling there all the rubbish, all the weeds and litter which he raked off the melon patch.

So you see how the Unclean Power takes a man in. I know that bit of ground well; later on, some neighbouring Cossacks hired it from Dad as a melon patch. It's capital ground and there is always a wonderful crop on it; but there has never been anything good grown on that bewitched place. They may sow it properly, but there's no saying what it is that comes up: a melon is not a melon, a pumpkin not a pumpkin, a cucumber not a cucumber . . . the devil only knows what to make of it!

Ivan Fyodorovitch Shponka
and his Aunt

THERE IS A STORY about this story: we were told it by Stepan Ivanovitch Kurotchka, who came over from Gadyatch. You must know that my memory is incredibly poor: you may tell me a thing or not tell it, it is all the same. It is just pouring water into a sieve. Being aware of this failing, I purposely begged him to write the story down in an exercise-book. Well, God give him good health, he was always a kind man to me, he set to work and wrote it down. I put it in the little table; I expect you know it; it stands in the corner as you come in by the door . . . But there, I forgot that you had never been in my house. My old woman, with whom I have lived thirty years, has never learned to read – no use hiding one's shortcomings. Well, I noticed that she baked the pies on paper of some sort. She bakes pies beautifully, dear readers; you will never taste better pies anywhere. I happened to look on the underside of a pie – what do I see? Written words! My heart seemed to tell me at once: I went to the table, only half the notebook was there! All the other pages she had pinched for the pies! What could I do? There is no fighting at our age! Last year I happened to be passing through Gadyatch. Before I reached the town I purposely tied a knot in my handkerchief that I might not forget to ask Stepan Ivanovitch about it. That was not all; I vowed to myself that as soon as ever I sneezed in the town I would be sure to think of it. It was all no use. I drove through the town and sneezed and blew my nose into my handkerchief too, but still I forgot it; and I only thought of it nearly five miles after I had passed through the town-gate. There was no help for it, I had to print it without the end. However, if anyone particularly wants to know what happened later on in the story, he need only go on purpose to Gadyatch and ask Stepan Ivanovitch. He will be glad to tell the story, I dare say, all over again from the beginning. He lives not far from the stone church. There is a little lane close by, and as soon as you turn into the lane it is the second or third gate. Or better still, when you see a big post with a quail on it in the yard and coming to meet you a stout peasant woman in a green petticoat (it may be as well to mention that he is a bachelor), that is his yard. Though indeed you may meet him in the market, where he is to be seen every morning before nine o'clock, choosing fish and vegetables for his table and talking to Father Antip or the Jewish contractor. You will know him at once, for there is no one else who has trousers of flowered linen and coat of yellow Chinese cotton. And another thing you may know him by – he always swings his arms as he walks. Denis Petrovitch, the assessor, now deceased, always used to say when he saw him in the distance, 'Look, look, here comes our windmill!'

1. Ivan Fyodorovitch Shponka

It is four years since Ivan Fyodorovitch retired from the army and came to live on his farm, Vytrebenki. When he was still Vanyusha, he was at the Gadyatch district school, and I must say he was a very well-behaved and industrious boy. Nikifor Timofyevitch Dyepritchastie, the teacher of Russian grammar, used to say that if all the boys had been as anxious to do their best as Shponka, he would not have brought into the classroom the maple-wood ruler with which, as he owned himself, he was tired of hitting the lazy and mischievous boys' hands. His exercise-book was always neat, with a ruled margin, and not the tiniest blot anywhere. He always sat quietly with his arms folded and his eyes fixed on the teacher, and he never used to stick scraps of paper on the back of the boy sitting in front of him, never carved the bench and never played at shoving the other boys off the bench before the master came in. If anyone wanted a penknife to mend his pen, he immediately applied to Ivan Fyodorovitch knowing that he always had a penknife, and Ivan Fyodorovitch, at that time simply Vanyusha, would take it out of a little leather case attached to a buttonhole of his grey coat, and would only request that the sharp edge should not be used for scraping the pen, pointing out that there was a blunt side for the purpose. Such good conduct soon attracted the attention even of the Latin master, whose cough in the corridor was enough to reduce the class to terror, even before his frieze coat and pockmarked countenance had appeared in the doorway. This terrible master, who always had two birches lying on his desk and half of whose pupils were always on their knees, made Ivan Fyodorovitch monitor, although there were many boys in the class of much greater ability.

Here I cannot omit an incident which had an influence on the whole of his future life. One of the boys entrusted to his charge tried to induce his monitor to write *scit* on his report, though he had not learned his lesson, by bringing into class a pancake soaked in butter and wrapped in paper. Though Ivan Fyodorovitch was usually conscientious, on this occasion he was hungry and could not resist the temptation: he took the pancake, held a book up before him and began eating it. He was so absorbed in this occupation that he did not observe that a deathly silence had fallen upon the classroom. He only woke up with horror when a terrible hand protruding from a frieze overcoat seized him by the ear and dragged him into the middle of the room. 'Hand over that pancake! Hand it over, I tell you, you rascal!' said the terrible master; he seized the buttery pancake in his fingers and flung it out of window, sternly forbidding the boys running about in the yard to pick it up. Then he proceeded on the spot to whack Ivan Fyodorovitch very painfully on the hands. And quite rightly: the hands were responsible for taking it and no other part of the body. Anyway, the timidity which had always been characteristic of him was more marked from that time forward. Possibly the same incident was the reason that he never had any desire to enter the civil service, having learned by experience that one is not always successful in hiding one's misdeeds.

He was very nearly fifteen when he moved up into the second class, where instead of the four rules of arithmetic and the abridged catechism, he went on to the longer one, the book of the duties of man, and fractions. But seeing that the further you went into the forest, the thicker the wood became, and receiving the news that his father had departed this life, he stayed only two years longer at school, and with his mother's consent went into the P— infantry regiment.

The P— infantry regiment was not at all of the class to which many infantry regiments belong, and, although it was for the most part stationed in country places, it was in no way inferior to many cavalry regiments. The majority of the officers drank neat spirit and were quite as good at dragging about Jews by their curls as any Hussars; some of them even danced the mazurka, and the colonel of the regiment never missed an opportunity to mention the fact when he was talking to anyone in company. 'Among my officers,' he used to say, patting himself on the belly after every word, 'a number dance the mazurka, quite a number of them, really a great number of them indeed.' To show our readers the degree of culture of the P— infantry regiment, we must add that two of the officers were passionately fond of the game of 'bank' and used to gamble away their uniforms, caps, overcoats, sword-knots and even their underclothes, which is more than you could find in every cavalry regiment.

Contact with such comrades did not, however, diminish Ivan Fyodorovitch's timidity; and as he did not drink neat spirit, preferring to it a wineglassful of ordinary vodka before dinner and supper, did not dance the mazurka or play 'bank', naturally he was bound to be always left alone. And so it came to pass that while the others were driving about with hired horses, visiting the less important landowners, he was sitting at home spending his time in pursuits peculiar to a mild and gentle soul: he either polished his buttons, or read a book of dreams or set mousetraps in the corners of his room, or failing everything, he would take off his uniform and lie on his bed.

On the other hand, no one in the regiment was more punctual in his duties than Ivan Fyodorovitch, and he drilled his platoon in such a way that the commander of the company always held him up as a model to the others. Consequently in a short time, eleven years after becoming an ensign, he was promoted to second lieutenant.

During that time he had received the news that his mother was dead, and his aunt, his mother's sister, whom he only knew from her bringing him in his childhood – and even sending him when he was at Gadyatch – dried pears and extremely nice honey cakes which she made herself (she was on bad terms with his mother and so Ivan Fyodorovitch had not seen her in later years), this aunt, in the goodness of her heart, undertook to look after his little estate and in due time informed him of the fact by letter.

Ivan Fyodorovitch, having the fullest confidence in his aunt's good sense, continued to perform his duties as before.

Some men in his position would have grown conceited at such promotion, but pride was a feeling of which he knew nothing, and as lieutenant he was the same Ivan Fyodorovitch as he had been when an ensign. He spent another four years in the regiment after the event of so much consequence to him, and was about to leave the Mogilyev district for Great Russia with his regiment when he received a letter as follows:

MY DEAR NEPHEW, IVAN FYODOROVITCH — I am sending you some linen: five pairs of thread socks and four shirts of fine linen; and what is more I want to talk to you of something serious; since you have already a rank of some importance, as I suppose you are aware, and have reached a time of life when it is fitting to take up the management of your land, there is no reason for you to remain longer in military service. I am getting old and can no longer see to everything on your farm; and in fact there is a great deal that I want to talk to you about in person.

Come, Vanyusha! Looking forward to the real pleasure of seeing you, I remain your very affectionate Aunt,

VASSILISSA TSUPTCHEVSKA

PS — There is a wonderful turnip in our kitchen garden, more like a potato than a turnip.

23

A week after receiving this letter Ivan Fyodorovitch wrote an answer as follows:

HONOURED MADAM, AUNTIE, VASSILISSA KASH-PAROVNA — Thank you very much for sending the linen. My socks especially are very old, my orderly has darned them four times and that has made them very tight. As to your views in regard to my service in the army, I completely agree with you, and the day before yesterday I sent in my papers. As soon as I get my discharge I will engage a chaise. As to your commission in regard to the seed wheat and Siberian corn, I cannot carry it out; there is none in all the Mogilyev province. About here pigs are mostly fed on brewers' grains together with a little beer when it has grown flat. With the greatest respect, honoured madam and auntie, I remain your nephew,

IVAN SHPONKA

At last Ivan Fyodorovitch received his discharge with the grade of lieutenant, hired for forty roubles a Jew to drive from Mogilyev to Gadyatch, and set off in the chaise just at the time when the trees are clothed with young and still scanty leaves, the whole earth is bright with fresh green, and there is the fragrance of spring over all the fields.

2. The Journey

Nothing of great interest occurred on the journey. They were travelling a little over a fortnight. Ivan Fyodorovitch might have arrived a little sooner than that, but the devout Jew kept the Sabbath on the Saturdays and, putting his horse-cloth over his head, prayed the whole day. Ivan Fyodorovitch, however, as I have had occasion to mention already, was a man who did not give way to being bored. During these intervals he undid his trunk, took out his underclothes, inspected them thoroughly to see whether they were properly washed and folded; carefully removed the fluff from his new uniform, which had been made without epaulettes, and repacked it all in the best possible way. He was not fond of reading in general; and if he did sometimes look into a book of dreams, it was because he liked to meet again what he had already read several times. In the same way one who lives in the town goes every day to the club, not for the sake of hearing anything new there, but in order to meet there friends with whom it has been his habit to chat at the club from time immemorial. In the same way a government clerk will read a directory of addresses with immense satisfaction several times a day with no ulterior object, he is simply entertained by the printed list of names. 'Ah! Ivan Gavrilovitch So-and-so . . .' he murmurs mutely to himself. 'And here again am I! Hm . . . !' and next time he reads it over again with exactly the same exclamations.

After a fortnight's journey Ivan Fyodorovitch reached a little village some eighty miles from Gadyatch. This was on Friday. The sun had long set when with the chaise and the Jew he reached an inn.

This inn differed in no respects from other little village inns. As a rule the traveller is zealously regaled in them with hay and oats, as though he were a post-horse. But should he want to lunch as decent people do lunch, he keeps his appetite intact for some future opportunity. Ivan Fyodorovitch, knowing all this, had provided himself beforehand with two bundles of bread-rings and a sausage, and asking for a glass of vodka, of which there is never a shortage in any inn, he began his supper, sitting down on a bench before an oak table which was fixed immovably in the clay floor.

Meanwhile he heard the rattle of a chaise. The gates creaked but it was a long while before the chaise drove into the yard. A loud voice was engaged in scolding the old woman who kept the inn. 'I will drive in,' Ivan Fyodorovitch heard, 'but if I am bitten by a single bedbug in your inn, I will beat you, on my soul I will, you old witch! And I will give you nothing for your hay!'

A minute later the door opened and there walked – or rather squeezed himself – in a stout man in a green frock-coat. His head rested immovably on his short neck, which seemed even thicker, from a double chin. To judge from his appearance, he belonged to that class of men who do not trouble their heads about trifles and whose whole life had been well-oiled.

'I wish you good day, honoured sir!' he pronounced on seeing Ivan Fyodorovitch.

Ivan Fyodorovitch bowed in silence.

'Allow me to ask, to whom have I the honour of speaking?' the stout newcomer continued.

At such an examination Ivan Fyodorovitch involuntarily got up and stood at attention as he usually did when the colonel asked him a question.

'Retired Lieutenant Ivan Fyodorovitch Shponka,' he answered.

'And may I ask what place you are bound for?'

'My own farm, Vytrebenki.'

'Vytrebenki!' cried the stern examiner. 'Allow me, honoured sir, allow me!' he said, going towards him, and, waving his arms as though someone were hindering him or as though he were making his way through a crowd, he folded Ivan Fyodorovitch in an embrace and kissed him first on the right cheek and then on the left and then on the right again. Ivan Fyodorovitch was much gratified by this kiss, for his lips were pressed against the stranger's fat cheeks as though against soft cushions.

'Allow me to make your acquaintance, my dear sir!' the fat man continued: 'I am a landowner of the same district of Gadyatch and your neighbour; I live not more than four miles from your Vytrebenki in the village of Hortyshtche; and my name is Grigory Grigoryevitch Stortchenko. You really must, sir, you really must pay me a visit at Hortyshtche. I won't speak to you if you don't. I am in haste now on business . . . Why, what's this?' he said in a mild voice to his postilion, a boy in a Cossack tunic with patched elbows and a bewildered expression, who came in and put bags and boxes on the table. 'What's this, what's the meaning of it?' And by degrees Grigory Grigoryevitch's voice grew more and more threatening. 'Did I tell you to put them here, my good lad? Did I tell you to put them here, you rascal? Didn't I tell you to heat the chicken up first, you scoundrel? Be off!' he shouted, stamping. 'Stay, you fright! Where's the basket with the bottles? Ivan Fyodorovitch!' he said, pouring out a glass of liqueur, 'I beg you take some cordial!'

'Oh, really, I cannot . . . I have already had occasion . . .' Ivan Fyodorovitch began hesitatingly.

'I won't hear a word, sir!' The gentleman raised his voice. 'I won't hear a word! I won't budge till you drink it . . .'

Ivan Fyodorovitch, seeing that it was impossible to refuse, not without gratification emptied the glass.

'This is fowl, sir,' said the fat Grigory Grigoryevitch, carving it inside a wooden box.

'I must tell you that my cook Yavdoha is fond of a drop at times and so she often dries up things. Hey, lad!' Here he turned to the boy in the Cossack tunic who was bringing in a feather-bed and pillows. 'Make my bed on the floor in the middle of the room! Mind you put plenty of hay under the pillow! And pull a bit of hemp from the woman's distaff to stop up my ears for the night! I must tell you, sir, that I have the habit of stopping up my ears at night ever since the damnable occasion when a cockroach crawled into my left ear in a Great Russian inn. The confounded long-beards, as I found out afterwards, eat their cabbage soup with cockroaches in it. Impossible to describe what happened to me; there was such a tickling, such a tickling in my ear . . . I was downright crazy! I was cured by a simple old woman in our district, and by what do you suppose? Simply by whispering to it. What do you think, my dear sir, about doctors? What I think is that they simply hoax us and make fools of us: some old women know a dozen times as much as all these doctors.'

'Indeed, what you say is perfectly true, sir. There certainly are cases . . .' Here Ivan Fyodorovitch paused as though he could not find the right word. It may not be amiss to mention here that he was at no time lavish of words. This may have been due to timidity, or it may have been due to a desire to express himself elegantly.

'Shake up the hay properly, shake it up properly!' said Grigory Grigoryevitch to his servant. 'The hay is so bad about here that you may come upon a twig in it any minute. Allow me, sir, to wish you a good night! We shall not see each other tomorrow. I am setting off before dawn. Your Jew will keep the Sabbath because tomorrow is Saturday, so it is no good for you to get up early. Don't forget my invitation; I won't speak to you if you don't come to see me at Hortyshtche.'

At this point Grigory Grigoryevitch's servant pulled off his coat and high boots and gave him his dressing-gown instead, and Grigory Grigoryevitch stretched on his bed, and it looked as though one huge feather-bed were lying on another.

'Hey, lad! Where are you, rascal? Come here and arrange my quilt. Hey, lad, prop up my head with hay! Have you watered the horses yet? Some more hay! Here, under this side! And do arrange the quilt properly, you rascal! That's right, more! Ough . . . !'

Then Grigory Grigoryevitch heaved two sighs and filled the whole room with a terrible whistling through his nose, snoring so loudly at times that the old woman who was snoozing on the settle, suddenly waking up, looked about her in all directions, but, seeing nothing, subsided and went to sleep again.

When Ivan Fyodorovitch woke up next morning, the fat gentleman was no longer there. This was the only noteworthy incident that occurred on the journey. Two days later he drew near his little farm.

He felt his heart begin to throb when the windmill waving its sails peeped out and, as the Jew drove his nags up the hill, the row of willows came into sight below. The pond gleamed bright and shining through them and a breath of freshness rose from it. Here he used to bathe in old days; in that pond he used to wade with the peasant lads up to his neck after crayfish. The covered cart mounted the dam and Ivan Fyodorovitch saw the little old-fashioned house thatched with reeds, and the apple trees and cherry trees which he used to climb on the sly. He had no sooner driven into the yard than dogs of all kinds, brown, black, grey, spotted, ran up from every side. Some flew under the horse's hoofs, barking, others ran behind the cart, noticing that the axle was smeared with bacon fat; one, standing near the kitchen and keeping his paw on a bone, uttered a volley of shrill barks; and another gave tongue in the distance, running to and fro wagging his tail and seeming to say: 'Look, good Christians! What a fine young fellow I am!' Boys in grubby shirts ran out to stare. A sow who was promenading in the yard with sixteen little pigs lifted her snout with an inquisitive air and grunted louder than usual. In the yard a number of hempen sheets were lying on the ground covered with wheat, millet and barley drying in the sun. A good many different kinds of herbs, such as wild chicory and swine-herb, were drying on the roof.

Ivan Fyodorovitch was so occupied in scrutinising all this that he was only roused when a spotted dog bit the Jew on the calf of his leg as he was getting down from the box. The servants who ran out, that is the cook and another woman and two girls in woollen petticoats, after the first exclamations – 'It's our young master!' – informed him that his aunt was sowing sweet corn together with the girl Palashka and Omelko the coachman, who often performed the duties of a gardener and watchman also. But his aunt, who had seen the sack-covered cart in the distance, was already on the spot. And Ivan Fyodorovitch was astonished when she almost lifted him from the ground in her arms, hardly able to believe that this could be the aunt who had written to him of her old age and infirmities.

3. Auntie

Auntie Vassilissa Kashparovna was at this time about fifty. She had never been married, and commonly declared that she valued her maiden state above everything. Though, indeed, to the best of my memory, no one ever courted her. This was due to the fact that all men felt a certain timidity in her presence, and never had the spirit to make her an offer. 'A girl of great character, Vassilissa Kashparovna!' all the young men used to say, and they were quite right, too, for there was no one Vassilissa Kashparovna could not get the whip hand of. With her own manly hand, tugging every day at his top-knot of curls, she could, unaided, turn the drunken miller, a worthless fellow, into a perfect treasure. She was of almost gigantic stature, and her breadth and strength were fully in proportion. It seemed as though nature had made an unpardonable mistake in condemning her to wear a dark brown gown with little flounces on weekdays and a red cashmere shawl on Sunday and on her name-day, though a dragoon's moustaches and high top-boots would have suited her better than anything. On the other hand, her pursuits completely corresponded with her appearance: she rowed the boat herself and was more skilful with the oars than any fisherman; shot game; stood over the mowers all the while they were at work; knew the exact number of the melons, of all kinds, in the kitchen garden; took a toll of five kopecks from every waggon that crossed her dam; climbed the trees and shook down the pears; beat lazy vassals with her terrible hand and with the same menacing hand bestowed a glass of vodka on the deserving. Almost at the same moment she was scolding, dyeing yarn, racing to the kitchen, brewing kvass, making jam with honey; she was busy all day long and everywhere in the nick of time. The result of all this was that Ivan Fyodorovitch's little property, which had consisted of eighteen souls at the last census, was flourishing in the fullest sense of the word. Moreover, she had a very warm affection for her nephew and carefully accumulated kopecks for him.

From the time of his arrival at his home Ivan Fyodorovitch's life was completely transformed and took an entirely different turn. It seemed as though nature had designed him expressly for looking after an estate of eighteen souls. Auntie herself observed that he would make an excellent farmer, though she did not yet permit him to meddle in every branch of the management. 'He's but a young child yet,' she used commonly to say, though Ivan Fyodorovitch was as a fact not far off forty. 'How should he know it all!'

However, he was always in the fields with the reapers and mowers, and this was a source of unutterable pleasure to his gentle heart. The sweep of a dozen or more gleaming scythes in unison; the sound of the grass falling in even swathes; the carolling songs of the reapers at intervals, at one time joyous as the welcoming of a guest, at another mournful as parting; the calm pure evening – and what an evening! How free and fresh the air! How everything revived; the steppe flushed red, then turned dark blue and gleamed with flowers; quails, bustards, gulls, grasshoppers, thousands of insects, and all of them whistling, buzzing, churring, calling and suddenly blending into a harmonious chorus; nothing silent for an instant, while the sun sets and is hidden.

Oh, how fresh and delightful it was! Here and there, about the fields, camp-fires are built and cauldrons set over them, and mowers with moustaches sit round the fires; the steam from the dumplings floats upwards; the twilight turns greyer . . . It is hard to say what passed in Ivan Fyodorovitch at such times. When he joined the mowers, he forgot to try their dumplings, though he liked them particularly, and stood motionless, watching a gull disappear in the sky or counting the sheaves of wheat dotted over the field.

In a short time Ivan Fyodorovitch was spoken of as a great farmer. Auntie was never tired of rejoicing over her nephew and never lost an opportunity of boasting of him. One day – it was just after the end of the arable harvest, that is at the end of July – Vassilissa Kashparovna took Ivan Fyodorovitch by the arm with a mysterious air, and said she wanted now to speak to him of a matter which had long been on her mind.

'You are aware, dear Ivan Fyodorovitch,' she began, 'that there are eighteen souls on your farm, though, indeed, that is by the census register, and in reality they may reckon up to more, they may be twenty-four. But that is not the point. You know the copse that lies behind our vegetable ground, and no doubt you know the broad meadow behind it; there are very nearly sixty acres in it; and the grass is so good that it is worth a hundred roubles every year, especially if, as they say, a cavalry regiment is to be stationed at Gadyatch.'

'To be sure, Auntie, I know: the grass is very good.'

'You needn't tell me the grass is very good, I know it; but do you know that all that land is by rights yours? Why do you look so surprised? Listen, Ivan Fyodorovitch! You remember Stepan Kuzmitch? What am I saying: "you remember"! You were so little that you could not even pronounce his name. Yes, indeed! How could you remember! When I came on the very eve of St Philip's Fast and took you in my arms, you almost ruined my dress; luckily I was just in time to hand you to your nurse, Matryona; you were such a horrid little thing then . . . ! But that is not the point. All the land beyond our farm, and the village of Hortyshtche itself belonged to Stepan Kuzmitch. I must tell you that before you were in this world he used to visit your mamma – though, indeed, only when your father was not at home. Not that I say it in blame of her – God rest her soul! – though your poor mother was always unfair to me! But that is not the point. Be that as it may, Stepan Kuzmitch made a deed of gift to you of that same estate of which I have been speaking. But your poor mamma, between ourselves, was a very strange character. The devil himself (God forgive me for the nasty word!) would have been puzzled to understand her. What she did with that deed of gift – God only knows. It's my opinion that it is in the hands of that old bachelor, Grigory Grigoryevitch Stortchenko. That pot-bellied rascal has got hold of the whole estate. I'd bet anything you like that he has hidden that deed.'

'Allow me to ask, Auntie: isn't he the Stortchenko whose acquaintance I made at the inn?' Hereupon Ivan Fyodorovitch described his meeting with Stortchenko.

'Who knows,' said his aunt after a moment's thought, 'perhaps he is not a rascal. It's true that it's only six months since he came to live among us; there's no finding out what a man is in that time. The old lady, his mother, is a very sensible woman, so I hear, and they say she is a great hand at salting cucumbers; her own serf-girls can make capital rugs. But as you say he gave you such a friendly welcome, go and see him, perhaps the old sinner will listen to his conscience and will give up what is not his. If you like you can go in the chaise, only those confounded brats have pulled out all the nails at the back; you must tell the coachman, Omelko, to nail the leather on better everywhere.'

'What for, Auntie? I will take the trap that you sometimes go out shooting in.'

With that the conversation ended.

4. The Dinner

It was about dinner-time when Ivan Fyodorovitch drove into the hamlet of Hortyshtche and he felt a little timid as he approached the manor-house. It was a long house, not thatched with reeds like the houses of many of the neighbouring landowners, but with a wooden roof. Two barns in the yard also had wooden roofs; the gate was of oak. Ivan Fyodorovitch felt like a dandy who, on arriving at a ball, sees everyone more smartly dressed than himself. He stopped his trap by the barn as a sign of respect and went on foot towards the front door.

'Ah, Ivan Fyodorovitch!' cried the fat man Grigory Grigoryevitch, who was crossing the yard in his coat but without cravat, waistcoat and braces. But apparently this attire weighed oppressively on his bulky person, for the perspiration was streaming down him.

'Why, you said you would come as soon as you had seen your aunt, and all this time you have not been here?' After these words Ivan Fyodorovitch's lips found themselves again in contact with the same cushions.

'Chiefly occupied with land management . . . I have come just for a minute to see you on business . . .'

'For a minute? Well, that won't do. Hey, lad!' shouted the fat gentleman, and the same boy in the Cossack tunic ran out of the kitchen. 'Tell Kassyan to shut the gate tight, do you hear! Make it fast! And take this gentleman's horse out of the shafts this minute. Please come indoors; it is so hot out here that my shirt's soaked.'

On going indoors Ivan Fyodorovitch made up his mind to lose no time and in spite of his shyness to act with decision.

'My aunt had the honour . . . she told me that a deed of gift of the late Stepan Kuzmitch . . .'

It is difficult to describe the unpleasant grimace made by the broad countenance of Grigory Grigoryevitch at these words.

'Oh dear, I hear nothing!' he responded. 'I must tell you that a cockroach got into my left ear (those bearded Russians breed cockroaches in all their huts); no pen can describe what agony it was, it kept tickling and tickling. An old woman cured me by the simplest means . . .'

'I meant to say . . .' Ivan Fyodorovitch ventured to interrupt, seeing that Grigory Grigoryevitch was intentionally changing the subject, 'that in the late Stepan Kuzmitch's will mention is made, so to speak, of a deed of gift . . . According to it I ought . . .'

'I know; so your aunt has told you that story already. It's a lie, upon my soul it is! My uncle made no deed of gift. Though, indeed, some such deed is referred to in the will. But where is it? No one has produced it. I tell you this because I sincerely wish you well. Upon my soul it is a lie!'

Ivan Fyodorovitch said nothing, reflecting that possibly his aunt really might be mistaken.

'Ah, here comes Mother with my sisters,' said Grigory Grigoryevitch, 'so dinner is ready. Let us go!'

Thereupon he drew Ivan Fyodorovitch by the hand into a room in which vodka and savouries were laid out on the table.

At the same time a short little old lady, a regular coffee pot in a cap, with two young ladies, one fair and one dark, came in. Ivan Fyodorovitch, like a well-bred gentleman, went up to kiss the old lady's hand and then to kiss the hands of the two young ladies.

'This is our neighbour, Ivan Fyodorovitch Shponka, Mother,' said Grigory Grigoryevitch.

The old lady looked intently at Ivan Fyodorovitch, or perhaps it only seemed that she looked intently at him. She was good-natured simplicity itself, though; she looked as though she would like to ask Ivan Fyodorovitch: 'How many cucumbers have you salted for the winter?'

'Have you had some vodka?' the old lady asked.

'You can't have had enough sleep, Mother,' said Grigory Grigoryevitch. 'Who asks a visitor whether he has had anything? You offer it to him, that's all: whether we have had any or not, that is our business. Ivan Fyodorovitch! The centaury-flavoured vodka or the Trofimov brand? Which do you prefer? And you, Ivan Ivanovitch, why are you standing there?' Grigory Grigoryevitch announced, turning round, and Ivan Fyodorovitch saw the gentleman so addressed approaching the vodka, in a frock-coat with long skirts and an immense stand-up collar, which covered the whole back of his head, so that his head sat in it, as though it were a chaise.

Ivan Ivanovitch went up to the vodka and rubbed his

hands, carefully examined a liqueur glass, filled it, held it up to the light, and poured all the vodka at once into his mouth. He did not, however, swallow it at once, but rinsed his mouth thoroughly with it first before finally swallowing it, and then, after eating some bread and salted mushrooms, he turned to Ivan Fyodorovitch.

'Is it not Ivan Fyodorovitch, Mr Shponka, I have the honour of addressing?'

'Yes, certainly,' answered Ivan Fyodorovitch.

'You have changed a great deal, sir, since I saw you last. Why!' he continued, 'I remember you that high!' As he spoke he held his hand a yard from the floor. 'Your poor father, God grant him the kingdom of Heaven, was a rare man. He used to have melons such as you never see anywhere now. Here, for instance,' he went on, drawing him aside, 'they'll set melons before you on the table. But such melons – you wouldn't want to look at them! Would you believe it, sir, he used to have watermelons,' he pronounced with a mysterious air, flinging out his arms as if he were about to embrace a stout tree-trunk, 'upon my soul as big as this!'

'Come to dinner!' said Grigory Grigoryevitch, taking Ivan Fyodorovitch by the arm.

Grigory Grigoryevitch sat down in his usual place at the end of the table, draped with an enormous table-napkin which made him resemble the Greek heroes depicted by barbers on their signs. Ivan Fyodorovitch, blushing, sat down in the place assigned to him, facing the two young ladies; and Ivan Ivanovitch did not let slip the chance of sitting down beside him, inwardly rejoicing that he had someone to whom he could impart his various items of information.

'You shouldn't take the bishop's nose, Ivan Fyodorovitch! It's a turkey!' said the old lady, addressing Ivan Fyodorovitch, to whom the rustic waiter in a grey swallowtail patched with black was offering a dish. 'Take the back!'

'Mother! No one asked you to interfere!' commented Grigory Grigoryevitch. 'You may be sure our visitor knows what to take himself! Ivan Fyodorovitch! Take a wing, the other one there with the gizzard! But why have you taken so little? Take a leg! Why do you stand gaping with the dish? Ask him! Go down on your knees, rascal! Say, at once, "Ivan Fyodorovitch, take a leg!"'

'Ivan Fyodorovitch, take a leg!' the waiter with the dish howled, kneeling down.

'Hm! Do you call this a turkey?' Ivan Ivanovitch muttered in a low voice, turning to his neighbour with an air of disdain. 'Is that what a turkey ought to look like? If you could see my turkeys! I assure you there is more fat on one of them than on a dozen of these. Would you believe me, sir, they

43

are really a repulsive sight when they walk about my yard, they are so fat . . . !'

'Ivan Ivanovitch, you are telling lies!' said Grigory Grigoryevitch, overhearing these remarks.

'I tell you,' Ivan Ivanovitch went on talking to his neighbour, affecting not to hear what Grigory Grigoryevitch had said, 'last year when I sent them to Gadyatch, they offered me fifty kopecks apiece for them, and I wouldn't take even that.'

'Ivan Ivanovitch! I tell you, you are lying!' observed Grigory Grigoryevitch, dwelling on each syllable for greater distinctness and speaking more loudly than before.

But Ivan Ivanovitch behaved as though the words could not possibly refer to him; he went on as before, but in a much lower voice: 'Yes, sir, I would not take it. There is not a gentleman in Gadyatch . . .'

'Ivan Ivanovitch! You are a fool, and nothing else,' Grigory Grigoryevitch said in a loud voice. 'Ivan Fyodorovitch knows it all better than you do, and won't believe you.'

At this Ivan Ivanovitch was really offended: he said no more, but fell to gobbling the turkey, even though it was not as fat as those of his that were so fat as to be a repulsive sight.

The clatter of knives, spoons and plates took the place of conversation for a time, but loudest of all was the sound made by Grigory Grigoryevitch, smacking his lips over the marrow out of the mutton bones.

'Have you,' enquired Ivan Ivanovitch after an interval of silence, poking his head out of the chaise, 'read the *Travels of Korobeynikov in the Holy Land*? It's a real delight to heart and soul! Such books aren't published nowadays. I very much regret that I did not notice in what year it was written.'

Ivan Fyodorovitch, hearing mention of a book, applied himself diligently to taking sauce.

'It is truly marvellous, sir, when you think that a humble artisan visited all those places: over two thousand miles, sir! Over two thousand miles! Truly, it was by divine grace that it was vouchsafed him to reach Palestine and Jerusalem.'

'So you say,' said Ivan Fyodorovitch, who had heard a great deal about Jerusalem from his orderly, 'that he visited Jerusalem.'

'What are you saying, Ivan Fyodorovitch?' Grigory Grigoryevitch enquired from the end of the table.

'I had occasion to observe what distant lands there are in the world!' said Ivan Fyodorovitch, genuinely gratified that he had succeeded in uttering so long and difficult a sentence.

'Don't you believe him, Ivan Fyodorovitch!' said Grigory Grigoryevitch, who had not quite caught what he said. 'He always tells fibs!'

Meanwhile dinner was over. Grigory Grigoryevitch went to his own room for a little nap, as was his habit; and the visitors followed their elderly hostess and the young ladies into the drawing-room, where the same table on which they had left vodka when they went out to dinner was now as though by some magical transformation covered with little saucers of jam of various sorts and dishes of cherries and different kinds of melon.

The absence of Grigory Grigoryevitch was perceptible in everything: the old lady became more disposed to talk and, of her own accord, without being asked, revealed several secrets in regard to the making of apple cheese, and the drying of pears. Even the young ladies began talking, though the fair one, who looked some six years younger than her sister and who was apparently about five-and-twenty, was rather silent.

But Ivan Ivanovitch was more talkative and livelier than anyone. Feeling secure that no one would snub or contradict him, he talked of cucumbers and of planting potatoes and of how much more sensible people were in the old days – no comparison with what people are now! – and of how, as time goes on, everything improves and the most intricate inventions are discovered.

He was, indeed, one of those persons who take great pleasure in relieving their souls by conversation and will talk of anything that possibly can be talked about. If the conversation touched upon grave and solemn subjects, Ivan Ivanovitch sighed after each word and nodded his head slightly: if the subject were of a more homely character, he would pop his head out of his chaise and make faces from which one could almost, it seemed, read how to make pear kvass, how large were the melons of which he was speaking and how fat were the geese that were running about in his yard.

At last, with great difficulty and not before evening, Ivan Fyodorovitch succeeded in taking his leave, and although he was usually ready to give way and they almost kept him for the night by force, he persisted in his intention of going – and went.

5. Auntie's New Plans

'Well, did you get the deed of gift out of the old reprobate?' Such was the question with which Ivan Fyodorovitch was greeted by his aunt, who had been expecting him for some hours in the porch and had at last been unable to resist going out to the gate.

'No, Auntie,' said Ivan Fyodorovitch, getting out of the trap. 'Grigory Grigoryevitch has no deed of gift!'

'And you believed him? He was lying, the confounded fellow! Some day I shall come across him and I will give him a drubbing with my own hands. Oh, I'd get rid of some of his fat for him! Though perhaps we ought first to consult our court assessor and see if we couldn't get the law of him . . . But that's not the point now. Well, was the dinner good?'

'Very . . . yes, excellent, Auntie!'

'Well, what did you have? Tell me. The old lady, I know, is a great hand at looking after the cooking.'

'Curd fritters with sour cream, Auntie. A stew of pigeons, stuffed with . . .'

'And a turkey with pickled plums?' asked his aunt, for she was herself very skilful in the preparation of that dish.

'Yes, there was a turkey, too . . . ! Very handsome young ladies Grigory Grigoryevitch's sisters, especially the fair one!'

'Ah!' said Auntie, and she looked intently at Ivan Fyodorovitch, who dropped his eyes, blushing. A new idea flashed into her mind. 'Come, tell me,' she said eagerly and with curiosity, 'what are her eyebrows like?' It may not be amiss to observe that Auntie considered fine eyebrows as the most important item in a woman's looks.

'Her eyebrows, Auntie, are exactly like what you described yours as being when you were young. And there are little freckles all over her face.'

'Ah,' commented his aunt, well pleased with Ivan Fyodorovitch's observation, though he had had no idea of paying her a compliment. 'What sort of dress was she wearing? Though, indeed, it's hard to get good material nowadays, such as I have here, for instance, in this gown. But that's not the point. Well, did you talk to her about anything?'

'Talk . . . How do you mean, Auntie? Perhaps you are imagining . . .'

'Well, what of it, there would be nothing strange in that? Such is God's will! It may have been ordained at your birth that you should make a match of it.'

'I don't know how you can say such a thing, Auntie. That shows that you don't know me at all . . .'

'Well, well, now he is offended,' said his aunt. 'He's still only a child!' she thought to herself. 'He knows nothing! We must bring them together – let them get to know each other!'

Hereupon Auntie went to have a look at the kitchen and left Ivan Fyodorovitch alone. But from that time forward she thought of nothing but seeing her nephew married as soon as possible and fondling his little ones. Her brain was absorbed in making preparations for the wedding, and it was noticeable that she bustled about more busily than ever, though the work was the worse rather than the better for it. Often when she was making the pies, a job which she never left to

49

the cook, she would forget everything, and imagining that a tiny great-nephew was standing by her asking for some pie, would absently hold out her hands with the nicest bit for him, and the yard-dog taking advantage of this would snatch the dainty morsel and by its loud munching rouse her from her reverie, for which it was always beaten with the oven fork. She even abandoned her favourite pursuits and did not go out shooting, especially after she shot a crow by mistake for a partridge, a thing which had never happened to her before.

At last, four days later, everyone saw the chaise brought out of the carriage-house into the yard. The coachman Omelko (he was also the gardener and the watchman) had been hammering from early morning, nailing on the leather and continually chasing away the dogs who licked the wheels. I think it my duty to inform my readers that this was the very chaise in which Adam used to drive; and therefore, if anyone gives out that some other chaise was Adam's, it is an absolute lie, and his chaise is certainly not the genuine article. It is impossible to say how it survived the Deluge. It must be supposed that there was a special coach-house for it in Noah's Ark. I am very sorry that I cannot give a living picture of it for my readers. It is enough to say that Vassilissa Kashparovna was very well satisfied with its structure and always expressed regret that the old style of carriages had gone out of fashion.

The chaise had been constructed a little on one side, so that the right half stood much higher than the left, and this pleased her particularly, because, as she said, a stout person could sit on one side and a tall person on the other. Inside the chaise, however, there was room for five small persons or three such as Auntie herself.

About midday Omelko, having finished with the chaise, brought out of the stable three horses which were a little younger than the chaise, and began harnessing them with cord to the magnificent equipage. Ivan Fyodorovitch and his aunt, one on the left side and the other on the right, stepped in and the chaise drove off. The peasants they met on the road seeing this sumptuous turn-out (Vassilissa Kashparovna rarely drove out in it) stopped respectfully, taking off their caps and bowing low.

Two hours later the chaise stopped at the front door — I think I need not say — of Stortchenko's house. Grigory Grigoryevitch was not at home. His old mother and the two young ladies came into the dining-room to receive the guests. Auntie walked in with a majestic step, with a great air stopped short with one foot in front, and said in a loud voice: 'I am delighted, dear madam, to have the honour to offer you my respects in person; and at the same time to thank you for your hospitality to my nephew, who has been warm in his praises of it. Your buckwheat is very good, madam – I saw it as we drove into the village. May I ask how many sheaves you get to the acre?'

After that followed kisses all round. As soon as they were seated in the drawing-room, the old lady began: 'About the buckwheat I cannot tell you: that's Grigory Grigoryevitch's department; it's long since I have had anything to do with the farming; indeed, I am not equal to it, I am old now! In old days I remember the buckwheat stood up to my waist; now goodness knows what it is like, though they do say everything is better now.' At that point the old lady heaved a sigh, and some observers would have heard in that sigh the sigh of a past age, of the eighteenth century.

'I have heard, madam, that your own maids can make excellent carpets,' said Vassilissa Kashparovna, and with that touched on the old lady's most sensitive chord: at those words she seemed to brighten up, and she talked readily of the way to dye the yarn and prepare the thread.

From carpets the conversation passed easily to the salting of cucumbers and drying of pears. In short, before the end of an hour the two ladies were talking together as though they had been friends all their lives. Vassilissa Kashparovna had already said a great deal to her in such a low voice that Ivan Fyodorovitch could not hear what she was saying.

'Yes, would not you like to have a look at them?' said the old lady, getting up.

The young ladies and Vassilissa Kashparovna also got up and all moved towards the maids' room. Auntie made a sign, however, to Ivan Fyodorovitch to remain and said something in an undertone to the old lady.

'Mashenka,' said the latter, addressing the fair-haired young lady, 'stay with our visitor and talk with him, that he may not be dull.'

The fair-haired young lady remained and sat down on the sofa. Ivan Fyodorovitch sat on his chair as though on thorns, blushed and cast down his eyes; but the young lady appeared not to notice this and sat unconcernedly on the sofa, carefully scrutinising the windows and the walls, or watching the cat timorously running round under the chairs.

Ivan Fyodorovitch grew a little bolder and would have begun a conversation; but it seemed as though he had lost all his words on the way. Not a single idea came into his mind.

The silence lasted for nearly a quarter of an hour. The young lady went on sitting as before.

At last Ivan Fyodorovitch plucked up his courage. 'There are a great many flies in summer, madam!' he brought out in a half-trembling voice.

'A very great many!' answered the young lady. 'My brother

has made a flapper out of an old slipper of Mamma's on purpose to kill them, but there are lots of them still.'

Here the conversation dropped again, and Ivan Fyodorovitch was utterly unable to find anything to say.

At last the old lady together with his aunt and the dark-haired young lady came back again. After a little more conversation, Vassilissa Kashparovna took leave of the old lady and her daughters in spite of their entreaties that they would stay the night. The three ladies came out on the steps to see their visitors off, and continued for some time nodding to the aunt and nephew, as they looked out of the chaise.

'Well, Ivan Fyodorovitch, what did you talk about when you were alone with the young lady?' Auntie asked him on the way home.

'A very discreet and well-behaved young lady, Marya Grigoryevna!' said Ivan Fyodorovitch.

'Listen, Ivan Fyodorovitch, I want to talk seriously to you. Here you are, thirty-eight, thank God; you have obtained a good rank in the service – it's time to think about children! You must have a wife . . .'

'What, Auntie?' cried Ivan Fyodorovitch panic-stricken. 'A wife! No, Auntie, for goodness' sake . . . You make me quite ashamed . . . I've never had a wife . . . I shouldn't know what to do with her!'

'You'll find out, Ivan Fyodorovitch, you'll find out,' said his aunt, smiling, and she thought to herself: 'What next, he is a perfect baby, he knows nothing!' 'Yes, Ivan Fyodorovitch!' she went on aloud. 'We could not find a better wife for you than Marya Grigoryevna. Besides, you are very much attracted by her. I have had a good talk with the old lady about it: she'll be delighted to see you her son-in-law. It's true that we don't know what that reprobate Grigoryevitch will say to it; but we won't consider him, and if he takes it into his head not to give her a dowry, we'll have the law of him . . .'

At that moment the chaise drove into the yard and the ancient nags grew more lively, feeling that their stable was not far off.

'Mind, Omelko! Let the horses have a good rest first, and don't take them down to drink the minute they are unharnessed; they are overheated.'

'Well, Ivan Fyodorovitch,' his aunt went on as she got out of the chaise, 'I advise you to think it over well. I must run to the kitchen: I forgot to tell Soloha what to get for supper, and I expect the wretched girl won't have thought of it herself.'

But Ivan Fyodorovitch stood as though thunderstruck. It was true that Marya Grigoryevna was a very nice-looking young lady; but to get married . . . ! It seemed to him so strange, so peculiar, he couldn't think of it without horror.

Living with a wife . . . ! Unthinkable! He would not be alone in his own room, but they would always have to be two together . . . ! Perspiration came out on his face as he sank more deeply into meditation.

He went to bed earlier than usual but in spite of all his efforts he could not go to sleep. But at last sleep, that universal comforter, came to him; but such sleep! He had never had such incoherent dreams. First, he dreamed that everything was whirling with a noise around him, and he was running and running, as fast as his legs could carry him . . . Now he was at his last gasp . . . All at once someone caught him by the ear.

'Aïe! Who is it?'

'It is I, your wife!' a voice resounded loudly in his ear – and he woke up. Then he imagined that he was married, that everything in their little house was so peculiar, so strange: a double bed stood in his room instead of a single one; his wife was sitting on a chair. He felt queer: he did not know how to approach her, what to say to her, and then he noticed that she had the face of a goose. He happened to turn aside and saw another wife, also with the face of a goose. Turning in another direction, he saw yet a third wife; and behind him was still another. Then he was seized by panic: he dashed away into the garden: but there it was hot, he took off his hat, and . . . saw a wife sitting in his hat. Drops of sweat came out on his face. He put his hand in his pocket for his handkerchief and in his pocket too there was a wife; he took some cotton-wool out of his ear – and there too sat a wife . . . Then he suddenly began hopping on one leg, and Auntie, looking at him, said with a dignified air: 'Yes, you must hop on one leg now, for you are a married man.'

He went towards her, but his aunt was no longer an aunt but a belfry, and he felt that someone was dragging him by a rope on the belfry.

'Who is it pulling me?' Ivan Fyodorovitch asked plaintively.

'It is I, your wife. I am pulling you because you are a bell.'

'No, I am not a bell, I am Ivan Fyodorovitch,' he cried.

'Yes, you are a bell,' said the colonel of the P— infantry regiment, who happened to be passing. Then he suddenly dreamed that his wife was not a human being at all but a sort of woollen material; that he went into a shop in Mogilyev.

'What sort of stuff would you like?' asked the shopkeeper.

'You had better take a wife, that is the most fashionable material! It wears well! Everyone is having coats made of it now.' The shopkeeper measured and cut off his wife. Ivan Fyodorovitch put her under his arm and went off to a Jewish tailor.

'No,' said the Jew, 'that is poor material! No one has coats made of that now . . .'

Ivan Fyodorovitch woke up in terror, not knowing where he was; he was dripping with cold perspiration.

As soon as he got up in the morning, he went at once to his fortune-teller's book, at the end of which a virtuous book-seller had in the rare goodness of his heart and unselfishness inserted an abridged book of dreams. But there was absolutely nothing in it that remotely resembled this incoherent dream.

Meanwhile a quite new plot, of which you shall hear more in the following chapter, was being matured in Auntie's brain.

A Madman's Diary

3 October

Today an extraordinary event occurred. I got up rather late in the morning, and when Mavra brought me my cleaned boots I asked her the time. Hearing that it was long past ten I made haste to dress. I own I wouldn't have gone to the department at all, knowing the sour face the chief of our section will make me. For a long time past he has been saying to me: 'How is it, my man, your head always seems in a muddle? Sometimes you rush about as though you were crazy and do your work so that the devil himself could not make head or tail of it, you write the title with a small letter, and you don't put in the date or the number.' The damned heron! To be sure he is jealous because I sit in the director's room and mend pens for his Excellency. In short I wouldn't have gone to the department if I had not hoped to see the counting-house clerk and to find out whether maybe I could not get something of my month's salary in advance out of that wretched Jew. That's another creature! Do you suppose he would ever let one have a month's pay in advance? Good gracious! The heavens would fall before he'd do it! You may ask till you burst, you may be at your last farthing, but the grey-headed devil won't let you have it – and when he is at home his own cook slaps him in the face; everybody knows it. I can't see the advantage of serving in a department; there are absolutely no possibilities in it. In the provincial government, or in the civil and crown offices, it's quite a different matter: there you may see some wretched man squeezed into the corner, copying away, with a nasty old coat on and such a face that it nearly makes you sick, but look what a villa he takes! It's no use offering him a gilt china cup: 'That's a doctor's present,' he will say. You must give him a pair of trotting horses or a droshky or a beaver fur worth three hundred roubles. He is such a quiet fellow to look at, and says in such a refined way: 'Oblige me with a penknife just to mend a pen,' but he fleeces the petitioners so that he scarcely leaves them a shirt to their backs. It is true that ours is a gentlemanly office, there is a cleanliness in everything such as is never seen in provincial offices, the tables are mahogany and all the heads address you formally . . . I must confess that if it were not for the gentlemanliness of the service I should have left the department long ago.

I put on my old greatcoat and took my umbrella, as it was raining in torrents. There was no one in the streets; some women pulling their skirts up to cover themselves, and some Russian merchants under umbrellas and some messengers met my eye. I saw none of the better class except one of ourselves. I saw him at the crossroads. As soon as I saw him I said to myself: 'No, my dear man, you are not on your way to the department; you are running after that girl who is racing ahead and looking at her feet.' What sad dogs clerks are! Upon my soul, they are as bad as any officer: if any female goes by in a hat they are bound to be after her. While I was making this reflection I saw a carriage driving up to the shop which I was passing. I recognised it at once. It was our director's carriage. 'But he can have nothing to go to the shop for,' I thought; 'I suppose it must be his daughter.' I flattened myself against the wall. The footman opened the carriage door and she darted out like a bird. How she glanced from right to left, how her eyes and eyebrows gleamed . . . Good God, I am done for, done for utterly! And why does she drive out in such rain! Don't tell me that women have not a passion for all this frippery. She didn't know me, and, indeed, I tried to muffle myself up all I could, because I had on a very muddy greatcoat of an old-fashioned cut. Now people wear cloaks with long collars while I had short collars one above the other, and, indeed, the cloth was not at all rainproof. Her little dog, who had been too late to dash in at the door, was left in the street. I know the dog – her name is Madgie. I had hardly been there a minute when I heard a thin little voice: 'Good morning, Madgie.'

'Well, upon my soul! Who's that speaking?'

I looked round me and saw two ladies walking along under an umbrella: one old and the other young; but they had passed already and again I heard beside me: 'It's too bad of you, Madgie!'

What the devil! I saw that Madgie was sniffing at a dog that was following the ladies. 'Aha,' I said to myself, 'but come, surely I am drunk! Only I fancy that very rarely happens to me.'

'No, Fido, you are wrong there,' said Madgie – I saw her say it with my own eyes. 'I have been, wow, wow, I have been very ill, wow, wow, wow!'

'Oh, so it's you, you little dog! Goodness me!' I must own I was very much surprised to hear her speaking like a human being; but afterwards, when I thought it was all over, I was no longer surprised. A number of similar instances have as a fact occurred. They say that in England a fish popped up and uttered two words in such a strange language that the learned men have been for three years trying to interpret them and have not succeeded yet. I have read in the papers of two cows also who went into a shop and asked for a pound of tea. But I must own I was much more surprised when Madgie said: 'I did write to you, Fido; I expect Polkan did not take my letter.' Dash it all! I never in all my life heard of a dog being able to write. No one but a gentleman born can write correctly. It's true, of course, that some shopmen and even serfs can sometimes write a little; but their writing is for the most part mechanical: they have no commas, no stops, no style.

It amazed me. I must confess that of late I have begun seeing and hearing things such as no one has ever seen or heard before. 'I'll follow that dog,' I said to myself, 'and find out what she is like and what she thinks.' I opened my umbrella and set off after the two ladies. They passed into Gorohovy Street, turned into Myeshtchansky and from there into Stolyarny Street; at last they reached Kokushin Bridge and stopped in front of a big edifice. 'I know that building,' I said to myself. 'That's Zvyerkov's Buildings. What a huge mechanism! All sorts of people live in it: such a lot of cooks, of visitors from all parts! And our friends the clerks, one on the top of another, with a third trying to squeeze in, like dogs. I have a friend living there, who plays capitally on the horn.' The ladies went up to the fifth storey. 'Good,' I thought, 'I won't go in now, but I will note the place and I will certainly take advantage of the first opportunity.'

4 October

Today is Wednesday, and so I was in our chief's study. I came a little early on purpose and, sitting down, began mending the pens. Our director must be a very clever man. His whole study is lined with bookshelves. I have read the titles of some of them: they are all learned, so learned that they are quite beyond anyone like me – they are all either in French or in German. And just look into his face! Ough! What importance shining in his eyes! I have never heard him say a word too much. Only sometimes when one hands him the papers he'll ask: 'What's it like out of doors?' 'Damp, your Excellency.' Yes, he is a cut above anyone like me! He's a statesman. I notice, however, he is particularly fond of me. If his daughter, too, were ... Ah, you rascal! ... Never mind, never mind, silence! I read *The Bee*. They are stupid people, the French! What do they want? I'd take the lot of them, upon my word I would, and thrash them all soundly! In it I read a very pleasant description of a ball written by a country gentleman of Kursk. The country gentlemen of Kursk write well. Then I noticed it was half-past twelve and that our chief had not come out of his bedroom. But about half-past one an event occurred which no pen could describe. The door opened, I thought it was the director and jumped up from my chair with my papers, but it was she, she herself! Holy saints, how she was dressed! Her dress was white as a swan – ough, how sumptuous! And the look in her eye – like sunshine, upon my soul, like sunshine. She bowed and said: 'Hasn't Papa been here?' Aïe, aïe, aïe, what a voice! A canary, a regular canary. 'Your Excellency,' I was on the point of saying, 'do not bid them punish me, but if you want to punish, then punish with your own illustrious hand.' But devil take it, my tongue would not obey me, and all I said was: 'No, madam.'

She looked at me, looked at the books, and dropped her handkerchief. I dashed forward, slipped on the damned parquet and almost smashed my nose but recovered myself and picked up the handkerchief. Saints, what a handkerchief! The most delicate batiste – amber, perfect amber! You would know from the very scent that it belonged to a general's daughter. She thanked me and gave a faint smile, so that her sugary lips scarcely moved, and after that went away. I stayed on another hour, when a footman came in and

65

said: 'You can go home, Aksenty Ivanovitch, the master has gone out.' I cannot endure the flunkey set: they are always lolling about in the vestibule and don't as much as trouble themselves to nod. That's nothing: once one of the beasts had the effrontery to offer me his snuffbox without even getting up from his seat. Don't you know, you dull fellow, that I am a government clerk, that I am a gentleman by birth! However, I took my hat and put on my greatcoat myself, for these gentry never help me on with it, and went off. At home I spent most of the time lying on my bed. Then I copied out some very good verses:

> *My love for one hour I did not see,*
> *And a whole year it seemed to me.*
> *My life is now a hated task,*
> *How can I live this life, I ask.*

It must have been written by Pushkin.

In the evening, wrapping myself up in my greatcoat, I went to the front door of her Excellency's house and waited about for a long time on the chance of her coming out to get into her carriage, that I might snatch another glimpse of her, but she never came out.

6 November

The head of our section put me in such a fury today. When I came into the department he called me into his room and began like this: 'Come, kindly tell me what you are doing?'

'How do you mean?' I said. 'I am doing nothing.'

'Come, think what you are about! Why, you are over forty. It's time you had a little sense. What do you imagine yourself to be? Do you suppose I don't know all the tricks you are up to? Why, you are dangling after the director's daughter! Come, look at yourself; just think what you are! Why, you are a nonentity and nothing else! Why, you haven't a penny to bless yourself with. And just look at yourself in the looking-glass – how could you think of such a thing!'

Dash it all, because his face is rather like a medicine bottle and he has a clump of hair on his head curled in a tuft, and pomades it into a kind of rosette, and holds his head in the air, he imagines he is the only one who may do anything. I understand, I understand why he is in such a rage with me. He is envious: he has seen perhaps signs of preference shown to me. But I spit on him! As though a court councillor were of so much consequence! He hangs a gold chain on his watch and orders boots at thirty roubles – but deuce take him! Am I some plebeian – a tailor or a son of a non-commissioned

67

officer? I am a gentleman. Why, I may rise in the service too. I am only forty-two, a time of life in which a career in the service is really only just beginning. Wait a bit, my friend! We too shall be a colonel and perhaps, please God, something better. We shall establish a reputation, and better maybe than your own. A queer notion you have got into your head that no one is a gentleman but yourself. Give me a fashionably cut coat and let me put on a cravat like yours – and then you wouldn't hold a candle to me. I haven't the means, that's the trouble.

8 November

I have been to the theatre. It was a performance of the Russian fool Filatka. I laughed very much. There was a vaudeville too, with some amusing verses about lawyers, and especially about a collegiate registrar, very freely written so that I wondered that the censor had passed it; and about the merchants they openly said that they cheat people and that their sons are debauched and ape the gentry. There was a very amusing couplet about the journalists too; saying that they abused everyone and that an author begged the public to defend him against them. The authors do write amusing plays nowadays. I love going to the theatre. As soon as I have a coin in my pocket I can't resist going. And among our dear friends the officials there are such pigs; they positively won't go to the theatre, the louts; unless perhaps you give them a free ticket. One actress sang very nicely. I thought of her . . . ah, you rascal! . . . Never mind, never mind . . . silence!

9 November

At eight o'clock I went to the department. The head of our section put on a look as though he did not see me come in. On my side, too, I behaved as though nothing had passed between us. I looked through and checked some papers. I went out at four o'clock. I walked by the director's quarters, but no one was to be seen. After dinner for the most part lay on my bed.

11 November

Today I sat in our director's study. I mended twenty-three pens for him and for her . . . aïe, aïe! For her Excellency four pens. He likes to have a lot of pens. Ooh, he must have a head! He always sits silent, and I expect he is turning over everything in his head. I should like to know what he thinks most about. What is going on in that head? I should like to get a close view of the life of these gentlemen, of all these *équivoques* and court ways. How they go on and what they do in their circle – that's what I should like to find out! I have several times thought of beginning a conversation with his Excellency, but, dash it all! I couldn't bring my tongue to it; one says it's cold or warm today and can't utter another word. I should like to look into the drawing-room, of which one sees the open door and another room beyond it. Ah, what sumptuous furniture! What mirrors and china! I long to have a look in there, into the part of the house where her Excellency is, that's where I should like to go! Into her boudoir where there are all sorts of little jars, little bottles and such flowers that one is frightened even to breathe on them, to see her dresses lying scattered about, more like ethereal gossamer than dresses. I long to glance into her bedroom, there I fancy there must be marvels . . . a paradise, such as is not to be found in the heavens. To look at the little stool on which she puts her little foot when she gets out of bed and the way she puts a stocking on that little snow-white foot . . . Aïe, aïe, aïe! Never mind, never mind . . . silence.

But today a light as it were dawned upon me. I remembered the conversation between the two dogs that I heard on Nevsky Prospect. 'Good,' I thought to myself, 'now I will learn all. I must get hold of the correspondence that these wretched dogs have been carrying on. Then I shall certainly learn something.' I must own I once called Madgie to me and said to her: 'Listen, Madgie; here we are alone. If you like, I will shut the door too, so that no one shall see you; tell me all you know about your young lady; what she is like and how she behaves. I swear I won't tell anyone.' But the sly little dog put her tail between her legs, doubled herself up and went quickly to the door as though she hadn't heard. I have long suspected that dogs are far more intelligent than men; I am even convinced that they can speak, only there is a certain doggedness about them. They are extremely diplomatic: they notice everything, every step a man takes. Yes, whatever happens I will go tomorrow to Zvyerkov's Buildings, I will question Fido, and if I am successful I will seize all the letters Madgie has written her.

12 November

At two o'clock in the afternoon I set out determined to see Fido and question her. I can't endure cabbage, the smell of which reeks from all the little shops in Myetchansky Street; moreover, such a hellish reek rises from under every gate that I raced along at full speed holding my nose. And the nasty workmen let off such a lot of soot and smoke from their workshops that a gentleman cannot walk there. When

I climbed up to the sixth storey and rang the bell, a girl who was not at all bad-looking, with little freckles, came to the door. I recognised her: it was the girl who was with the old lady. She turned a little red, and I said to myself at once: 'You are on the look-out for a young man, my dear.'

'How can I be of help?' she asked.

'I want to have a few words with your doggie.'

The girl was silly. I saw at once that she was silly. At that moment the doggie ran out barking; I tried to catch hold of her, but the nasty wretch almost snapped at my nose. However, I saw her bed in the corner. Ah, that was just what I wanted.

I went up to it, rummaged in the straw in the wooden box, and to my indescribable delight pulled out a packet of little slips of paper. The wretched dog, seeing this, first bit my calf, and then when she perceived that I had taken her letters began to whine and fawn on me, but I said, 'No, my dear, goodbye,' and took to my heels. I believe the girl thought I was a madman, as she was very much frightened. When I got home I wanted to set to work at once to decipher the letters, for I don't see very well by candlelight; but Mavra had taken it into her head to wash the floor. These stupid Finnish women always clean at the wrong moment. And so I went out to walk about and think over the incident. Now

I shall find out all their doings and ways of thinking, all the hidden springs, and shall get to the bottom of it all. These letters will reveal everything. Dogs are a clever people, they understand all the diplomatic relations, and so no doubt I shall find there everything about our gentleman: the portrait and all the doings of the man. There will be something in them too about her who . . . never mind, silence! Towards evening I came home. For the most part I lay on my bed.

13 November

Well, we shall see! The writing is fairly distinct, at the same time there is something doggy about the hand. Let us read:

> DEAR FIDO – I never can get used to your plebeian name. As though they could not have given you a better one? Fido, Rose – what vulgarity! No more about that, however. I am very glad we thought of writing to each other.

The letter is very well written. The punctuation and even the spelling are quite correct. Even the chief of our section could not write like this, though he does talk of having studied at some university. Let us see what comes next.

'It seems to me that to share one's ideas, one's feelings and one's impressions with others is one of the greatest blessings on earth.'

Hm! . . . an idea taken from a work translated from the German. I don't remember the name of it.

'I say this from experience, though I have not been about the world, beyond the gates of our house. Is not my life spent in comfort? My young lady, whom her papa calls Sophie, loves me passionately.'

Aïe, aïe! Never mind, never mind! Silence!

'Papa, too, often caresses me. I drink tea and coffee with cream. Ah, *ma chère*, I ought to tell you that I see nothing agreeable at all in big, gnawed bones such as our Polkan crunches in the kitchen. The only bones that are nice are those of game, and then only when the marrow hasn't been sucked out of them by someone. What is very good is several sauces mixed together, only they must be free from capers and green stuff; but I know of nothing worse than giving dogs little balls of bread. A gentleman sitting at the table who has been touching all sorts of nasty things with his hands begins with those hands rolling up bread, calls one up and thrusts the ball upon one. To refuse seems somehow discourteous – well, one eats it – with repulsion, but one eats it . . .'

What the devil's this! What nonsense! As though there

were nothing better to write about. Let us look at another page and see if there is nothing more sensible.

'I shall be delighted to let you know about everything that happens here. I have already told you something about the chief gentleman, whom Sophie calls Papa. He is a very strange man.'

Ah, here we are at last! Yes, I knew it; they have a very diplomatic view of everything. Let us see what Papa is like.

'. . . a very strange man. For the most part he says nothing; he very rarely speaks. But about a week ago he was continually talking to himself: "Shall I receive it or shall I not?" He would take a paper in one hand and close the other hand empty and say: "Shall I receive it or shall I not?" Once he turned to me with the question: "What do you think, Madgie, shall I receive it or not?" I couldn't understand a word of it, I sniffed at his boots and walked away. A week later, *ma chère*, he came in in high glee. All the morning gentlemen in uniform were coming to see him and congratulating him on something. At table he was merrier than I have ever seen him; he kept telling stories. And after dinner, he lifted me up to his neck and said: "Look, Madgie, what's this?" I saw a little ribbon. I sniffed it, but could discover no aroma whatever; at last I licked it on the sly: it was a little bit salt.'

Hm! This doggie seems to me to be really too . . . She

ought to be thrashed! And so he is ambitious! One must take that into consideration.

'Farewell, *ma chère*! I fly, and so on . . . and so on . . . I will finish my letter tomorrow. Well, good day, I am with you again. Today my young lady Sophie . . .'

Oh come, let us see about Sophie. Ah, you rascal . . . Never mind, never mind . . . let us go on.

'My young lady Sophie was in a great fluster. She was getting ready to go to a ball, and I was delighted that in her absence I could write to you. My Sophie is always very glad to go to a ball, though she always gets almost angry when she is being dressed. I cannot understand why people dress. Why don't they go about as we do, for instance? It's nice and it's comfortable. I can't understand, *ma chère*, what pleasure there is in going to balls. Sophie always comes home from balls at six o'clock in the morning, and I can almost always guess from her pale and exhausted face that they had given the poor thing nothing to eat. I must own I couldn't live like that. If I didn't get grouse and gravy or the roast wing of a chicken, I don't know what would become of me. Gravy is nice too with grain in it, but carrots, turnips and artichokes are never good.'

Extraordinary inequality of style! You can see at once that it is not a man writing; it begins as it ought and ends with dogginess. Let us look at one more letter. It's rather long. Hm! And there's no date on it.

'Ah, my dear, how one feels the approach of spring! My heart beats as though I were always expecting someone. There is always a noise in my ears so that I often stand for some minutes with my foot in the air listening at doors. I must confide to you that I have a number of suitors. I often sit at the window and look at them. Oh, if only you knew what ugly creatures there are among them. One is a very ungainly yard-dog, fearfully stupid, stupidity is painted on his face; he walks about the street with an air of importance and imagines that he is a distinguished person and thinks that everybody is looking at him. Not a bit of it. I don't take any notice of him – I behave exactly as though I didn't see him. And what a terrible Great Dane stops before my window! If he were to stand upon his hind legs, which I expect the clumsy fellow could not do, he would be a whole head taller than my Sophie's papa, though he is fairly tall and stout. That blockhead must be a frightfully insolent fellow. I growled at him, but much he cared: he hardly frowned, he put out his tongue, dangled his huge ears and looked up at the window – such a country bumpkin! But can you suppose, *ma chère*, that my heart makes no response to any overture? Ah no . . . If only you could see one of my suitors climbing over the fence next door, by name Tresor . . . Ah, *ma chère*, what a face he has! . . .'

Ough, the devil! . . . What rubbish! How can anyone fill a letter with such foolishness! Give me a man! I want to see a man. I want spiritual sustenance – in which my soul might find food and enjoyment; and instead of that I have this nonsense . . . Let us turn over the page and see whether it is better!

'Sophie was sitting at the table sewing something, I was looking out of the window because I am fond of watching passers-by, when all at once the footman came in and said "Teplov!" "Ask him in," cried Sophie, and rushed to embrace me. "Ah, Madgie, Madgie! If only you knew who that is: a dark young man, a kammer-junker, and such eyes, black and bright as fire!" And Sophie ran off to her room. A minute later a kammer-junker with black whiskers came in, walked up to the looking-glass, smoothed his hair and looked about the room. I growled and sat in my place. Sophie soon came in and bowed gaily in response to his scraping; and I just went on looking out of the window as though I were noticing nothing. However, I bent my head a little on one side and tried to hear what they were saying. Oh, *ma chère*, the nonsense they talked! They talked about a lady who had mistaken one figure for another at the dance; and said that someone called

Bobov with a ruffle on his shirt looked just like a stork and had almost fallen down on the floor, and that a girl called Lidin imagined that her eyes were blue when they were really green – and that sort of thing. "Well," I thought to myself, "if one were to compare that kammer-junker to Tresor, heavens, what a difference!" In the first place, the kammer-junker has a perfectly flat face with whiskers all round as though he had tied it up in a black handkerchief; while Tresor has a delicate little countenance with a white patch on the forehead. It's impossible to compare the kammer-junker's figure with Tresor's. And his eyes, his ways, his manners are all quite different. Oh, what a difference! I don't know, *ma chère*, what she sees in her Teplov. Why she is so enthusiastic about him . . .'

Well, I think myself that there is something wrong about it. It's impossible that she can be fascinated by the kammer-junker. Let us see what next.

'It seems to me that if she is attracted by that kammer-junker she will soon be attracted by that clerk that sits in Papa's study. Oh, *ma chère*, if you know what an ugly fellow that is! A regular tortoise in a bag . . .'

What clerk is this?

'He has a very queer surname. He always sits mending the pens. The hair on his head is very much like hay. Papa sometimes sends him out instead of a servant . . .'

I do believe the nasty little dog is alluding to me. But my hair isn't like hay!

'Sophie can never help laughing when she sees him.'

That's a lie, you damned little dog! What an evil tongue! As though I didn't know that that is the work of envy! As though I didn't know whose tricks were at the bottom of that! This is all the doing of the chief of my section. The man has vowed eternal hatred, and here he tried to injure me again and again, at every turn. Let us look at one more letter though. Perhaps the thing will explain itself.

MY DEAR FIDO, – Forgive me for not writing for so long. I have been in a perfect delirium. How truly has some writer said that love is a second life. Moreover, there are great changes in the house here. The kammer-junker is here every day. Sophie is frantically in love with him. Papa is very good-humoured. I have even heard from our Grigory, who sweeps the floor and almost always talks to himself, that there will soon be a wedding because Papa is set on seeing Sophie married to a general or a kammer-junker or to a colonel in the army . . .

Deuce take it! I can't read any more . . . It's always a kammer-junker or a general. Everything that's the best in the world falls to the kammer-junkers or the generals. If you find some poor treasure and think it is almost within your grasp, a kammer-junker or a general will snatch it from you. The devil take it! I should like to become a general myself, not in order to receive her hand and all the rest of it; no, I should like to be a general only to see how they would wriggle and display all their court manners and *équivoques* and then to say to them: I spit on you both. Deuce take it, it's annoying! I tore the silly dog's letters to bits.

3 December

It cannot be. It's idle talk! There won't be a wedding! What if he is a kammer-junker? Why, that is nothing but a dignity, it's not a visible thing that one could pick up in one's hands. You don't get a third eye in your head because you are a kammer-junker. Why, his nose is not made of gold but is just like mine and everyone else's; he sniffs with it and doesn't eat with it, he sneezes with it and doesn't cough with it. I have often tried to make out from what all these differences arise. Why am I a titular councillor and on what grounds am I a titular councillor? Perhaps I am not a titular councillor at all? Perhaps I am a count or a general, and only somehow appear to be a titular councillor. Perhaps I don't know myself who

I am. How many instances there have been in history: some simple, humble tradesman or peasant, not even a nobleman, is suddenly discovered to be a grand gentleman or the sovereign, or what do you call it . . . If a peasant can sometimes turn into something like that, what may not a nobleman turn into? I shall suddenly, for instance, enter wearing a general's uniform: with an epaulette on my right shoulder and an epaulette on my left shoulder, and a blue ribbon across my chest; well, my charmer will sing a different tune then, and what will her papa, our director, himself say? Ah, he is very ambitious! He is a mason, he is certainly a mason; though he does pretend to be this and that, but I noticed at once that he was a mason: if he shakes hands with anyone, he only offers him two fingers. Might I not be appointed a governor-general this very minute or an intendant, or something of that sort? I should like to know why I am a titular councillor. Why precisely a titular councillor?

5 December

I spent the whole morning reading the newspaper. Strange things are going on in Spain. In fact, I can't really make it out. They write that the throne is vacant, and that they are in a difficult position about choosing an heir, and that there are insurrections in consequence. It seems to me that it is extremely queer. How can the throne be vacant? They say that some *doña* ought to ascend to the throne. A *doña* cannot ascend the throne, she cannot possibly. There ought to be a king on the throne. 'But,' they say, 'there is not a king.' It cannot be that there is no king. A kingdom cannot exist without a king. There is a king, only probably he is in hiding somewhere. He may be there, but either family reasons or danger from some neighbouring State, such as France or some other country, may compel him to remain in hiding, or there may be some other reasons.

8 December

I quite wanted to go to the department, but various reasons and considerations detained me. I cannot get the affairs of Spain out of my head. How can it be that a *doña* should be made queen? They won't allow it. England in the first place won't allow it. And besides, the politics of all Europe, the Emperor of Austria and our Tsar . . . I must own these events have so overwhelmed and shaken me that I haven't been able to do anything all day. Mavra remarked that I was extremely absent-minded at table. And I believe I did accidentally throw two plates on the floor, which smashed immediately. After dinner I went for a walk to the winter festival: I could deduce nothing edifying from it. For the most part I lay on my bed and reflected on the affairs of Spain.

43 April 2000 AD

This is the day of the greatest public rejoicing! There is a king of Spain! He has been discovered. I am that king. I only heard of it this morning. I must own it burst upon me like a flash of lightning. I can't imagine how I could believe and imagine myself to be a titular councillor. How could that crazy, mad idea ever have entered my head? It's a good thing that no one thought of putting me in a madhouse. Now everything has been revealed to me. Now it is all as plain as possible. But until now I did not understand, everything was in a sort of mist. And I believe it all arose from believing that the brain is in the head. It's not so at all; it comes with the wind from the direction of the Caspian Sea. First of all, I told Mavra who I am. When she heard that the King of Spain was standing before her, she threw up her hands and almost died of horror; the silly woman had never seen a king of Spain before. I tried to reassure her, however, and in gracious words tried to convince her of my benevolent feeling towards her, saying that I was not angry with her for having sometimes cleaned my boots so badly. Of course they are benighted people; it is no good talking of elevated subjects to them. She is frightened because she is convinced that all kings of Spain are like Philip II. But I assured her that there was no resemblance between me and Philip II and that I have not even one Capuchin. I didn't go to the department. The devil take it! No, my friends, you won't lure me there again; I am not going to copy your nasty papers!

Martober 86, Between Day and Night

Our office messenger arrived today to tell me to go to the department, and to say that I had not been there for more than three weeks.

But people are unjust: they do their reckoning by weeks. It's the Jews brought that in because their Rabbi washes once a week. However, I did go to the department for a joke. The head of our section thought that I should bow to him and apologise, but I looked at him indifferently, not too angrily and not too graciously, and sat down in my place as though I did not notice anything. I looked at all the scum of the office and thought: 'If only you knew who is sitting among you!' Good gracious! Wouldn't there be an upset! And the head of our section would bow to me as he bows now to the director. They put a paper before me to make some sort of an extract from it. But I didn't touch it. A few minutes later everyone was in a bustle. They said the director was coming. A number of clerks ran forward to show off to him, but I didn't stir. When he walked through our room they all buttoned up their coats, but I didn't do anything at all. What's a director? Am I going to tremble before him? Never! He's a fine director! He is a cork, he is not a director. An ordinary cork, a simple cork and nothing else – such as you cork a bottle with. What amused me most of all was when they put a paper before me to sign. They thought I should write at the bottom of the paper, 'So-and-so, head clerk of the table' – how else should it be! But in the most important place, where the director of the department signs his name, I wrote 'Ferdinand VIII'. You should have seen the awe-struck silence that followed; but I only waved my hand and said, 'I don't insist on any signs of allegiance!' and walked out. From there I walked straight to the director's. He was not at home. The footman did not want to let me in, but I spoke to him in such a way that he let his hands drop. I went straight to her dressing-room. She was sitting before the looking-glass, she jumped up and stepped back on seeing me. I did not tell her that I was the King of Spain, however; I only told her that there was a happiness awaiting her such as she could not imagine, and that in spite of the wiles of our enemies we should be together. I didn't care to say more and walked out. Oh, woman is a treacherous creature! I have discovered now what women are. Hitherto no one has found out with whom woman is in love: I have been the first to discover it. Woman is in love with the devil. Yes, joking apart. Scientific men write nonsense saying that she is this or that – she cares for nothing but the devil. You will see her from a box in the first tier fixing her lorgnette. You imagine she is looking at the fat man with decorations. No, she is looking at the devil who is standing behind his back. There he is, hidden in his coat. There he is, making signs to her! And she will marry him, she will marry him.

And all these people, their dignified fathers who fawn on everybody and push their way to court and say that they are patriots and one thing and another: profit, profit is all that these patriots want! They would sell their father and their mother and God for money, ambitious creatures, Judases! All this is ambition, and the ambition is because of a little pimple under the tongue and in it a little worm no bigger than a pin's head, and it's all the doing of a barber who lives in Gorohovy Street, I don't remember his name; but I know for a fact that, in collusion with a midwife, he is trying to spread Mahometanism all over the world, and that is how it is, I am told, that the majority of people in France profess the Mahometan faith.

No date. The day had no number.

I walked incognito along Nevsky Prospect. His Majesty the Tsar drove by. All the people took off their caps and I did the same, but I made no sign that I was the King of Spain. I thought it improper to discover myself so suddenly before everyone, because I ought first to be presented at court. The only thing that has prevented my doing so is the lack of a royal dress. If only I could get hold of a royal mantle. I should have liked to order it from a tailor, but they are perfect asses; besides, they neglect their work so, they have given themselves up to speculating and for the most part are employed in laying the pavement in the street. I determined to make the mantle out of my new uniform, which I had only worn twice. And that the scoundrels should not ruin it I decided to make it myself, shutting the door that no one might see me at it. I ripped it all up with the scissors because the cut has to be completely different.

I don't remember the date. There was no month either. Goodness knows what to make of it.

The mantle is completely finished. Mavra gave a shriek when she saw me in it. However, I can't make up my mind to present myself at court, for so far there is no deputation from Spain. It wouldn't be proper to go without deputies: there would be nothing to give weight to my dignity. I expect them from hour to hour.

The 1st

I am extremely surprised at the tardiness of the deputies. What can be detaining them? Can it be the machinations of France? Yes, that is the most malignant of States. I went to enquire at the post office whether the Spanish deputies had not arrived; but the postmaster was excessively stupid and knew nothing. 'No,' he said, 'there are no deputies here, but if you care to write a letter I will send it off in accordance with the regulations.' Dash it all, what's the use of a letter? A letter is nonsense. Letters are written by chemists, and even then they have to moisten their tongues with vinegar or else their faces would be all over scabs.

Madrid, February Thirtieth

And so here I am in Spain, and it happened so quickly that I can hardly realise it yet. This morning the Spanish deputies arrived and I got into a carriage with them. The extraordinary rapidity of our journey struck me as strange. We went at such a rate that within half an hour we had reached the frontiers of Spain. But of course now there are railroads all over Europe, and steamers go very rapidly. Spain is a strange land! When we went into the first room I saw a number of people with shaven heads. I guessed at once that these were either grandees or soldiers because they do shake their heads. I thought the behaviour of the High Chancellor, who led me by the hand, extremely strange. He thrust me into a little room and said: 'Sit there, and if you persist in calling yourself King Ferdinand, I'll knock the inclination out of you.' But knowing that this was only to try me, I answered in the negative, whereupon the Chancellor hit me twice on the back with the stick and it hurt so that I almost cried out, but I restrained myself, remembering that this is the custom of chivalry on receiving any exalted dignity, for customs of chivalry persist in Spain to this day.

When I was alone I decided to occupy myself with the affairs of state. I discovered that Spain and China are one and the same country, and it is only through ignorance that they are considered to be a different kingdoms. I recommend everyone to try and write 'Spain' on a bit of paper and it will always turn out 'China'. But I was particularly distressed by an event which will take place tomorrow. Tomorrow at seven o'clock a strange phenomenon will occur: the earth will sit on the moon. The celebrated English chemist Wellington has written about it. I must confess that I experience a tremor in my heart when I reflect on the extreme softness and fragility of the moon. You see, the moon is generally made in Hamburg, and very badly made too. I am surprised that England hasn't taken notice of it. It was made by a lame cooper, and it is evident that the fool had no idea what a moon should be. He put in tarred cord and one part of olive oil; and that is why there is such a fearful stench all over the world that one has to stop up one's nose. And that's how it is that the moon is such a soft globe that man cannot live on it and that nothing lives there but noses. And it is for that very reason that we can't see our noses, because they are all in the moon. And when I reflected that the earth is a heavy body and when it sits down may ground our noses to powder, I was overcome by such uneasiness that, putting on my shoes and stockings, I hastened to the hall of the Imperial Council to give orders to the police not to allow the earth to sit on the moon. The grandees with shaven heads whom I found in great numbers in the hall of the Imperial Council were very intelligent people, and when I said, 'Gentlemen, let us save the moon, for the earth is trying to fall upon it!' they all rushed to carry out my sovereign wishes, and several climbed up the walls to try and get at the moon, but at that moment the High Chancellor walked in. Seeing him they all ran in different directions. I as King remained alone. But, to my amazement, the Chancellor struck me with his stick and drove me back to my room! So great is the power of national customs in Spain.

January of the same year (it came after February)

So far I have not been able to make out what sort of a country Spain is. The national traditions and the customs of the court are quite extraordinary. I can't make it out, I can't make it out, I absolutely can't make it out. Today they shaved my head, although I shouted at the top of my voice that I didn't want to become a monk. But I can't even remember what happened afterwards when they poured cold water on my head. I have never endured such hell. I was almost going frantic so that they had a difficulty in holding me. I cannot understand the meaning of this strange custom. It's a stupid, senseless practice! The lack of good sense in the kings who have not abolished it to this day is beyond my comprehension. Judging from all the circumstances, I wonder whether I have not fallen into the hands of the Spanish Inquisition, and whether the man I took to be the Grand Chancellor isn't the Grand Inquisitor. Only I cannot understand how a king can be subject to the Inquisition. It can only be through the influence of France, especially of Polignac. Oh, that beast of a Polignac! He has sworn to me enmity to the death. And he pursues me and pursues me; but I know, my friend, that you are the tool of England. The English are great politicians. They poke their noses into everything. All the world knows that when England takes a piece of snuff, France sneezes.

The Twenty-Fifth

Today the Grand Inquisitor came into my room again, but hearing his steps in the distance I hid under a chair. Seeing I wasn't there, he began calling me. At first he shouted 'Popristchin!' I didn't say a word. Then: 'Aksenty Ivanov! Titular councillor! Nobleman!' I still remained silent. 'Ferdinand VIII, King of Spain!' I was on the point of sticking out my head, but then I thought: 'No, my friend, you won't take me in. I know you: you will be pouring cold water on my head again.' However, he caught sight of me and drove me from under the chair with a stick. That damned stick does hurt. However, I was rewarded for all this by the discovery I made today. I found out that every cock has a Spain, that it is under his wings not far from his tail.

The Grand Inquisitor went away, however, very wroth,

threatening me with some punishment. But I disdain his impotent malice, knowing that he is simply an instrument, a tool of England.

34 Еspıñαλλ Yrae 349

No, I haven't the strength to endure more. My God! The things they are doing to me! They pour cold water on my head! They won't listen to me, they won't see me, they won't hear me. What have I done to them? Why do they torture me? What do they want of a poor creature like me? What can I give them? I have nothing. It's too much for me, I can't endure these agonies, my head is burning and everything is going round. Save me, take me away! Give me a troika and horses swift as a whirlwind! Take your seat, my driver, ring out, my bells, fly upwards, my steeds, and bear me away from this world! Far away, far away, so that nothing can be seen, nothing. Yonder the sky whirls before me, a star sparkles in the distance; the forest floats by with dark trees and the moon, blue-grey mist lies stretched under my feet; a chord resounds in the mist; on one side the sea, on the other Italy, yonder the huts of Russia can be seen. Is that my home in the distance? Is it my mother sitting before the window? Mother, save your poor son! Drop a tear on his sick head! See how they torment him! Press your poor orphan to your bosom! There is nowhere in the world for him! He is persecuted! Mother, have pity on your sick child!

And do you know that the King of France has a boil just under his nose?

The Overcoat

IN THE DEPARTMENT OF . . . but I had better not mention in what department. There is nothing in the world more readily moved to wrath than a department, a regiment, a government office, and in fact any sort of official body. Nowadays every private individual considers all society insulted in his person. I have been told that very lately a petition was handed in from a police captain of what town I don't recollect, and that in this petition he set forth clearly that the institutions of the State were in danger and that its sacred name was being taken in vain; and, in proof thereof, he appended to his petition an enormously long volume of some work of romance in which a police captain appeared on every tenth page, occasionally, indeed, in an intoxicated condition. And so, to avoid any unpleasantness, we had better call the department of which we are speaking a certain department.

And so, in a certain department there was a government clerk; a clerk of whom it cannot be said that he was very remarkable; he was short, somewhat pockmarked, with rather reddish hair and rather dim, bleary eyes, with a small bald patch on the top of his head, with wrinkles on both sides of his cheeks and the sort of complexion which is usually associated with haemorrhoids . . . no help for that, it is the Petersburg climate. As for his grade in the service (for among us the grade is what must be put first), he was what is called a perpetual titular councillor, a class at which, as we all know, various writers who indulge in the praiseworthy habit of attacking those who cannot defend themselves jeer and jibe to their hearts' content. This clerk's surname was Bashmatchkin. From the very name it is clear that it must have been derived from a shoe (*bashmak*); but when and under what circumstances it was derived from a shoe, it is impossible to say. Both his father and his grandfather and even his brother-in-law, and all the Bashmatchkins without exception wore boots, which they simply resoled two or three times a year. His name was Akaky Akakyevitch. Perhaps it may strike the reader as a rather strange and far-fetched name, but I can assure him that it was not far-fetched at all, that the circumstances were such that it was quite out of the question to give him any other name. Akaky Akakyevitch was born towards nightfall, if my memory does not deceive me, on the twenty-third of March. His mother, the wife of a government clerk, a very good woman, made arrangements in due course to christen the child. She was still lying in bed, facing the door, while on her right hand stood the godfather, an excellent man called Ivan Ivanovitch Yeroshkin, one of the head clerks in the Senate, and the godmother, the wife of a police official, and a woman of rare qualities, Arina Semyonovna Byelobryushkov.

Three names were offered to the happy mother for selection – Moky, Sossy or the name of the martyr Hozdazat. 'No,' thought the poor lady, 'they are all such names!' To satisfy her, they opened the calendar at another place, and the names which turned up were: Trifily, Dula, Varahasy. 'What an infliction!' said the mother. 'What names they all are! I really never heard such names. Varadat or Varuh would be bad enough, but Trifily and Varahasy! They turned over another page and the names were: Pavsikahy and Vahtisy. 'Well, I see,' said the mother, 'it is clear that it is his fate. Since that is how it is, he had better be called after his father, his father is Akaky, let the son be Akaky, too.' This was how he came to be Akaky Akakyevitch. The baby was christened, and cried, and made wry faces during the ceremony, as though he foresaw that he would be a titular councillor. So that was how it all came to pass. We have recalled it here so that the reader may see for himself that it happened quite inevitably and that to give him any other name was out of the question. No one has been able to remember when and how long ago he entered the department, nor who gave him the job.

However many directors and higher officials of all sorts came and went, he was always seen in the same place, in the same position and at the very same duty, precisely the same copying clerk, so that they used to declare that he must have been born a copying clerk, in uniform all complete and with a bald patch on his head. No respect at all was shown him in the department.

The porters, far from getting up from their seats when he came in, took no more notice of him than if a simple fly had flown across the vestibule. His superiors treated him with a sort of domineering chilliness. The head clerk's assistant used to thrust papers under his nose without even saying, 'Copy this,' or, 'Here is an interesting, nice little case,' or some agreeable remark of the sort, as is usually done in well-behaved offices. And he would take it, gazing only at the paper without looking to see who had put it there and whether he had the right to do so; he would take it and at once set to work to copy it. The young clerks jeered and made jokes at him to the best of their clerkly wit, and told before his face all sorts of stories of their own invention about him; they would say of his landlady, an old woman of seventy, that she beat him, would enquire when the wedding was to take place, and would scatter bits of paper on his head, calling them snow. Akaky Akakyevitch never answered a word, however, but behaved as though there were no one there. It had no influence on his work, even; in the midst of all this teasing, he never made a single mistake in his copying. Only when the jokes were too unbearable, when they jolted his arm and prevented him from going on with his work, he would bring out 'Leave me alone! Why do you insult me?' and there was something strange in the words and in the voice in which they were uttered. There was a note in it of something that aroused compassion, so that one young man, new to the office, who, following the example of the rest, had allowed himself to mock at him, suddenly stopped as though cut to the heart, and from that time forth, everything was, as it were, changed and appeared in a different light to him. Some unnatural force seemed to push him away from the companions with whom he had become acquainted, accepting them as well-bred, polished people. And long afterwards, at moments of the greatest gaiety, the figure of the humble little clerk with a bald patch on his head rose before him with his heart-rending words, 'Leave me alone!

Why do you insult me?' and in those heart-rending words he heard others: 'I am your brother.' And the poor young man hid his face in his hands, and many times afterwards in his life he shuddered, seeing how much inhumanity there is in man, how much savage brutality lies hidden under refined, cultured politeness, and – my God! – even in a man whom the world accepts as a gentleman and a man of honour . . .

It would be hard to find a man who lived in his work as did Akaky Akakyevitch. To say that he was zealous in his work is not enough; no, he loved his work. In it, in that copying, he found a varied and agreeable world of his own. There was a look of enjoyment on his face; certain letters were favourites with him, and when he came to them he was delighted; he chuckled to himself and winked and moved his lips, so that it seemed as though every letter his pen was forming could be read in his face. If rewards had been given according to the measure of zeal in the service, he might to his amazement have even found himself a civil councillor; but all he gained in the service, as the wits, his fellow clerks, expressed it, was a buckle in his buttonhole and a pain in his back. It cannot be said, however, that no notice had ever been taken of him. One director, being a good-natured man and anxious to reward him for his long service, sent him something a little more important than his ordinary copying;

he was instructed from a finished document to make some sort of report for another office; the work consisted only of altering the headings and in places changing the first person into the third. This cost him such an effort that it threw him into a regular perspiration: he mopped his brow and said at last, 'No, better let me copy something.' From that time forth they left him to go on copying forever. It seemed as though nothing in the world existed for him outside his copying. He gave no thought at all to his clothes; his uniform was – well, not green but some sort of rusty, muddy colour. His collar was very short and narrow, so that, although his neck was not particularly long, yet, standing out of the collar, it looked as immensely long as those of the plaster kittens that wag their heads and are carried about on trays by the dozen on the heads of foreign traders. And there were always things sticking to his uniform, either bits of hay or threads; moreover, he had a special art of passing under a window at the very moment when various rubbish was being flung out into the street, and so was continually carrying off bits of melon rind and similar litter on his hat. He had never once in his life noticed what was being done and going on in the streets, all those things at which, as we all know, his colleagues, the young clerks, always stare, carrying their sharp sight so far even as to notice anyone on the other side of the pavement with a trouser strap hanging loose – a detail which always calls forth a sly grin.

Whatever Akaky Akakyevitch looked at, he saw nothing anywhere but his clear, evenly written lines, and only perhaps when a horse's head suddenly appeared from nowhere just on his shoulder, and its nostrils blew a perfect gale upon his cheek, did he notice that he was not in the middle of his writing, but rather in the middle of the street.

On reaching home, he would sit down at once to the table, hurriedly sup his cabbage soup and eat a piece of beef with an onion; he did not notice the taste at all, but ate it all up together with the flies and anything else that Providence chanced to send him. When he felt that his stomach was beginning to stick out, he would rise up from the table, get out a bottle of ink and set to copying the papers he had brought home with him. When he had none to do, he would make a copy expressly for his own pleasure, particularly if the document were remarkable not for the beauty of its style but for the fact of its being addressed to some new or important personage.

Even at those hours when the grey Petersburg sky is completely overcast and the whole population of clerks have dined and eaten their fill, each as best he can, according to the salary he receives and his personal tastes; when they are all resting after the scratching of pens and bustle of the office, their own necessary work and other people's, and all the tasks that an over-zealous man voluntarily sets himself even beyond what is necessary; when the clerks are hastening to devote what is left of their time to pleasure; some more enterprising are flying to the theatre, others to the street to spend their leisure, staring at women's hats, some to spend the evening at a party paying compliments to some attractive girl, the star of a little official circle, while some – and this is the most frequent of all – go simply to a fellow clerk's flat on the third or fourth storey, two little rooms with an entry hall or a kitchen, with some pretensions to style, with a lamp or some such article that has cost many sacrifices of dinners and excursions – at the time when all the clerks are scattered about the little flats of their friends, playing a tempestuous game of whist, sipping tea out of glasses to the accompaniment of biscuits, sucking in smoke from long pipes, telling, as the cards are dealt, some scandal that has floated down from higher circles, a pleasure which the Russian can never by any possibility deny himself, or, when there is nothing better to talk about, repeating the everlasting anecdote of the commanding officer who was told that the tail had been cut off the horse on the Falconet monument – in short, even when everyone was eagerly seeking entertainment, Akaky Akakyevitch did not give himself up to any amusement. No one could say that they had ever seen him at an evening party. After working to his heart's content, he would go to bed, smiling at the thought of the next day and wondering what God would send him to copy.

So flowed on the peaceful life of a man who knew how to be content with his fate on a salary of four hundred roubles, and so perhaps it would have flowed on to extreme old age, had it not been for the various calamities that bestrew the path through life, not only of titular, but even of privy, actual court, and all other councillors, even those who neither give counsel to others nor accept it themselves.

There is in Petersburg a mighty foe for all who receive a salary of four hundred roubles or about that sum. That foe is none other than our northern frost, although it is said to be very good for the health. Between eight and nine in the morning, precisely at the hour when the streets are full of clerks going to their departments, the frost begins giving such sharp and stinging flips at all their noses indiscriminately that the poor fellows don't know how to hide them. At that time, when even those in the higher grade have a pain in their brows and tears in their eyes from the frost, the poor titular councillors are sometimes almost defenceless. Their only protection lies in running as fast as they can through five or six streets in a wretched, thin little overcoat and then stomping their feet thoroughly in the porter's room to warm them, till all their faculties and qualifications for their various duties thaw again after being frozen on the way. Akaky Akakyevitch had for some time been feeling that his back and shoulders were particularly nipped by the cold, although he did try to run the regular distance as fast as he could. He wondered at last whether there were any defects in his overcoat. After examining it thoroughly in the privacy of his home, he discovered that in two or three places, to wit on the back and the shoulders, it had become a regular sieve; the cloth was so worn that you could see through it and the lining was coming out. I must observe that Akaky Akakyevitch's overcoat had also served as a butt for the jibes of the clerks. It had even been deprived of the honourable name of overcoat and had been referred to as the 'dressing-jacket'. It was indeed of rather a strange cut. Its collar had been growing smaller year by year as it served to patch the other parts. The patches were not good specimens of the tailor's art, and they certainly looked clumsy and unappealing. On seeing what was wrong, Akaky Akakyevitch decided that he would have to take the overcoat to Petrovitch, a tailor who lived on a fourth storey up a back staircase, and, in spite of having only one eye and being pockmarked all over his face, was rather successful in repairing the trousers and coats of clerks and others – that is, when he was sober, be it understood, and had no other enterprise in his mind.

Of this tailor I ought not, of course, to say much, but since it is now the rule that the character of every person in a novel must be completely drawn, well, there is no help for it, here is Petrovitch too. At first he was called simply Grigory, and was a serf belonging to some gentleman or other. He began to be called Petrovitch from the time that he got his freedom and began to drink rather heavily on every holiday, at first only on the chief holidays, but afterwards on all church holidays indiscriminately, wherever there is a cross in the calendar. On that side he was true to the customs of his forefathers, and when he quarrelled with his wife used to call her 'a worldly woman and a German'. Since we have now mentioned the wife, it will be necessary to say a few words about her too, but unfortunately not much is known about her, except indeed that Petrovitch had a wife and that she wore a cap and not a kerchief, but apparently she could not boast of beauty; anyway, none but soldiers of the Guards peeped under her cap when they met her, and they twitched their moustaches and gave vent to a rather peculiar sound.

As he climbed the stairs, leading to Petrovitch's – which, to do them justice, were all soaked with water and slops and saturated through and through with that smell of spirits which makes the eye smart, and is, as we all know, inseparable from the back stairs of Petersburg houses – Akaky Akakyevitch was already wondering how much Petrovitch would ask for the job, and inwardly resolving not to give more than two roubles. The door was open, for Petrovitch's wife was frying some fish and had so filled the kitchen with smoke that you could not even see the cockroaches. Akaky Akakyevitch crossed the kitchen unnoticed by the good woman, and walked at last into a room where he saw Petrovitch sitting on a big, wooden, unpainted table with his legs tucked under him like a Turkish pasha. The feet, as is usual with tailors when they sit at work, were bare; and the first object that caught Akaky Akakyevitch's eye was the big toe, with which he was already familiar, with a misshapen nail as thick and strong as the shell of a tortoise. Round Petrovitch's neck hung a skein of silk and another of thread and on his knees was a rag of some sort. He had for the last three minutes been trying to thread his needle, but could not get the thread into the eye and so was very angry with the darkness and indeed with the thread itself, muttering in an undertone 'It won't go in, the savage! You wear me out, you rascal.' Akaky Akakyevitch was vexed that he had come just at the minute when Petrovitch was in a bad humour; he liked to give him an order when he was a little 'elevated', or, as his wife expressed it, 'had fortified himself with home-brew, the one-eyed devil'.

In such circumstances Petrovitch was as a rule very ready

to give way and agree, and invariably bowed and thanked. Afterwards, it is true, his wife would come wailing that her husband had been drunk and so had asked too little, but adding a single ten-kopeck piece would settle that. But on this occasion Petrovitch was apparently sober and consequently curt, unwilling to bargain, and the devil knows what price he would be ready to lay on. Akaky Akakyevitch perceived this, and was, as the saying is, beating a retreat, but things had gone too far, for Petrovitch was screwing up his solitary eye very attentively at him and Akaky Akakyevitch involuntarily brought out: 'Good day, Petrovitch!'

'I wish you a good day, sir,' said Petrovitch, and squinted at Akaky Akakyevitch's hands, trying to discover what sort of goods he had brought. 'Here I have come to you, Petrovitch, do you see . . . !'

It must be noticed that Akaky Akakyevitch for the most part explained himself by prepositions, adverbs and lexical items which have absolutely no significance whatsoever. If the subject were a very difficult one, it was his habit indeed to leave his sentences quite unfinished, so that very often after a sentence had begun with the words, 'It really is, don't you know . . .' nothing at all would follow and he himself would be quite oblivious, supposing he had said all that was necessary.

'What is it?' said Petrovitch, and at the same time with

his solitary eye he scrutinised the man's whole uniform from the collar to the sleeves, the back, the skirts, the buttonholes – with all of which he was very familiar as they were all his own work. Such scrutiny is habitual with tailors, it is the first thing they do on meeting one.

'It's like this, Petrovitch . . . the overcoat, the broadcloth . . . you see everywhere else it is quite strong; it's a little dusty and looks as though it were old, but it is new and it is only in one place just a little . . . on the back, and just a little worn on one shoulder and on this shoulder, too, a little . . . do you see? That's all, and it's not much work . . .' Petrovitch took the 'dressing-jacket', first spread it out over the table, examined it for a long time, shook his head and put his hand out to the window for a round snuffbox with a portrait on the lid of some general – which precisely I can't say, for a finger had been thrust through the spot where a face should have been, and the hole had been pasted up with a square bit of paper.

After taking a pinch of snuff, Petrovitch held the 'dressing-jacket' up in his hands and looked at it against the light, and again he shook his head; then he turned it with the lining upwards and once more shook his head; again he took off the lid with the general pasted up with paper and stuffed a pinch into his nose, shut the box, put it away and at last said: 'No, it can't be repaired; a wretched garment!'

Akaky Akakyevitch's heart skipped a beat with these words.

'Why can't it, Petrovitch?' he said, almost in the imploring voice of a child. 'Why, the only thing is it is a bit worn on the shoulders; why – you have got some little pieces . . .'

'Yes, the pieces will be found all right,' said Petrovitch, 'but it can't be patched, the stuff is quite rotten; if you put a needle in it, it would give way.'

'Let it give way, but you just put a patch on it.'

'There is nothing to put a patch on. There is nothing for it to hold on to; there is a great strain on it, it is not worth calling broadcloth, it would fly away at a breath of wind.'

'Well, then, underpin it with something – upon my word, really, this is . . . !'

'No,' said Petrovitch resolutely, 'there is nothing to be done, the thing is no good at all. You had far better, when the cold winter weather comes, make yourself leg wrappings out of it, for there is no warmth in stockings, the Germans invented them just to make money.' (Petrovitch was fond of a dig at the Germans occasionally.) 'And as for the overcoat, it is clear that you will have to have a new one.'

At the word 'new' there was a mist before Akaky Akakyevitch's eyes, and everything in the room seemed muddled. He could see nothing clearly but the general with the piece of paper over his face on the lid of Petrovitch's snuffbox.

'A new one?' he said, still feeling as though he were in a dream. 'Why, I haven't the money for it.'

'Yes, a new one,' Petrovitch repeated with barbarous composure.

'Well, and if I did have a new one, how much would it . . .'

'You mean what will it cost?'

'Yes.'

'Well, three fifty-rouble notes or more,' said Petrovitch, and he compressed his lips significantly. He was very fond of making an effect; he was fond of suddenly disconcerting a man completely and then squinting sideways to see what sort of a face he made.

'A hundred and fifty roubles for an overcoat,' screamed poor Akaky Akakyevitch – it was perhaps the first time he had screamed in his life, for he was always distinguished by the softness of his voice.

'Yes,' said Petrovitch, 'and even then it's according to the coat. If I were to put marten on the collar, and add a hood with silk linings, it would come to two hundred.'

'Petrovitch, please,' said Akaky Akakyevitch in an imploring voice, not hearing and not trying to hear what Petrovitch said, and missing all his effects, 'do repair it somehow, so that it will serve a little longer.'

'No, that would be wasting work and spending money for

nothing,' said Petrovitch, and after that Akaky Akakyevitch went away completely crushed, and when he had gone, Petrovitch remained standing for a long time with his lips pursed up significantly before he took up his work again, feeling pleased that he had not demeaned himself nor lowered the dignity of the tailor's art.

When he got into the street, Akaky Akakyevitch was as though in a dream. 'So that is how it is,' he said to himself. 'So the thing is, this is the thing . . .' And then after a pause he added, 'So that's it! So, in the end, that's how it is! And I really could never have supposed it would have been so.' There followed another long silence, after which he brought out: 'So there it is! Well, it really is, exactly, utterly unexpected, that . . . it couldn't have . . . What a circumstance . . .'

Saying this, instead of going home he walked off in quite the opposite direction without suspecting what he was doing. On the way a clumsy sweep brushed the whole of his sooty side against him and blackened all his shoulder; a regular hatful of plaster scattered upon him from the top of a house that was being built. He noticed nothing of this, and only after he had jostled against a sentry who had set his halberd down beside him and was shaking some snuff out of his horn into his rough fist, he came to himself a little and then only because the sentry said, 'Why are you poking yourself right in one's face, haven't you got the pavement to yourself?' This made him look round and turn homeward; only there did he begin to collect his thoughts, to see his position in a clear and true light and began talking to himself no longer incoherently but reasonably and openly as with a sensible friend with whom one can discuss the most intimate and vital matters. 'No, indeed,' said Akaky Akakyevitch, 'it is no use talking to Petrovitch now; just now he really is . . . His wife must have been giving it to him. I had better go to him on Sunday morning; after the Saturday evening he will be squinting and sleepy, so he'll want a little drink to carry it off and his wife won't give him a penny. I'll slip ten kopecks into his hand and then he will be more accommodating and maybe take the overcoat . . .'

So reasoning with himself, Akaky Akakyevitch cheered up and waited until the next Sunday; then, seeing from a distance Petrovitch's wife leaving the house, he went straight in. Petrovitch was certainly squinting vigorously after the Saturday. He could hardly hold his head up and was very drowsy: but, for all that, as soon as he heard what he was speaking about, it seemed as though the devil had nudged him. 'I can't,' he said, 'you must kindly order a new one.' Akaky Akakyevitch at once slipped a ten-kopeck piece into his hand. 'I thank you, sir, I will have just a drop to your health, but don't trouble yourself about the overcoat; it is not a bit of good for anything. I'll make you a fine new coat, you can trust me for that.'

Akaky Akakyevitch would have said more about repairs, but Petrovitch, without listening, said: 'A new one now I'll make you without fail; you can rely upon that, I'll do my best. It could even be like the fashion that has come in with the collar to button with silver claws under appliqué.'

Then Akaky Akakyevitch saw that there was no escape from a new overcoat and he was utterly depressed. How indeed, for what, with what money could he get it? Of course, he could to some extent rely on the bonus for the coming holiday, but that money had long ago been appropriated and its use determined beforehand. It was needed for new trousers and to pay the cobbler an old debt for putting some new tops to some old boot-legs, and he had to order three shirts from a seamstress as well as two specimens of an undergarment which it is improper to mention in print; in short, all that money absolutely must be spent, and even if the director were to be so gracious as to assign him a gratuity of forty-five or even fifty, instead of forty roubles, there would be still left a mere trifle, which would be but as a drop in the ocean beside the fortune needed for an overcoat. Though, of course, he knew that Petrovitch had a strange craze for suddenly putting on the devil knows what enormous price, so that at times his own wife could not help crying out 'Why, you are out of your wits, you idiot! Another time he'll undertake a job for nothing, and here the devil has bewitched him to ask more than he is worth himself!' – though, of course, he knew that Petrovitch would undertake to make it for eighty roubles; still, where would he get those eighty roubles? He might manage half of that sum; half of it could be found, perhaps even a little more; but where could he get the other half? . . . But, first of all, the reader ought to know where that first half was to be found. Akaky Akakyevitch had the habit every time he spent a rouble of putting aside two kopecks in a little locked-up box with a slit in the lid for slipping the money in.

At the end of every half-year he would inspect the pile of coppers there and change them for small silver. He had done this for a long time, and in the course of many years the sum had mounted up to forty roubles and so he had half the money in his hands, but where was he to get the other half – where was he to get another forty roubles? Akaky Akakyevitch pondered and pondered, and decided at last that he would have to diminish his ordinary expenses, at least for a year: chase away his need for tea in the evenings, give up burning candles in the evening, and if he had to do anything he must go into the landlady's room and work by her candle;

that as he walked along the streets he must walk as lightly and carefully as possible, almost on tiptoe, on the cobbles and flagstones, so that his soles might last a little longer than usual; that he must send his linen to the wash less frequently, and that, to preserve it from being worn, he must take it off every day when he came home and sit in a thin cotton-shoddy dressing-gown, a very ancient garment which Time itself had spared. To tell the truth, he found it at first rather hard to get used to these privations, but after a while it became a habit and went smoothly enough – he even became quite accustomed to being hungry in the evening; on the other hand, he had spiritual nourishment, for he carried ever in his thoughts the idea of his future overcoat. His whole existence had in a sense become fuller, as though he had married, as though some other person was present with him, as though he were no longer alone, but an agreeable companion had consented to walk the path of life hand in hand with him, and that companion was no other than the new overcoat with its thick wadding and its strong, durable lining. He became, as it were, more animated, even more assertive, like a man who has set before himself a definite aim. Uncertainty, indecision, in fact all the hesitating and vague characteristics vanished from his face and his manners. At times there was a gleam in his eyes; indeed, the most bold and audacious ideas flashed through his mind. Why not really have marten on the collar? Meditation on the subject always made him absent-minded, On one occasion when he was copying a document, he very nearly made a mistake, so that he almost cried out 'Ough!' aloud and crossed himself. At least once every month he went to Petrovitch to talk about the overcoat, where it would be best to buy the broadcloth, and what colour it should be, and what price, and, though he returned home a little anxious, he was always pleased at the thought that at last the time was at hand when everything would be bought and the overcoat would be made. Things moved even faster than he had anticipated.

Contrary to all expectations, the director bestowed on Akaky Akakyevitch a gratuity of no less than sixty roubles. Whether it was that he had an inkling that Akaky Akakyevitch needed a greatcoat, or whether it happened so by chance, owing to this he found he had twenty roubles extra. This circumstance hastened the course of affairs. Another two or three months of partial fasting and Akaky Akakyevitch had actually saved up nearly eighty roubles. His heart, as a rule very tranquil, began to throb. The very first day he set off in company with Petrovitch to the shops. They bought some very good broadcloth, and no wonder, since they had been thinking of it for more than six months before, and scarcely a month had passed without their going to the shop to compare prices; now Petrovitch himself declared that there was no better cloth to be had. For the lining they chose calico, but of a stout quality, which in Petrovich's words was even better than silk, and actually as strong and handsome to look at. Marten they did not buy, because it certainly was dear, but instead they chose cat fur, the best to be found in the shop – cat which in the distance might almost be taken for marten. Petrovitch was busy over the coat for a whole fortnight, because there were a great many stitches needed, otherwise it would have been ready sooner. Petrovitch asked twelve roubles for the work; less than that it hardly could have been, everything was sewn with silk, with fine double seams, and Petrovitch went over every seam afterwards with his own teeth imprinting various figures with them. It was . . . it is hard to say precisely on what day, but probably on the most triumphant day of the life of Akaky Akakyevitch that Petrovitch at last brought the overcoat.

He brought it in the morning, just before it was time to set off for the department. The overcoat could not have arrived more in the nick of time, for rather sharp frosts were just beginning and seemed threatening to be even more severe. Petrovitch brought the greatcoat himself as a good tailor should. There was an expression of importance on his face, such as Akaky Akakyevitch had never seen there before. He seemed fully conscious of having completed a work of no little moment and of having shown in his own person the gulf that separates tailors who only put in linings and do repairs from those who make up new garments. He took the greatcoat out of the napkin in which he had brought it (the napkin had just come home from the wash); he then folded it up and put it in his pocket for future use. After taking out the overcoat, he looked at it with much pride and, holding it in both hands, threw it very deftly over Akaky Akakyevitch's shoulders, then pulled it down and smoothed it out behind with his hands; then draped it about Akaky Akakyevitch with somewhat jaunty carelessness.

The latter, as a man advanced in years, wished to try it with his arms in the sleeves. Petrovitch helped him to put it on, and it appeared that it looked splendid, too, with his arms in the sleeves. In fact it turned out that the overcoat was exactly a perfect fit. Petrovitch did not let slip the occasion for observing that it was only because he lived in a small street and had no signboard, and because he had known Akaky Akakyevitch so long, that he had done it so cheaply, but on Nevsky Prospect they would have asked him seventy-five roubles for the work alone. Akaky Akakyevitch had no inclination to discuss this with Petrovitch; besides, he was frightened of the big sums that Petrovitch was fond of flinging airily about in conversation.

He paid him, thanked him and went off on the spot, with his new overcoat on, to the department. Petrovitch followed him out and stopped in the street, staring for a good time at the coat from a distance, and then purposely turned off and, taking a short cut by a side alley, ran into the street and got another view of the coat from the other side, that is, from the front.

Meanwhile Akaky Akakyevitch walked along with every emotion in its most holiday mood. He felt every second that he had a new overcoat on his shoulders, and several times he actually smirked from inward satisfaction. Indeed, it had two advantages: one that it was warm, and the other that it was good. He did not notice the way at all and found himself all at once at the department; in the porter's room he took off the overcoat, looked it over and put it in the porter's special care. I cannot tell how it happened, but all at once everyone in the department learned that Akaky Akakyevitch had a new overcoat and that the 'dressing-jacket' no longer existed. They all ran out at once into the porter's room to look at Akaky Akakyevitch's new overcoat; they began welcoming him and congratulating him so that at first he could do nothing but smile and afterwards felt positively abashed. When, coming up to him, they all began saying that he must christen the new overcoat and that he ought at least to stand them all a supper, Akaky Akakyevitch lost his head completely and did not know what to do, how to get out of it, nor what to answer. A few minutes later, flushing crimson, he even began assuring them with great simplicity that it was not a new overcoat at all, that it was just nothing, that it was an old overcoat. At last one of the clerks – indeed, the assistant of the head clerk of the room – probably in order to show that he was not proud and was able to get on with those beneath him, said, 'So be it, I'll give a party instead of Akaky Akakyevitch and invite you all to tea with me this evening; as luck would have it, it is my name-day.' The clerks naturally congratulated the assistant of the head clerk and eagerly accepted the invitation. Akaky Akakyevitch was beginning to make excuses, but they all declared that it was uncivil of him, that it was simply a shame and a disgrace and that he could not possibly refuse. However, he felt pleased about it afterwards when he remembered that through this he would have the opportunity of going out in the evening, too, in his new overcoat.

That whole day was, for Akaky Akakyevitch, the most triumphant and festive day in his life. He returned home in the happiest frame of mind, took off the overcoat and hung it carefully on the wall, admiring the cloth and lining once more, and then pulled out his old 'dressing-jacket', now completely coming to pieces, on purpose to compare them. He glanced at it and positively laughed, the difference was so immense! And long afterwards he went on laughing at dinner, as he recalled the position in which the 'dressing-jacket' was placed. He dined in excellent spirits and after dinner wrote nothing, no papers at all, but just took his ease for a little while on his bed, till it got dark, then, without putting things off, he dressed, put on his overcoat, and went out into the street. Where precisely the clerk who had invited him lived we regret to say that we cannot tell; our memory is beginning to fail sadly, and everything there in Petersburg, all the streets and houses, are so blurred and muddled in our head that it is a very difficult business to put anything in orderly fashion. However that may have been, there is no doubt that the clerk lived in the better part of the town and consequently a very long distance from Akaky Akakyevitch. At first, the latter had to walk through deserted streets, scantily lit, but as he approached his destination the streets became more lively, more full of people, and more brightly lit; passers-by began to be more frequent; ladies began to appear, here and there, beautifully dressed; beaver collars were to be seen on the men. Cabmen with wooden trelliswork sledges, studded with gilt nails, were less frequently to be met; on the other hand, jaunty drivers in raspberry-coloured velvet caps with varnished sledges and bearskin rugs appeared, and carriages with decorated boxes dashed along the streets, their wheels crunching through the snow. Akaky Akakyevitch looked at all this as a novelty; for several years he had not gone out into the streets in the evening. He stopped with curiosity before a lit shop-window to look at a picture in which a beautiful woman was represented in the act of taking off her shoe and displaying as she did so the whole of a very shapely leg, while behind her back a gentleman with whiskers and a handsome imperial on his chin was putting his head in at the door. Akaky Akakyevitch shook his head and smiled, and then went on his way. Why did he smile? Was it because he had come across something quite unfamiliar to him, though every man retains some instinctive feeling on the subject, or was it that he reflected, like many other clerks, as follows: 'Well, upon my soul, those Frenchmen! It's beyond anything! If they try anything of the sort, it really is . . . !' Though possibly he did not even think that; there is no creeping into a man's soul and finding out all that he thinks.

At last he reached the house in which the assistant of the head clerk lived in fine style; there was a lamp burning on the stairs, and the flat was on the second floor. As he went into the entry, Akaky Akakyevitch saw whole rows of galoshes. Amongst them in the middle of the room stood a samovar hissing and letting off clouds of steam. On the walls hung coats and cloaks, among which some actually had beaver collars or velvet revers. The other side of the wall there was noise and talk, which suddenly became clear and loud when the door opened and the footman came out with a tray full of empty glasses, a jug of cream and a basket of biscuits. It was evident that the clerks had arrived long before and had already drunk their first glass of tea. Akaky Akakyevitch, after hanging up his coat with his own hands, went into the room, and at the same moment there flashed before his eyes a vision of candles, clerks, pipes and card tables, together with the confused sounds of conversation rising up on all sides and the noise of moving chairs. He stopped very awkwardly in the middle of the room, looking about and trying to think what to do, but he was observed and received with a shout, and they all went at once into the entry and again took a look at his overcoat. Though Akaky Akakyevitch was somewhat embarrassed, yet, being a simple-hearted man, he could not help being pleased at seeing how they all admired his coat. Then of course they all abandoned him and his coat, and turned their attention as usual to the tables set for whist. All this – the noise, the talk, and the crowd of people – was strange to Akaky Akakyevitch. He simply did not know how to behave, what to do with his arms and legs and his whole figure; at last he sat down beside the players, looked at the cards, stared first at one and then at another of the faces, and in a little while began to yawn and felt that he was bored – especially as it was long past the time at which he usually went to bed. He tried to take leave of his hosts, but they would not let him go, saying that he absolutely must have a glass of champagne in honour of the new coat. An hour later supper was served, consisting of salad, cold veal, pasties, pies and tarts from the confectioner's, and champagne. They made Akaky Akakyevitch drink two glasses, after which he felt that things were much more cheerful, though he could not forget that it was twelve o'clock and that he ought to have been home long ago. That his host might not take it into his head to detain him, he slipped out of the room, hunted in the entry for his greatcoat, which he found, not without regret, lying on the floor, shook it, removed every last bit of fluff from it, put it on and went down the stairs into the street.

It was still light in the streets. Some little general shops, those perpetual clubs for house-serfs and all sorts of people, were open; others which were closed showed, however, a long streak of light at every crack of the door, proving that they were not yet deserted, and probably maids and menservants were still finishing their conversation and discussion, driving their masters to utter perplexity as to their whereabouts. Akaky Akakyevitch walked along in a cheerful state of mind; he was even on the point of running, goodness knows why, after a lady of some sort who passed by like lightning with every part of her frame in violent motion. He checked himself at once, however, and again walked along very gently, feeling positively surprised, himself, at the inexplicable impulse that had seized him. Soon the deserted streets, which are not particularly cheerful by day and even less so in the evening, stretched before him.

Now they were still more dead and deserted; the street lamps were scantier, the oil was evidently running low; then came wooden houses and fences; not a soul anywhere; only the snow gleamed on the streets and the low-pitched slumbering hovels looked black and gloomy with their closed shutters. He approached the spot where the street was intersected by an endless square, which looked like a fearful desert with houses scarcely visible on the further side. In the distance, goodness knows where, there was a gleam of light from some sentry-box which seemed to be standing at the end of the world. Akaky Akakyevitch's light-heartedness grew somehow sensibly less at this place. He stepped into the square, not without an involuntary uneasiness – as though his heart had a foreboding of evil. He looked behind him and to both sides – it was as though the sea were all round him. 'No, better not look,' he thought, and walked on, shutting his eyes, and when he opened them to see whether the end of the square were near, he suddenly saw standing before him, almost under his very nose, some men with moustaches; just what they were like he could not even distinguish. There was a mist before his eyes and a throbbing in his chest. 'I say the overcoat is mine!' said one of them in a voice like a clap of thunder, seizing him by the collar. Akaky Akakyevitch was on the point of shouting 'Help!' when another put a fist the size of a clerk's head against his very lips, saying, 'You just shout now.' Akaky Akakyevitch felt only that they took the overcoat off, and gave him a kick with their knees, and he fell on his face in the snow and was conscious of nothing more. A few minutes later he came to himself and got to his feet, but there was no one there. He felt that it was cold on the ground and that he had no overcoat, and began screaming, but it seemed as though his voice could not carry to the end of the square.

Overwhelmed with despair and continuing to scream, he ran across the square straight to the sentry-box, beside which stood a sentry leaning on his halberd and, so it seemed, looking with curiosity to see who the devil the man was who was screaming and running towards him from the distance. As Akaky Akakyevitch reached him, he began breathlessly shouting that he was asleep and not looking after his duty not to see that a man was being robbed. The sentry answered that he had seen nothing, that he had only seen him stopped in the middle of the square by two men, and supposed that they were his friends, and that, instead of abusing him for nothing, he had better go the next day to the superintendent and that he would find out who had taken the overcoat. Akaky Akakyevitch ran home in a terrible state: his hair, which was still comparatively abundant on his temples and the back of his head, was completely dishevelled; his sides and chest and his trousers were all covered with snow. When his old landlady heard a fearful knock at the door she jumped hurriedly out of bed and, with only one slipper on, ran to open it, modestly holding her shift across her bosom; but when she opened it she stepped back, seeing what a state Akaky Akakyevitch was in. When he told her what had happened, she clasped her hands in horror and said that he must go straight to the superintendent, that the police constable of the quarter would deceive him, make promises and lead him a dance; that it would be best of all to go to the superintendent, and that she knew him indeed, because Anna the Finnish girl who was once her cook was now in service as a nurse at the superintendent's, and that she often saw him himself when he passed by their house, and that he used to be every Sunday at church too, saying his prayers and at the same time looking good-humouredly at everyone, and that therefore by every token he must be a kind-hearted man. After listening to this advice, Akaky Akakyevitch made his way very gloomily to his room, and how he spent that night I leave to the imagination of those who are in the least able to picture the position of others. Early in the morning he set off to the police superintendent's, but was told that he was asleep. He came at ten o'clock, he was told again that he was asleep; he came at eleven and was told that the superintendent was not at home; he came at dinner-time, but the clerks in the anteroom would not let him in, and insisted on knowing what was the matter and what business had brought him and exactly what had happened; so that at last Akaky Akakyevitch for the first time in his life tried to show the strength of his character and said curtly that he must see the superintendent himself, that they dare not refuse to admit him, that he had come from the department on government business, and that if he made complaint of them they would see. The clerks dared say nothing to this, and one of them went to summon the superintendent. The latter received his story of being robbed of his overcoat in an extremely strange way.

Instead of attending to the main point, he began asking Akaky Akakyevitch questions. Why had he been coming home so late? Wasn't he going, or hadn't he been, to some house of ill-fame? Akaky Akakyevitch was overwhelmed with confusion, and went away without knowing whether or not the proper measures would be taken in regard to his overcoat. He was absent from the office all that day (the only time that it had happened in his life). Next day he appeared with a pale face, wearing his old 'dressing-jacket', which had become a still more pitiful sight. The tidings of the theft of the overcoat – though there were clerks who did not let even this chance slip of jeering at Akaky Akakyevitch – touched many of them. They decided on the spot to get up a subscription for him, but collected only a very trifling sum, because the clerks had already spent a good deal on subscribing to the director's portrait and on the purchase of a book, at the suggestion of the head of their department, who was a friend of the author, and so the total realised was very insignificant. One of the clerks, moved by compassion, ventured at any rate to assist Akaky Akakyevitch with good advice, telling him not to go to the district police inspector, because, though it might happen that the latter might be sufficiently zealous of gaining the approval of his superiors to succeed in finding the overcoat, it would remain in the possession of the police unless he presented legal proofs that it belonged to him; he urged that far the best thing would be to appeal to a Person of Consequence; that the Person of Consequence, by writing and getting into communication with the proper authorities, could push the matter through more successfully. There was nothing else for it. Akaky Akakyevitch made up his mind to go to the Person of Consequence. What precisely was the nature of the functions of the Person of Consequence has remained a matter of uncertainty. It must be noted that this Person of Consequence had only lately become a person of consequence, and until recently had been a person of no consequence. Though, indeed, his position even now was not reckoned of consequence in comparison with others of still greater consequence. But there is always to be found a circle of persons to whom a person of little consequence in the eyes of others is a person of consequence. It is true that he did his utmost to increase the consequence of his position in various ways, for instance by insisting that his subordinates should come out on to the stairs to meet him when he arrived at his office; that no one should venture to approach him directly but all proceedings should be by the strictest order of precedence, that a collegiate registration clerk should report the matter to the provincial secretary, and the provincial secretary to the titular councillor or whomsoever it might be, and that business should only reach him by this channel. Everyone in Holy Russia has a craze for imitation, everyone apes and mimics his superiors.

I have actually been told that a titular councillor who was put in charge of a small separate office, immediately partitioned off a special room for himself, calling it the head office, and set special porters at the door with red collars and gold braid, who took hold of the handle of the door and opened it for everyone who went in, though the 'head office' was so tiny that it was with difficulty that an ordinary writing-table could be squeezed into it. The manners and habits of the Person of Consequence were dignified and majestic, but not complex. The chief foundation of his system was strictness, 'strictness, strictness, and – strictness!' he used to say, and at the last word he would look very significantly at the person he was addressing, though, indeed, he had no reason to do so, for the dozen clerks who made the whole administrative mechanism of his office stood in befitting awe of him; any clerk who saw him in the distance would leave his work and remain standing at attention till his superior had left the room. His conversation with his subordinates was usually marked by severity and almost confined to three phrases: 'How dare you?'; 'Do you know to whom you are speaking?'; 'Do you understand who I am?' He was, however, at heart a good-natured man, pleasant and obliging with his colleagues; but the rank of general had completely turned his head. When he received it, he was perplexed, thrown off his balance, and quite at a loss how to behave. If he chanced to be with his equals, he was still quite a decent man, a very gentlemanly man, in fact, and in many ways even an intelligent man, but as soon as he was in company with men who were even one grade below him, there was simply no doing anything with him: he sat silent and his position excited compassion, the more so as he himself felt that he might have been spending his time to incomparably more advantage. At times there could be seen in his eyes an intense desire to join in some interesting conversation, but he was restrained by the doubt whether it would not be too much on his part, whether it would not be too great a familiarity and lowering of his dignity, and in consequence of these reflections he remained everlastingly in the same mute condition, only uttering from time to time monosyllabic sounds, and in this way he gained the reputation of being a very tiresome man.

So this was the Person of Consequence to whom our friend Akaky Akakyevitch appealed, and he appealed to him at a most unpropitious moment, very unfortunate for himself, though fortunate, indeed, for the Person of Consequence. The latter happened to be in his study, talking in the very best of spirits with an old friend of his childhood who had only just arrived and whom he had not seen for several years. It was at this moment that he was informed that a man called Bashmatchkin was asking to see him. He asked abruptly, 'What sort of man is he?' and received the answer, 'A government clerk.'

'Ah! He can wait, I haven't time now,' said the Person of

Consequence. Here I must observe that this was a complete lie on the part of the Person of Consequence: he had time; his friend and he had long ago said all they had to say to each other, and their conversation had begun to be broken by very long pauses during which they merely slapped each other on the knee, saying, 'So that's how things are, Ivan Abramovitch!' – 'There it is, Stepan Varlamovitch!' but, for all that, he told the clerk to wait in order to show his friend, who had left the service years before and was living at home in the country, how long clerks had to wait in his anteroom. At last, after they had talked, or rather been silent to their hearts' content, and had smoked a cigar in very comfortable armchairs with sloping backs, he seemed suddenly to recollect, and said to the secretary, who was standing at the door with papers for his signature, 'Oh, by the way, there is a clerk waiting, isn't there? Tell him he can come in.' When he saw Akaky Akakyevitch's meek appearance and old uniform, he turned to him at once and said, 'What do you want?' in a firm and abrupt voice, which he had purposely practised in his own room in solitude before the looking-glass for a week before receiving his present post and the rank of general. Akaky Akakyevitch, who was overwhelmed with befitting awe beforehand, was somewhat confused and, as far as his tongue would allow him, explained to the best of his powers, with even more frequent 'ers' than usual, that he had had a perfectly new overcoat and now he had been robbed of it in the most inhuman way, and that now he had come to beg him by his intervention either to correspond with his Honour the Head Police-Master or anybody else, and find the overcoat. This mode of proceeding struck the general for some reason as taking a great liberty. 'What next, sir?' he went on as abruptly. 'Don't you know the way to proceed? To whom are you addressing yourself? Don't you know how things are done? You ought first to have handed in a petition to the office; it would have gone to the head clerk of the room, and to the head clerk of the section, then it would have been handed to the secretary and the secretary would have brought it to me . . .'

'But, your Excellency,' said Akaky Akakyevitch, trying to collect all the small allowance of presence of mind he possessed and feeling at the same time that he was getting into a terrible perspiration, 'I ventured, your Excellency, to trouble you because secretaries . . . er . . . are people you can't depend on . . .'

'What? what? what?' said the Person of Consequence. 'Where did you get hold of that spirit? Where did you pick up such ideas? What insubordination is spreading among young men against their superiors and betters!'

The Person of Consequence did not apparently observe that Akaky Akakyevitch was well over fifty, and therefore if he could have been called a young man it would only have been in comparison with a man of seventy. 'Do you know to whom you are speaking? Do you understand who I am? Do you understand that, I ask you?' At this point he stamped, and raised his voice to such a powerful note that Akaky Akakyevitch would not have been alone in being terrified. Akaky Akakyevitch was positively petrified; he staggered, trembling all over, and could not stand; if the porters had not run up to support him, he would have flopped upon the floor; he was carried out almost unconscious. The Person of Consequence, pleased that the effect had surpassed his expectations and enchanted at the idea that his words could even deprive a man of consciousness, stole a sideways glance at his friend to see how he was taking it, and perceived not without satisfaction that his friend was feeling very uncertain and even beginning to be a little terrified himself. How he got downstairs, how he went out into the street – of all that Akaky Akakyevitch remembered nothing, he had no feeling in his arms or his legs. In all his life he had never been so severely reprimanded by a general, and this was by one of another department, too. He went out into the snowstorm, that was whistling through the streets, with his mouth open, and as he went he stumbled off the pavement; the wind, as its way is in Petersburg, blew upon him from all points of the compass and from every side street. In an instant it had blown a quinsy into his throat, and when he got home he was not able to utter a word; with a swollen face and throat he went to bed. So violent is sometimes the effect of a suitable reprimand!

Next day he was in a high fever. Thanks to the gracious assistance of the Petersburg climate, the disease made more rapid progress than could have been expected, and when the doctor came, after feeling his pulse he could find nothing to do but prescribe a fomentation, and that simply that the patient may not be left without the benefit of medical assistance; however, at the same time, he said that within two days the patient would be kaput, after which he turned to the landlady and said: 'And you had better lose no time, my good woman, but order him now a pine coffin – an oak one will be too dear for him.' Whether Akaky Akakyevitch heard these fateful words or not, whether they produced a shattering effect upon him, and whether he regretted his pitiful life, no one can tell, for he was all the time in delirium and fever.

Apparitions, each stranger than the one before, were continually haunting him: first, he saw Petrovitch and was ordering him to make a greatcoat trimmed with some sort of traps for robbers, who were, he fancied, continually under the bed, and he was calling his landlady every minute to pull out a thief who had even got under the quilt; then he kept asking why his old 'dressing-jacket' was hanging before him when he had a new overcoat, then he fancied he was standing before the general listening to the appropriate reprimand and saying, 'I am sorry, your Excellency,' then finally he became abusive, uttering the most awful language, so that his old landlady positively crossed herself, having never heard anything of the kind from him before, and the more horrified because these dreadful words followed immediately upon the phrase 'your Excellency'. Later on, his talk was a mere medley of nonsense, so that it was quite unintelligible; all that could be seen was that his incoherent words and thoughts were concerned with nothing but the overcoat. At last poor Akaky Akakyevitch gave up the ghost. No seal was put upon his room nor upon his things, because, in the first place, he had no heirs and, in the second, the property left was very small, to wit: a bundle of goose-feathers, a quire of white government paper, three pairs of socks, two or three buttons that had come off his trousers, and the 'dressing-jacket' with which the reader is already familiar. Who came into all this wealth God only knows; even I who tell the tale must own that I have not troubled to enquire. And Petersburg remained without Akaky Akakyevitch, as though, indeed, he had never been in the city. A creature had vanished and departed whose cause no one had championed, who was dear to no one, of interest to no one, who never even attracted the attention of the student of natural history, though the latter does not disdain to fix a common fly upon a pin and look at him under the microscope – a creature who bore patiently the jeers of the office and for no particular reason went to his grave, though even he at the very end of his life was visited by a gleam of brightness in the form of an overcoat that for one instant brought colour into his poor life – a creature on whom calamity broke as insufferably as it breaks upon the heads of the mighty ones of this world . . . ! Several days after his death, the porter from the department was sent to his lodgings with instructions that he should go at once to the office, for his chief was asking for him; but the porter was obliged to return without him, explaining that he could not come, and to the enquiry 'Why?' he added, 'Well, you see: the fact is he is dead, he was buried three days ago.' This was how they learned at the office of the death of Akaky Akakyevitch, and the next day there was sitting in his seat a new clerk who was very much taller and who wrote not in the same upright hand but made his letters more slanting and crooked.

But who could have imagined that this was not all there was to tell about Akaky Akakyevitch, that he was destined for a few days to make a noise in the world after his death, as though to make up for his life having been unnoticed by anyone? But so it happened, and our poor story unexpectedly finishes with a fantastic ending. Rumours were suddenly floating about Petersburg that in the neighbourhood of Kalinkin Bridge and for a little distance beyond, a corpse had taken to appearing at night in the form of a clerk looking for a stolen overcoat, and stripping from the shoulders of all passers-by, regardless of rank and calling, overcoats of all descriptions – trimmed with cat fur or beaver, or wadded, lined with raccoon, fox and bear – made, in fact, of all sorts of skin which men have adapted for the covering of their own. One of the clerks of the department saw the corpse with his own eyes and at once recognised it as Akaky Akakyevitch; but it excited in him such terror, however, that he ran away as fast as his legs could carry him and so could not get a very clear view of him, and only saw him hold up his finger threateningly in the distance. From all sides complaints were continually coming that backs and shoulders, not of mere titular councillors, but even of upper-court councillors, had been exposed to taking chills, owing to being stripped of their greatcoats. Orders were given to the police to catch the corpse regardless of trouble or expense, alive or dead, and to punish him in the cruellest way, as an example to others, and, indeed, they very nearly succeeded in doing so. The sentry of one district police station in Kiryushkin Place snatched a corpse by the collar on the spot of the crime in the very act of attempting to snatch a frieze overcoat from a retired musician, who used in his day to play the flute. Having caught him by the collar, he shouted until he had brought two other comrades, whom he chargèd to hold him while he felt just a minute in his boot to get out a snuffbox in order to revive his nose which had six times in his life been frostbitten, but the snuff was probably so strong that not even a dead man could stand it. The sentry had hardly had time to put his finger over his right nostril and draw up some snuff in the left when the corpse sneezed violently right into the eyes of all three. While they were putting their fists up to wipe them, the corpse completely vanished, so that they were not even sure whether he had actually been in their hands. From that time forward, the sentries conceived such a horror of the dead that they were even afraid to seize the living and confined themselves to shouting from the distance, 'Hey, you there, be off!' and the dead clerk began to appear even on the other side of Kalinkin Bridge, rousing no little terror in all timid people. We have, however, quite deserted the Person of Consequence, who may in reality almost be said to be the cause of the fantastic ending of this perfectly true story.

To begin with, my duty requires me to do justice to the Person of Consequence by recording that soon after poor Akaky Akakyevitch had gone away crushed to powder, he felt something not unlike regret. Sympathy was a feeling not unknown to him; his heart was open to many kindly impulses, although his exalted grade very often prevented them from being shown. As soon as his friend had gone out of his study, he even began brooding over poor Akaky Akakyevitch, and from that time forward, he was almost every day haunted by the image of the poor clerk who had succumbed so completely to the befitting reprimand. The thought of the man so worried him that a week later he actually decided to send a clerk to find out how he was and whether he really could help him in any way. And when they brought him word that Akaky Akakyevitch had died suddenly in delirium and fever, it made a great impression on him, his conscience reproached him and he was in a bad mood all day. Anxious to distract his mind and to forget the unpleasant impression, he went to spend the evening with one of his friends, where he found a genteel company and, what was best of all, almost everyone was of the same grade so that he was able to be quite free from restraint. This had a wonderful effect on his spirits; he expanded, became affable and genial – in short, spent a very agreeable evening. At supper he drank a couple of glasses of champagne – a proceeding which we all know has a happy effect in inducing good humour. The champagne made him inclined to do something unusual, and he decided not to go home yet but to visit a lady of his acquaintance, one Karolina Ivanovna – a lady apparently of German extraction, for whom he entertained extremely friendly feelings. It must be noted that the Person of Consequence was a man no longer young, an excellent husband, and the respectable father of a family. He had two sons, one already serving in his office, and a nice-looking daughter of sixteen with a rather turned-up, pretty little nose, who used to come every morning to kiss his hand, saying: '*Bonjour*, Papa.' His wife, who was still blooming and decidedly good-looking, indeed, used first to give him her hand to kiss and then would kiss his hand, turning it the other side upwards. But though the Person of Consequence was perfectly satisfied with the kind amenities of his domestic life, he thought it proper to have a lady friend in another quarter of the town. This lady friend was not a bit better looking nor younger than his wife, but these mysterious facts exist in the world and it is not our business to criticise them.

And so the Person of Consequence went downstairs, got into his sledge, and said to his coachman, 'To Karolina

Ivanovna,' while, luxuriously wrapped in his warm fur coat, he remained in that agreeable frame of mind sweeter to a Russian than anything that could be invented; that is, when one thinks of nothing while thoughts come into the mind of themselves, one pleasanter than the other, without the labour of following them or looking for them. Full of satisfaction, he recalled all the amusing moments of the evening he had spent, all the phrases that had set the little circle laughing; many of them he repeated in an undertone and found them as amusing as before, and so, very naturally, chuckled very heartily at them again. From time to time, however, he was disturbed by a gust of wind which, blowing suddenly, God knows whence and wherefore, cut him in the face, pelting him with flakes of snow, puffing out his coat collar like a sack, or suddenly flinging it with unnatural force over his head and giving him endless trouble to extricate himself from it. All at once, the Person of Consequence felt that someone had clutched him very tightly by the collar. Turning round, he saw a short man in a shabby old uniform, and not without horror recognised him as Akaky Akakyevitch. The clerk's face was white as snow and looked like that of a corpse, but the horror of the Person of Consequence was beyond all bounds when he saw the mouth of the corpse distorted into speech and, breathing upon him the chill of the grave, it uttered the following words: 'Ah, so here you are at last! At last I've . . . er . . . caught you by the collar. It's your overcoat I want, you refused to help me and abused me into the bargain! So now give me yours!' The poor Person of Consequence very nearly died. Resolute and determined as he was in his office and before subordinates in general, and though anyone looking at his manly air and figure would have said, 'Oh, what a man of character!' yet in this plight he felt, like very many persons of athletic appearance, such terror that not without reason he began to be afraid he would have some sort of fit. He actually flung his overcoat off his shoulders as fast as he could and shouted to his coachman in a voice unlike his own, 'Drive home and make haste!' The coachman, hearing the tone which he had only heard in critical moments and then accompanied by something even more rousing, hunched his shoulders up to his ears in case of worse following, swung his whip and flew on like an arrow. In a little over six minutes the Person of Consequence was at the entrance of his own house. Pale, panic-stricken, and without his overcoat, he arrived home, instead of at Karolina Ivanovna's, dragged himself to his own room and spent the night in great perturbation, so that next morning his daughter said to him at breakfast, 'You look quite pale today, Papa,' but her papa remained mute and said/not a word to anyone of what had happened to him, where he had been, and where he had been going.

The incident made a great impression upon him. Indeed, it happened far more rarely that he said to his subordinates, 'How dare you? Do you understand who I am?' and he never uttered those words at all until he had first heard all the rights of the case.

What was even more remarkable is that from that time the apparition of the dead clerk ceased entirely. Apparently the general's overcoat had fitted him perfectly; anyway, nothing more was heard of overcoats being snatched from anyone. Many restless and anxious people refused, however, to be pacified, and still maintained that in remote parts of the town the ghost of the dead clerk went on appearing. One sentry in Kolomna, for instance, saw with his own eyes a ghost appear from behind a house; but, being by natural constitution somewhat feeble – so much so that on one occasion an ordinary, mature piglet, making a sudden dash out of some building, knocked him off his feet to the vast entertainment of the cabmen standing round, from whom he exacted two kopecks each for snuff for such rudeness – he did not dare to stop it, and so followed it in the dark until the ghost suddenly looked round and, stopping, asked him, 'What do you want?' displaying a fist such as you never see even among the living. The sentry said, 'Nothing,' and turned back on the spot. This ghost, however, was considerably taller and adorned with immense moustaches, and, directing its steps apparently towards Obuhov Bridge, vanished into the darkness of the night.

The Story of Captain Kopeykin

(from Chapter 10, *Dead Souls*)

WHEN THEY MET AT the house of the police-master, already known to the reader as the father and benefactor of the town, the officials had the opportunity of observing of each other that they had actually grown thin through all these worries and anxieties. And, indeed, the appointment of a new governor-general, and the two documents of so serious a character, and these extraordinary rumours, had, all taken together, left a perceptible imprint on their faces, and the dress-coats of some of them had become noticeably looser. Everything was changed for the worse: the president was thinner, and the inspector of the medical board was thinner, and the prosecutor was thinner, and one Semyon

Ivanovitch, who was never called by his surname, and wore on his first finger a ring which he used to show to ladies — even he was thinner. Of course there were some bold spirits, as there always are, who did not lose their presence of mind; but they were not many; in fact the postmaster was the only one. He alone was unchanged in his invariable composure, and always when such things happened was in the habit of saying:

'We know all about you governor-generals! You may be changed three or four times over, but I have been for thirty years in the same place, my good sir.'

To this the other officials usually answered: 'It's all very well for you, *Sprechen Sie Deutsch*, Ivan Andreitch: the post office is your job — receiving and dispatching the mail; the worst you can do is to close the post office an hour too early if you are in a bad temper, or to accept a late letter from some merchant at the wrong hour, or to send off some parcel which ought not to be sent off — anyone would be a saint, of course, in your place. But suppose you had the devil at your elbow every day, so that even what you don't want to take he thrusts upon you. You have not much to fear, to be sure; you have only one son; while God has been so bountiful to Praskovya Fyodorovna, my boy, that not a year passes but she presents me with a little Praskovya or a little Petrushka; in our place, you'd sing a different tune, my boy.'

So said the officials, but whether it is really possible to resist the devil it is not for the author to decide. In the council assembled on this occasion, there was a conspicuous absence of that essential thing which among the common people is called good sense. We seem somehow not made for representative institutions. In all our assemblies, from the meetings of the peasants up to all kinds of learned and other committees, there is a pretty thorough muddle, unless there is someone at the head who is managing it all. It is hard to say why it is. Apparently the nature of the Russian people is such, that the only successful committees are those formed to arrange entertainments, or dinners, such as clubs, or pleasure gardens in the German style. Yet we are always ready at any minute for anything. We fly like the wind to get up benevolent and philanthropic societies and goodness knows what. The aim may be excellent but nothing ever comes of it. Perhaps it is because we are satisfied at the very beginning and consider everything has already been done.

For instance, after organising a society for the benefit of the poor, and subscribing a considerable sum, we immediately spend half of the fund subscribed on giving a dinner to all the worthies of the town in celebration of our laudable enterprise; with what is left of our funds we promptly take a grand house with heating arrangements and porters for the use of the committee; after which five roubles and a half is all that is left for the poor, and over the distribution of that sum, the members of the committee cannot agree, each one urging the claims of some crony of his own. The committee that met on this occasion was of quite another kind: it was formed through urgent necessity. It was not a question of the poor or of outsiders at all: it concerned every official personally: the occasion was a calamity which threatened all alike, and so the meeting should have been more unanimous and more united. But for all that, the result was awfully queer. To say nothing of the differences of opinion that crop up at every meeting, an inexplicable indecisiveness was apparent in the views of all present; one said that Tchitchikov was a forger of government notes, and then added, 'Though perhaps he isn't a forger'; another declared that he was an official in the governor-general's office, and at once went on, 'Though the devil only knows, it is not branded on his forehead.' All were opposed to the suggestion that he was a brigand in disguise. They considered that, besides his appearance, which was highly respectable, there was nothing in his conversation to suggest a man given to deeds of violence. All at once the postmaster, who had been standing for some minutes lost in meditation, cried out suddenly from some inspiration or from something else:

'Do you know who he is, my friends?'

There was something so striking in the voice in which he uttered this, that it made them all cry out with one voice: 'Who?'

'He is no other than Captain Kopeykin, gentlemen!'

And when they all instantly asked with one voice, 'Who is Captain Kopeykin?' the postmaster said:

'Why, don't you know who Captain Kopeykin is?'

They all answered that they did not know who Captain Kopeykin was.

'Captain Kopeykin,' said the postmaster, opening his snuffbox only a little way for fear that some of his neighbours should take a pinch with fingers in whose cleanliness he had no confidence – he was, indeed, in the habit of saying, 'We know, my good sir, there is no telling where your fingers have been, and snuff's a thing that must be kept clean.'

'Captain Kopeykin,' he repeated as he took a pinch, 'why, you know if I were to tell you, it would make a regular romance after a fashion, very interesting to any author.'

Everyone present expressed a desire to hear this story, or as the postmaster expressed it, a regular romance after a fashion, very interesting to any author, and he began as follows:

'After the campaign of 1812, my good sir –' so the postmaster began his story, regardless of the fact that not one but six gentlemen were sitting in the room – 'after the campaign of 1812, Captain Kopeykin was sent back with the wounded. A hot-headed fellow, as whimsical as the devil, he had been punished in various ways and been under arrest – there was nothing he had not had a taste of. Whether it was at Krasnoe or at Leipzig I can't say but, can you fancy, he had an arm and a leg blown off. Well, at that time, no arrangements had been made, you know, about the wounded; that – what do you call it? – pension fund for the wounded was only set going, can you fancy, long afterwards. Captain Kopeykin saw that he would have to work, but he only had one arm, you understand, the left. He went home to his father's. His father said, "I can't keep you, I can scarcely –" only fancy – "get a crust of bread for myself." So my Captain Kopeykin made up his mind to go to Petersburg, my good sir, to see whether he could get help from the authorities, to put it to them, in a manner of speaking, that he had sacrificed his life and shed his blood . . . Well, in one way or another, on a train of waggons, you know, or on the government vans, he got at last to Petersburg, my good sir. Well, can you fancy, here what-do-you-call-him, I mean Captain Kopeykin, found himself in the capital, the like of which, in a manner of speaking, there is not in the world! All at once a world, in a manner of speaking, lies before him, a certain plane of life, a fairy tale of Scheherazade, you understand.

All at once, can you fancy, Nevsky Prospect or Gorohovaya, dash it all, or Liteiny; there is a spire of some sort in the air; the bridges hang there like the devil, only fancy, without any support, that is, in short, a Semiramis, sir, and that's the only word for it! He made some attempts to get lodgings, only it was all terribly dear: curtains, blinds, all sorts of devilry, you understand, carpets – Persia, sir, in short . . . in a manner of speaking, you trample fortunes under foot. You walk along the street and your very nose can sniff the thousands: and all my Captain Kopeykin's banking account consisted of was some fifty roubles and some small silver . . .

'Well, you can't buy an estate with that, you know, you might buy one perhaps, if you added forty thousand to it, but you would have to borrow the forty thousand from the King of France; well, he found a refuge in a tavern for a rouble a day; dinner – cabbage soup, a piece of beef-steak . . . He sees it won't do to stay there long. He makes enquiries where he is to apply. "Where are you to apply?" they say. "The higher authorities are not in Petersburg yet." They were all in Paris, you understand, the troops had not come back yet. "But there is a temporary committee," they tell him. "You had better try there, maybe they can do something." "I'll go to the committee," says Kopeykin. "I'll say that I have, in a manner of speaking, shed my blood, that in a sense I have sacrificed my life." So, sir, getting up early he combed his beard with his left hand, for to pay a barber would be in a certain sense to run up a bill, he pulled on his shabby uniform and stumped off, only fancy, on his wooden leg to the chief of the committee. He enquired where the chief lives. "Over yonder," they tell him, "a house on the embankment": a poor hovel, you understand, glass panes in the windows, only fancy, mirrors ten feet across, marbles, footmen, my good sir, in fact, enough to turn you giddy.

‘A metal handle on the door – a luxury of the highest class so that one would have to run to the shop, you know, and buy a ha'p'orth of soap and scrub away at one's hands for a couple of hours in a manner of speaking, and then perhaps one might venture to take hold of the handle. A porter at the door, you understand, with a stick in his hand, a face like a count's, a cambric collar, like some fat, overfed pug dog . . . My Kopeykin dragged himself somehow on his wooden leg to the reception room, squeezed himself into a corner for fear he might jerk his elbow against some American or Indian, only fancy, gilt china vase of some sort. Well, I need hardly say he had to wait till he had had enough, for he arrived at the hour when the chief was, in a manner of speaking, just getting out of bed, and his valet had just brought him a silver basin for washing and all that, don't you know. My Kopeykin waits for four hours, and then the clerk on duty comes in and says: "The director will be here directly." And the room was full up by then with epaulettes and shoulder knots, as many people as beans on a plate. At last, my good sir, the director comes in. Well . . . Can you imagine . . . The director! In his face, so to say . . . well in keeping, you understand, . . . with his position and his rank . . . such an expression, you know. He had a tip-top manner in every way; he goes up first to one and then to another: "What have you come about? What do you want? What is your business?"

'At last, my good sir, he goes up to Kopeykin. Kopeykin says one thing and another.

'"I have shed my blood, I have lost my arms and legs, I can't work – I make bold to ask, will there not be some assistance, some sort of an arrangement in regard to compensation, so to speak, a pension or something?" You understand.

'The director sees that the man has got a wooden leg and that his right sleeve is empty and pinned to his uniform.

'"Very good," he says, "come again in a day or two."

'My Kopeykin is highly delighted. "Come," he thinks, "the matter's settled." He hops along the pavement in such spirits as you can fancy, goes into the Palkinsky restaurant, drinks a glass of vodka, dines, my good sir, at the London restaurant, orders cutlets with caper sauce, a chicken with all sorts of trimmings, asks for a bottle of wine, and in the evening goes to the theatre – in fact he has a jolly good time, so to say. In the street he sees a graceful English girl, floating along like a swan, only fancy. My Kopeykin – his blood was a little heated, you understand – was just about to run after her on his wooden leg, tap-tap along the pavement. "But no," he thought, "to the devil with dangling after ladies for the time being! Better later on, when I get my pension. I have let myself go a little too much as it is." And meanwhile he had spent almost half his money in one day, I beg you to observe.

'Three or four days later he goes to the committee to see the director.

'"I have come," he said, "to hear what you have for me, owing to the illnesses and wounds I have sustained . . . I have in a sense shed my blood . . ." and that sort of thing, you understand, in the language suitable.

'"Well," said the director, "I must tell you first of all that we can do nothing in your case without instructions from the higher command. You see yourself the position. Military operations are, in a manner of speaking, not completely over yet. You must wait till the minister arrives, you must have patience. Then you may be sure you won't be overlooked. And if you have nothing to live upon, here," he said, "here is something to help you . . ."

'And what he gave him, you understand, was not very much, though with prudence it might have lasted till further instructions came. But that was not what my Kopeykin wanted. He had been reckoning on their paying him a thousand roubles down or something of the sort, with "There you are, my dear boy, drink and make merry," and instead of that, "You can wait," and no date fixed either. And already, you know, he had visions of the English girl and little suppers and cutlets. So he went down the steps as glum as an owl, looking like a poodle that has been drenched with water, with its ears drooping and its tail between its legs. Life in Petersburg had already got a hold on him, he had had some taste of it already. And now there was no knowing how he was to live, and he had no hope of any luxuries, you understand. And you know he was full of life and health and he had the appetite of a wolf. He passes some restaurant; and the cook there, only fancy, a Frenchman of some sort with an open countenance, with a linen shirt, an apron as white, in a manner of speaking, as snow, is making *fines herbes* or cutlets with truffles, in fact all sorts of such delicacies that it would give one appetite enough to eat oneself.

'He passes Milyutinsky's shop, there is a salmon looking out of the window, in a manner of speaking, cherries at five roubles the measure. A huge watermelon as big as an omnibus peeps out of the window and seems to be looking for someone fool enough to pay a hundred roubles for it – in short, there is temptation at every step, his mouth watering, so to speak, and he must wait. So imagine his position: here on one side, so to say, there is salmon and watermelon, while on the other side they present him with the bitter dish called "tomorrow". "Well," he thinks, "they can do as they like, but I will go," he says, "and rouse all the committee, everyone in authority. I shall say, 'Do as you like.'" And he certainly was a persistent, impudent fellow, no sense in his head, you understand, but plenty of bounce. He goes to the committee: "Well, what is it?" they say. "Why are you back again? You have been told already."

'"I can't scrape along anyhow," he says. "I want to eat a cutlet, have a bottle of French wine, enjoy myself in the theatre too, you understand . . ."

'"Well, you must excuse me," said the director. "For all that you must, in a manner of speaking, have patience. You have been given something to keep you for the time, till instructions arrive, and no doubt you will be properly pensioned, for it has never happened yet that among us in Russia a man who has, in a manner of speaking, deserved well of his country should be left without recognition. But if you want to pamper yourself with cutlets and the theatre, then you must excuse me. In that case, you must find the means and do what you can for yourself."

'But my Kopeykin, can you fancy, did not turn a hair. Those words bounced off him like peas against a wall. He made such an uproar, he did let them have it! He began going for them all and swearing at them, all of them, the head clerks and the secretaries. "You are this," he said, "you are that," he said, "you don't know your duties," he said. He gave them all a dressing. A general turned up, you know, from quite a different department; he went for him too, my good sir! He made such a row. What's to be done with a beggar like that? The director sees that they must have recourse, so to say, to stern measures.

'"Very good," he says, "if you won't be satisfied with what is given you, and wait quietly, in a manner of speaking, here in the capital for your case to be settled, I will find a lodging for you elsewhere. Call the attendant," he said, "take him to a place of detention!"

'And the attendant was there already, you understand, at the door, a man seven feet high, with a great fist made by nature for a driver, only fancy, a regular dentist, in fact . . . So they put him, the servant of God, into a cart, with the attendant. "Well," thinks Kopeykin, "I shan't have to pay my fare, anyway, that is something to be thankful for." He goes in the cart, and as he goes he thinks: "Very good," he thinks, "you told me I must find means for myself; very good, I will find them!" Well, how they took him to his destination and where he was taken, no one knows. All traces of Captain Kopeykin were lost, you understand, in the waters of oblivion, in Lethe, or whatever the poets call it. But here, gentlemen, allow me to point out, begins the gist of the story.

'What became of Kopeykin no one knows, but before two months had passed, would you believe it, a band of robbers made their appearance in the forests of Ryazan and the chief of that band, my good sir, was no other than . . .'

Nevsky Prospect

THERE IS NOTHING FINER than Nevsky Prospect, not in Petersburg anyway: it is the making of the city. What splendour does it lack, that fairest of our city thoroughfares? I know that no one among its pale and bureaucratic residents would exchange Nevsky Prospect for all the blessings of the world. Not only the young man of twenty-five summers with a fine moustache and a splendidly cut coat, but even the veteran with white hairs sprouting on his chin and a head as smooth as a silver dish is in ecstasy over Nevsky Prospect. And the ladies! Oh, Nevsky Prospect is even more attractive to the ladies. And indeed to whom is it not attractive? As soon as you step into Nevsky Prospect, there is a whiff of gaiety. Though you may have some necessary and urgent work to do, yet as soon as you are there you forget all about business. This is the one place where people put in an appearance without necessity, without being driven there by the needs and commercial interests that swallow up all Petersburg. A man met on Nevsky Prospect seems less of an egoist than on Morskaya, Gorokhovoy, Liteiny, Meshansky and other streets, where covetousness, self-interest and need are apparent in all those walking by or flying past in carriages and droshkies. Nevsky Prospect is the general channel of communication in Petersburg. The man who lives on the Petersburg or Viborg Side who hasn't seen his friend at Peski or at the Moscow Gate for years may reckon with certainty on meeting him in Nevsky Prospect. No directory list at an Address Enquiry Office gives such accurate information as Nevsky Prospect. All-powerful Nevsky Prospect! A unique place of entertainment in Petersburg, a city poor in such diversions! How cleanly swept are its pavements, and, my God, how many feet leave their traces on it! The clumsy, dirty boots of the discharged soldier, under whose weight the very granite seems to crack, and the miniature, ethereal little shoes of the young lady who turns her head towards the glittering shop-windows as the sunflower to the sun, and the clanking sabre of the hopeful lieutenant which marks a sharp scratch along it – all print the scars of strength or weakness on it! What rapid phantasms pass over it in a single day! What changes it goes through between one dawn and the next! Let us begin with the earliest morning when all Petersburg smells of hot, freshly baked bread and is filled with old women in ragged gowns and pelisses who are making their raids on the churches and on compassionate passers-by.

Then Nevsky Prospect is empty: the stout shopkeepers and their assistants are still asleep in their linen shirts or washing their genteel cheeks and drinking their coffee; beggars gather near the doors of the confectioners' shops where the drowsy Ganymede who the day before flew round like a fly with chocolate, walks out with no cravat on, broom in hand, and thrusts stale pies and scraps upon them. Working people move to and fro about the streets: sometimes *muzhiks* cross it, hurrying to their work, in high boots caked with mortar which even the Ekaterinsky canal, famous for its cleanness, could not wash off. At this hour it is not proper for ladies to walk out, because Russian people like to explain their meaning in rude expressions such as they would not hear even in a theatre. Sometimes a drowsy government clerk trudges along with a portfolio under his arm, if the way to his department lies through Nevsky Prospect. It may be confidently stated that at this period, that is, up to twelve o'clock, Nevsky Prospect is for no man the goal, but simply the means of reaching it:

it is gradually filled with people who have their occupations, their anxieties and their annoyances, and are thinking nothing about it. Russian *muzhiks* talk about ten kopecks or seven coppers, old men and women wave their hands or talk to themselves, sometimes with very striking gesticulations, but no one listens to them or laughs at them with the exception perhaps of street boys in homespun smocks, darting like lightning along Nevsky Prospect with empty bottles or pairs of boots from the cobblers in their arms. At that hour you may put on what you like, and even if you wear a cap instead of a hat, or the ends of your collar stick out too far from your cravat, no one notices it.

At twelve o'clock tutors of all nationalities make a descent upon Nevsky Prospect with their young charges in fine cambric collars. English Joneses and French Coques walk arm in arm with the nurselings entrusted to their parental care, and with becoming dignity explain to them that the signboards over the shops are put there that people may know what is to be found within. Governesses, pale Misses and rosy Slavs, walk majestically behind their light and nimble charges, bidding them hold themselves more upright or lift a shoulder slightly; in short, at this hour Nevsky Prospect is pedagogical Nevsky Prospect. But as two o'clock approaches, the governesses, tutors and children are fewer; and finally are crowded out by their tender papas walking arm in arm with their gaudy, variegated and hysterical spouses.

Gradually these are joined by all who have finished their rather important domestic duties, such as talking to the doctor about the weather and the pimple that has come out on their nose, enquiring after the health of their horses and their promising and gifted children, reading in the newspaper a leading article and the announcements of the arrivals and departures, and finally drinking a cup of tea or coffee. They are joined, too, by those whose enviable destiny has called them to the blessed vocation of clerks on special commissions. And they are joined, too, by those who serve in the Department of Foreign Affairs and are distinguished by the dignity of their pursuits and their habits. My God, what splendid positions and duties there are! How they elevate and sweeten the soul! But, alas, I am not in the service and am denied the pleasure of watching the refined behaviour of my superiors. Everyone you meet on Nevsky Prospect is brimming over with propriety: the men in long surtouts with their hands in their pockets, the ladies in pink, white or pale blue satin redingotes and hats. Here you meet unique whiskers, drooping with extraordinary and amazing elegance below the cravat, velvety, satiny whiskers, as black as sable or as coal, but, alas, invariably the property only of members of the Department of Foreign

Affairs. Providence has denied black whiskers to clerks in other departments; they are forced, to their great disgust, to wear red ones. Here you meet marvellous moustaches that no pen, no brush, could do justice to, moustaches to which the better part of a life has been devoted, the objects of prolonged care by day and by night; moustaches upon which enchanting perfumes are sprinkled and on which the rarest and most expensive kinds of pomade are lavished; moustaches which are twisted up at night in thin curl-papers; moustaches to which their possessors display the most touching devotion and which are the envy of passers-by. Thousands of varieties of hats, dresses and kerchiefs, flimsy and bright-coloured, for which their owners feel sometimes an adoration that lasts two whole days, dazzle everyone on Nevsky Prospect. A whole sea of butterflies seem to have flown up from their flower-stalks and to be floating in a glittering cloud above the black beetles of the male sex. Here you meet the waists of slim delicacy beyond one's dreams of elegance, no thicker than a bottle-neck, and respectfully step aside for fear of a careless nudge with a discourteous elbow; your heart beats with apprehension lest from an incautious breath the exquisite product of art and nature may be snapped in two. And the ladies' sleeves that you meet on Nevsky Prospect! Ah, how exquisite!

They are like two air balloons so that the lady might

suddenly float up into the air, were she not held down by the gentleman accompanying her; for it would be as easy and agreeable for a lady to be lifted into the air as for a glass of champagne to be lifted to the lips. Nowhere do people bow with such dignity and ease as on Nevsky Prospect. Here you meet with a unique smile, a smile that is the acme of art, that will sometimes melt you with pleasure, sometimes make you bow your head and feel lower than the grass, sometimes make you hold it high and feel loftier than the Admiralty spire. Here you meet people conversing about a concert or the weather with extraordinary dignity and sense of their own consequence. Here you meet a thousand incredible types and figures. Good heavens! What strange characters are met on Nevsky Prospect! There are numbers of people who, when they meet you, invariably stare at your boots, and when they have passed, turn around to have a look at the skirts of your coat. I have never been able to make out why it is. At first I thought they were bootmakers, but not a bit of it: they are for the most part clerks in various departments, many of them are very good at referring a case from one department to another; or they are people who spend their time walking about or reading the paper in restaurants – in fact they are usually very respectable people. In this blessed period between two and three o'clock in the afternoon, which might be called the moving centre of

Nevsky Prospect, there is a display of all the finest products of the wit of man. One exhibits a smart overcoat with the best beaver on it; the second – a lovely Greek nose; the third – superb whiskers; the fourth – a pair of pretty eyes and a marvellous hat; the fifth – a signet ring on a jaunty forefinger; the sixth – a foot in a bewitching shoe; the seventh – a cravat that excites wonder; and the eighth – a moustache that reduces one to stupefaction. But three o'clock strikes and the display is over, the crowd grows less dense . . . At three o'clock there is a fresh change. Suddenly it is like spring on Nevsky Prospect; it is covered with government clerks in green uniforms. Hungry titular, lower-court and other councillors do their best to quicken their pace. Young collegiate registrars and provincial and collegiate secretaries are in haste to be in time to parade Nevsky Prospect with a dignified air, trying to look as if they had not been sitting for the last six hours in an office.

But the elderly collegiate secretaries and titular and lower-court councillors walk quickly with bowed heads: they are not disposed to amuse themselves by looking at the passers-by; they have not yet completely torn themselves away from their office cares; in their heads is a regular list of work begun and not yet finished; for a long time instead of the signboards they seem to see a cardboard rack of papers or the full face of the head of their office.

From four o'clock Nevsky Prospect is empty, and you hardly meet a single government clerk. Some sewing-girl from a shop runs across Nevsky Prospect with a box in her hands. Some luckless victim of a benevolent attorney, cast adrift in a frieze overcoat; an eccentric visitor to whom all hours are alike; a tall, lanky Englishwoman with a reticule and a book in her hand; a foreman in a high-waisted coat of cotton-shoddy with a narrow beard, a figure barely held together in body and soul: his back, arms, legs and head all twisting and turning as he walks deferentially along the pavement; sometimes a humble craftsman. Those are all that we meet at that hour on Nevsky Prospect.

But as soon as dusk descends upon the houses and streets and the watchman covered with a sack-cloth climbs up his ladder to light the lamp, and engravings which do not venture to show themselves by day peep out of the lower windows of the shops, Nevsky Prospect revives again and begins to be astir. Then comes that mysterious time when the street lamps throw a marvellous alluring light upon everything. You meet a great number of young men, for the most part bachelors, in warm surtouts and overcoats. There is a suggestion at this time of some purpose, or rather something like a purpose, something extremely unaccountable; the steps of all become more rapid and altogether very uneven; long shadows flit over the walls and pavement and almost reach the heads on the Police Bridge. Young collegiate registrars, provincial and collegiate secretaries walk up and down for hours, but the elderly collegiate registrars, the titular and lower-court secretaries are for the most part at home, either because they are married, or because the German cook living in their house gives them a very good dinner. Here you may meet some of the respectable-looking old gentlemen who with such dignity and propriety walked on Nevsky Prospect at two o'clock. You may see them racing along like the young government clerks to peep under the hat of some lady descried in the distance, whose thick lips and fat cheeks plastered with rouge are so attractive to many, and above all to the shopmen, workmen and shopkeepers who promenade in crowds, always in German coats, and usually arm in arm.

'Stay!' cried Lieutenant Pirogov on such an evening, nudging a young man who walked beside him in a dress-coat and cloak; 'Did you see her?'

'I did; lovely, a perfect Bianca of Perugino.'

'But which do you mean?'

'The lady with the dark hair . . . And what eyes! Good God, what eyes! Her whole attitude and shape and the lines of the face – Exquisite!'

'I am talking of the fair girl who passed after her on the

other side. Why don't you go after the brunette if you find her so attractive?'

'Oh, how can you!' cried the young man in the dress-coat, turning crimson. 'As though she were one of the women who walk Nevsky Prospect at night. She must be a very distinguished lady,' he went on with a sigh. 'Why, her cloak alone is worth eighty roubles.'

'You simpleton!' cried Pirogov, giving him a hard shove in the direction in which the brilliant cloak was fluttering. 'Go along, you ninny, why are you lingering? And I will follow the fair one.'

The pair parted ways.

'We know what you all are,' Pirogov thought to himself with a self-satisfied and confident smile, convinced that no beauty could withstand him.

The young man in the dress-coat and the cloak with timid and tremulous step walked in the direction in which the bright-coloured cloak was fluttering, at one moment shining brilliantly as it approached a street lamp, at the next shrouded in darkness as it moved further away. His heart throbbed and he unconsciously quickened his pace. He dared not even imagine that he could have a claim on the attention of the beauty who was flying off into the distance, and still less could he admit the evil thought suggested by Lieutenant Pirogov.

All he wanted was to see the house, to discover where was the abode of this exquisite creature who seemed to have flown straight down from Heaven on to Nevsky Prospect, and who would probably fly away, no one could tell whither. He darted along so fast that he was continually jostling dignified, grey-whiskered gentlemen off the pavement. This young man belonged to a class which is a great exception among us, and he no more belonged to the common run of Petersburg citizens than a face that appears to us in a dream belongs to the world of actual fact. This exceptional class is very rare in the town where all are officials, shopkeepers or German craftsmen. He was an artist.

A strange phenomenon, is it not? A Petersburg artist. An artist in the land of snows. An artist in the land of the Finns where everything is wet, flat, pale, grey, even, foggy! These artists are utterly unlike the Italian artists, proud and ardent as Italy and her skies. The Russian artist on the contrary is, as a rule, mild, gentle, retiring, careless and quietly devoted to his art; he drinks tea with a couple of friends in his little room, modestly discusses his favourite subjects, and does not trouble his head at all about anything superfluous. He frequently engages some old beggar woman, and makes her sit for six hours on end in order to transfer to canvas her pitiful, almost inanimate countenance. He draws a sketch in perspective of his studio with all sorts of artistic litter lying about, copies plaster-of-Paris hands and feet, turned coffee-coloured by time and dust, a broken easel, a palette lying upside down, a friend playing the guitar, walls smeared with paint, with an open window through which there is a glimpse of the pale Neva and poor fishermen in red shirts. Almost all these artists paint in grey, muddy colours that bear the unmistakable imprint of the North. For all that, they all work with true enjoyment. They are often endowed with true talent, and if only they were breathing the fresh air of Italy, they would no doubt develop as freely, broadly and brilliantly as a plant at last brought out from indoors into the open air. They are, as a rule, very timid; stars and thick epaulettes reduce them to such an embarrassment that they ask less for their pictures than they had intended. They are sometimes fond of dressing smartly, but anything smart they wear always looks too startling and rather like something patched on to them. You sometimes see them dressed in an excellent coat and a grubby cloak, an expensive velvet waistcoat and a coat covered with paint, just as on one of their unfinished landscapes you sometimes see an upside-down nymph, for which the artist could find no other place, sketched on the background of an earlier work at which he had once painted with enjoyment. Such an artist never looks you straight in the face; or, if he does look at you, it is with a vague, indefinite expression. He does not transfix you with the vulture-like eye of an observer or the hawk-like glance of a cavalry officer. This is because he sees at the same time your features and the features of some plaster-of-Paris Hercules standing in his room, or because he is imagining a picture which he dreams of producing later on. This makes him often answer incoherently, sometimes quite at random, and the muddle in his head increases his shyness.

To this class belonged the young man we have described, an artist called Piskarev, retiring, shy, but bearing in his soul sparks of feelings, ready at a fitting opportunity to burst into flame. With a secret tremor he hastened after the lady who had made so strong an impression on him and seemed to be himself surprised at his audacity. The unknown being who had so captured his eyes, his thoughts and his feelings suddenly turned her head and glanced at him.

Good God, what divine features! The dazzling whiteness of the exquisite brow was framed by hair lovely as an agate. They curled, those marvellous tresses, and some of them strayed below the hat and caressed the cheek, flushed by the chill of evening with a delicate fresh colour. Her lips were locked in a swarm of exquisite visions. All the memories of childhood, all the visions that rise from dreaming and quiet inspiration in the lamplight – all seemed to be blended, mingled and reflected on her harmonious lips. She glanced at Piskarev and his heart quivered at that glance; her glance was severe, a look of indignation came into her face at the sight of this impudent pursuit; but on that lovely face even wrath was bewitching. Overcome by shame and timidity, he stood still, dropping his eyes; but how could he lose his divinity without even finding out the sanctuary in which she was enshrined? Such was the thought in the mind of the young dreamer, and he resolved to follow her. But, to avoid her notice, he fell back a good distance, looked carelessly from side to side and examined the signboards on the shops; at the same time he did not lose sight of a single step the unknown lady took. Passers-by were less frequent, the street became quieter. The beauty looked round and he fancied that her lips were curved in a faint smile. He was in a tremor all over and could not believe his eyes. No, it was the deceptive light of the street lamp which had thrown that semblance of a smile upon her lips; no, his own dreams were mocking him. But he held his breath and everything in him quivered in a vague tremor, all his feelings were in a glow and everything before him was lost in a sort of mist; the pavement seemed moving under his feet, the carriages with galloping horses seemed to stand still, the bridge stretched out and its arch seemed broken, a house was upside down, a sentry-box seemed reeling towards him, and the sentry's halberd, together with the gilt letters of the signboard and the scissors painted on it, all seemed to be gleaming on his very eyelash.

All this was produced by one glance, by one turn of a pretty head. Hearing nothing, seeing nothing, understanding nothing, he followed the light traces of the lovely feet, trying to moderate the swiftness of his own steps which moved in time with the throbbing of his heart. At moments he was overcome with doubt whether the look on her face was really so gracious; and then for an instant he stood still; but the beating of his heart, the irresistible violence and turmoil of his feelings drove him forward. He did not even notice a four-storey house that loomed before him, four rows of windows, all lit up, burst upon him all at once, and he was brought up suddenly by striking against the iron railing of the entrance. He saw the fair stranger fly up the stairs, look round, lay a finger on her lips and make a sign for him to follow her. His knees trembled, his feelings, his thoughts were aflame. A thrill of joy, unbearably acute, flashed like lightning through his heart. No, it was not a dream! Good God, what happiness in one instant! What a lifetime's rapture in two minutes!

But was it not all a dream? Could the being for one heavenly glance from whom he was ready to give his life, to approach whose dwelling he looked upon as unutterable bliss – could she have just been so gracious and attentive to him? He flew up the stairs. He was conscious of no earthly thought, he was not burning with the fire of earthly passion. No, at that moment he was pure and chaste as a virginal youth still aflame with the vague spiritual craving for love. And what would have awakened base thoughts in a dissolute man, in him made them still holier. This confidence, shown him by a weak and lovely creature, laid upon him the sacred duty of chivalrous austerity, the sacred duty slavishly to carry out all her commands. All that he desired was that those commands should be as difficult, as hard to carry out, as possible, that with more effort he might fly to overcome all obstacles. He did not doubt that some mysterious and at the same time important circumstance compelled the unknown lady to confide in him; that she would certainly require some important service from him, and he felt in himself strength and resolution enough for anything.

The staircase went round and round, and his thoughts whirled round and round with it.

'Be careful!' A voice rang out like a harp string, sending a fresh thrill all through him. On the dark landing of the fourth storey the fair stranger knocked at a door; it was opened and they went in together. A woman of rather attractive appearance met them with a candle in her hand, but she looked so strangely and impudently at Piskarev that he dropped his eyes.

They went into the room. Three female figures in different corners of the room met his eye.

One was laying out cards; another was sitting at the piano and with two fingers strumming out a pitiful travesty of an old polonaise; the third was sitting before a looking-glass, combing out her long hair and had apparently no intention of discontinuing her toilette on the arrival of an unknown visitor. An unpleasant untidiness, usually only seen in the neglected rooms of bachelors, was everywhere apparent. The furniture, which was fairly good, was covered with dust. Spiders' webs stretched over the carved cornice; through the open door of another room he caught the gleam of a spurred boot and the red edging of a uniform; a man's loud voice and a woman's laugh rang out without restraint.

Good God, where had he come! At first he would not believe it, and began looking more attentively at the objects that filled the room; but the bare walls and uncurtained windows betrayed the absence of a careful housewife; the faded faces of these pitiful creatures, one of whom was sitting just under his nose and examining him as coolly as though he were a spot on someone's dress – all convinced him that he had come into one of those revolting dens in which the pitiful vice that springs from a tawdry education and the terrible over-population of a capital city finds shelter, one of those dens in which man sacrilegiously tramples and derides all that is pure and holy, all that makes life fair, where woman, the beauty of the world, the crown of creation, is transformed into a strange, ambiguous creature, where she loses with purity of heart all that is womanly, revoltingly adopts the swagger and impudence of man and ceases to be the delicate, the lovely creature, so different from us. Piskarev scanned her from head to foot with perplexed eyes, as though trying to make sure whether this was really she who had so enchanted him and had brought him flying in from Nevsky Prospect. But she stood before him as lovely as ever; her eyes were still as heavenly. She was fresh, she was not more than seventeen; it could be seen that she had not long been in the grip of vice: it had as yet left no trace upon her cheeks, they were fresh and faintly flushed with colour; she was lovely.

He stood motionless before her and was ready to sink into the same simple-hearted forgetfulness as before. But the beauty was tired of this long silence and gave a meaningful smile, looking straight into his eyes. That smile was full of a sort of pitiful insolence; it was so strange and as incongruous with her face as a sanctimonious air with the brutal face of a bribe-taker or a manual of bookkeeping with a poet. He shuddered. She opened her lovely lips and began saying something, but all she said was so stupid, so vulgar . . . As though intelligence were lost with innocence! He wanted to hear no more.

He was extremely absurd and simple as a child. Instead of taking advantage of such graciousness, instead of rejoicing in such a chance, as anyone else in his place would probably have done, he rushed headlong away like a wild goat, and ran out into the street.

He sat in his room with his head bowed and his hands hanging loose, like a poor man who has found a precious pearl and at once dropped it into the sea. 'Such a beauty, such divine features! And where? In such a place . . .' That was all that he could articulate.

Nothing, indeed, moves us to such pity as the sight of beauty touched by the putrid breath of vice. Ugliness may go with it, but beauty, tender beauty . . . In our thoughts it blends with nothing but purity and innocence. The beauty who had so enchanted poor Piskarev really was a rare and marvellous exception. Her presence in those vile surroundings seemed even more marvellous. All her features were so purely moulded, the whole expression of her lovely face wore the stamp of such nobility, that it was impossible to think that vice already held her in its clutches. She should have been the priceless pearl, the whole world, the paradise, the wealth of a devoted husband; she should have been the lovely, gentle star of some quiet family circle, and with the faintest movement of her lovely lips have given her sweet commands there. She would have been a divinity in the crowded drawing-room, on the shining parquet, in the glare of candles surrounded by the silent adoration of a crowd of admirers at her feet; but, alas! by some terrible machination of the fiendish spirit, eager to destroy the harmony of life, she had been flung with mocking laughter into this fearful slough.

Wrung by heart-rending pity, he sat on before a candle that was burned low in the socket. Midnight was long past, the belfry chime rang out half-past twelve, and he sat on without stirring, neither asleep nor fully awake. Sleep, aided by his stillness, was beginning to steal over him, already the room was beginning to disappear, and only the light of the candle still shone through the dreams that were overpowering him, when all at once a knock at the door made him start and wake up. The door opened and a footman in a gorgeous livery walked in. Never had a gorgeous livery peeped into his lovely room, and at such an hour of the night! . . . He was amazed, and with impatient curiosity looked intently at the footman who entered.

'The lady,' the footman pronounced with a deferential bow, 'whom you visited some hours ago bade me invite you and sent the carriage to fetch you.'

Piskarev stood in speechless wonder: the carriage, a footman in livery! . . . No, there must be some mistake . . .

'My good man,' he said timidly, 'you must have come to the wrong door. Your mistress must have sent you for someone else and not for me.'

'No, sir, I am not mistaken. Did you not accompany my mistress home? It's in Liteyny Street, on the fourth storey.'

'I did.'

'Then, if so, pray make haste; my mistress is very anxious to see you, and begs you to come straight to her house.'

Piskarev ran down the stairs. A carriage was, in fact, standing in the courtyard. He got into it, the door was slammed, the cobbles of the pavement resounded under the wheels and the hoofs, and the illuminated perspective of houses with brightly coloured signboards passed by the carriage windows. Piskarev pondered all the way and could not explain this adventure. A house of her own, a carriage, a footman in gorgeous livery . . . He could not reconcile all this with the room on the fourth storey, the dusty windows and the jangling piano. The carriage stopped before a brightly lit entry, and he was at once struck by the procession of carriages, the talk of the coachmen, the brilliantly lit windows and the strains of music. The footman in gorgeous livery helped him out of the carriage and respectfully led him into a hall with marble columns, with a porter in gold lace, with cloaks and fur coats flung here and there and a brilliant lamp. An airy staircase with shining banisters, fragrant with perfume, led upwards. He was already mounting it; hesitating at the first step and startled at the crowds of people, he went into the first room. The extraordinary brightness and variety of the scene completely staggered him; it seemed to him as though some demon had crumbled the whole world into bits and mixed all these bits indiscriminately together. The gleaming shoulders of the ladies and the black dress-coats, the lustres, the lamps, the ethereal floating gauze, the filmy ribbons and the stout double-bass looking out from behind the railing of the orchestra – everything was dazzling to him.

He saw at the same instant such numbers of venerable old or half-old men with stars on their evening-coats and ladies sitting in rows or stepping so lightly, proudly and graciously over the parquet floor; he heard so many French and English words; moreover, the young men in black dress-coats were filled with such dignity, spoke or kept silence with such gentlemanly decorum, were so incapable of saying anything inappropriate, made jokes so majestically, smiled so politely, wore such superb whiskers, so skilfully displayed their elegant hands as they straightened their cravats, the ladies were so ethereal, so steeped in perfect gratification and beatitude, so enchantingly cast down their eyes, that ... but Piska-rev's subdued air, as he leaned timidly against a column, was enough to show that he was completely overwhelmed. At that moment the crowd stood round a group of dancers. They whirled around, draped in the transparent creations of Paris, in garments woven of air itself; carelessly they touched the parquet floor with their gleaming feet, as ethereal as though they trod on air. But one among them was lovelier, more splendid and more brilliantly dressed than the rest. An indescribable, subtle perfection of taste was apparent in all her attire, and at the same time it seemed as though she cared nothing for it, as though it had come unconsciously, of itself. She looked and did not look at the crowd of spectators crowding round her, she cast down her lovely long eyelashes indifferently, and the gleaming whiteness of her face was still more dazzling when she bent her head and a light shadow lay on her enchanting brow.

Piskarev did his utmost to make his way through the crowd and get a better look at her; but to his intense vexation a huge head of curly black hair was continually screening her from him; moreover, the crush was so great that he did not dare to press forward or to step back, for fear of jostling against some privy councillor. But at last he squeezed his way to the front and glanced at his clothes, anxious that everything should be neat. Heavenly Creator! What was his horror! He had on his everyday coat, and it was all smeared with paint; in his haste to set off, he had actually forgotten to change into suitable clothes. He blushed up to his ears and, dropping his eyes in confusion, would have disappeared, but there was absolutely nowhere he could go; kammer-junkers in gorgeous attire formed a compact wall behind him. By now his desire was to be as far away as possible from the beauty of the lovely brows and eyelashes. In terror he raised his eyes to see whether she were looking at him. Good God! She stood facing him . . . What did it mean? 'It is she!' he cried almost at the top of his voice. It really was she – the one he had met on Nevsky Prospect and had escorted home.

Meanwhile, she lifted her eyelashes and looked at all with her clear eyes. 'Aïe, aïe, aïe, how beautiful . . . !' was all he could say with bated breath. She scanned the faces around her, all eager to catch her attention, but with an air of weariness and indifference she looked away and met Piskarev's eyes. Oh heavens! What paradise! Oh God, for strength to bear this! Life cannot contain it, such rapture tears it asunder and bears away the soul! She made a sign, but not by hand nor by inclination of the head; no, the sign was a look in her ravishing eyes so subtle, so imperceptible, that no one else could see it, but he saw it, he understood it. The dance lasted long; the exhausted music seemed to flag and die away and again it broke out, shrilled and thundered; at last the dance was over. She sat down. Her panting bosom heaved under the light cloud of gossamer, her hand (Oh heavens! What a marvellous hand!) dropped on her knee, rested on her filmy gown which under it seemed breathing music, and its delicate lilac hue made that lovely hand look more dazzlingly white than ever. Only to touch it and nothing more! No other desires – they would be insolence . . . He stood behind her chair, not daring to speak, not daring to breathe. 'You have been bored?' she pronounced. 'I have been bored too. I see that you hate me . . .' she added, drooping her long eyelashes.

'Hate you? I? . . . I? . . .' Piskarev, completely over-whelmed, tried to articulate, and he would probably have poured out a stream of incoherent words, but at that moment a kammer-junker with a magnificent curled shock of hair came up making witty and polite remarks. He rather agreeably displayed a row of rather good teeth, and at every jest his wit drove a sharp nail into Piskarev's heart. At last someone fortunately addressed the kammer-junker with a question.

'How unbearable it is!' she said, lifting her heavenly eyes to him. 'I will sit at the other end of the room; be there!' She glided through the crowd and vanished. He pushed his way through the crowd like one possessed, and in a flash was there.

So this was she! She sat like a queen, finer than all, lovelier than all, and her eyes sought him.

'You are here,' she said softly. 'I will be open with you: no doubt you think the circumstances of our meeting strange. Can you imagine that I belong to the degraded class of beings among whom you met me? You think my conduct strange, but I will reveal a secret to you. Can you promise never to betray it?' she pronounced, fixing her eyes upon him.

'Oh, I will, I will, I will! . . .'

But at that moment an elderly man offered her his hand and began speaking in a language Piskarev did not understand. She looked at the artist with an imploring gaze, and signed to him to remain where he was and await her return: but in an access of impatience he could not obey a command even from her lips. He followed her, but the crowd parted them. He could no longer see the lilac dress; in consternation he forced his way from room to room and elbowed all he met mercilessly, but in all the rooms gentlemen were sitting at whist plunged in dead silence. In a corner of the room some elderly people were arguing about the superiority of military to civil service; in another some young men in superb dress-coats were making a few light remarks about the voluminous works of a poet. Piskarev felt that a gentleman of venerable appearance had taken him by the button of his coat and was submitting some very just observation to his criticism, but he rudely thrust him aside without noticing that he had a very distinguished order on his breast. He ran into another room — she was not there, into a third — she was not there either. 'Where is she? Give her to me! Oh, I cannot live without another look at her! I want to hear what she meant to tell me!' But all his search was in vain. Anxious and exhausted, he huddled in a corner and looked at the crowd. But everything seemed blurred to his strained eyes. At last the walls of his own room began to grow distinct. He raised his eyes: before him stood a candlestick with the light flickering in the socket; the whole candle had burned away and the melted grease lay on his table . . .

So he had been asleep! My God, what a dream! And why had he awakened? Why had it not lasted one minute longer? She would no doubt have appeared again! The unwelcome dawn was peeping in at his window with its unpleasant, dingy light. The room was in such a grey, untidy muddle . . . Oh, how revolting was reality! What was it beside dreams? He undressed quickly and got into bed, wrapping himself up in the coverlet, anxious to recapture the dream that had flown. Sleep certainly did not tarry, but it presented him with something quite different from what he wanted: at one time, Lieutenant Pirogov with his pipe, then a porter of the Academy, then an actual civil councillor, then the head of a Finnish woman who had sat to him for a portrait, and such foolish things.

He lay in bed till the middle of the day, longing to dream again, but she did not appear. If only for one minute she had shown her lovely features, if only for one minute her light step had rustled, if only her hand, shining white as driven snow, had for one minute gleamed before him!

Dismissing everything, forgetting everything, he sat with a crushed and hopeless expression, full of nothing but his dream. He never thought of touching anything; his eyes were fixed in a vacant, lifeless stare upon the windows that looked into the yard, where a dirty water-carrier was slopping water that froze in the air, and the cracked voice of a pedlar bleated like a goat, 'Old clothes for sale.' The sounds of everyday reality rang strangely in his ears. So he sat on till evening, and then flung himself eagerly into bed. For hours he struggled with sleeplessness; at last he overcame it. Again a dream, a vulgar, horrid dream. 'God, have mercy! For one minute, just for one minute, let me see her!'

Again he waited for the evening, again he fell asleep. He dreamed of a government clerk who was at the same time a government clerk and a bassoon. Oh, this was insufferable!

At last she appeared! Her head and her curls . . . she gazed at him . . . for – oh, how brief a moment, and then again mist, again some stupid dream.

At last, dreaming became his life and from that time his life was strangely turned upside down; he might be said to sleep when he was awake and to come to life when he was asleep. Anyone seeing him sitting dumbly before his empty table or walking along the street would certainly have taken him for a lunatic or a man deranged by drink: his eyes had a perfectly vacant look, his natural absent-mindedness developed and drove every sign of feeling and emotion out of his face. He only revived at the approach of night.

Such a condition destroyed his health, and the worst torture for him was the fact that sleep began to desert him altogether. Anxious to save the only treasure left him, he used every means to regain it. He had heard that there were means of inducing sleep – one need only take opium. But where could he get opium? He thought of a Persian who kept a shawl-shop and, whenever he saw Piskarev, asked him to paint a beautiful woman for him. He resolved to apply to him, assuming that he would be sure to have the drug he wanted.

The Persian received him, sitting on a sofa with his legs crossed under him. 'What do you want opium for?' he asked. Piskarev told him about his sleeplessness.

'Very well, you must paint me a beautiful woman, and I will give you opium. She must be a real beauty, let her eyebrows be black and her eyes be as big as olives; and let me be lying near her, smoking my pipe. Do you hear, let her be pretty! Let her be a beauty!'

Piskarev promised everything. The Persian went out for a minute and came back with a little jar filled with a dark liquid; he carefully poured some of it into another jar and gave it to Piskarev, telling him to take not more than seven drops in water. He greedily clutched the precious little jar, with which he would not have parted for a pile of gold, and ran headlong home.

When he got home he poured several drops into a glass of water and, swallowing it, lay down to sleep.

Oh God, what joy! She! She again, but now in quite a different world! Oh, how charmingly she sat at the window of a bright little country house! In her dress was the simplicity in which the poet's thought is clothed. And her hair! Merciful heavens! How simple it was and how it suited her! A short shawl was thrown lightly around her graceful neck; everything about her was modest, everything about her showed a mysterious, inexplicable sense of taste. How charming her graceful carriage! How musical the sound of her steps and the rustle of her simple gown! How lovely her hand, clasped by a hair bracelet! She said to him with a tear in her eye: 'Don't look down upon me; I am not at all what you take me for. Look at me, look at me more carefully and tell me: am I capable of what you imagine?' 'Oh no, no! May he who should dare to think it, may he . . .'

But he awoke, deeply moved, harassed, with tears in his eyes. 'Better that you had not existed! had not lived in this world, but had been an artist's creation! I would never have left the canvas, I would have gazed at you for ever and kissed you! I would have lived and breathed in you, as in the loveliest of dreams, and then I should have been happy. I should have desired nothing more, I would have called upon you as my guardian angel at sleeping and at waking, and I would have gazed on you, if ever I had to paint the divine and holy. But as it is . . . how terrible life is! What good is it that she lives? Does a madman's life rejoice his friends and family who once loved him? My God! What is our life! An everlasting disharmony between dream and reality!' Such ideas absorbed him continually. He thought of nothing, he almost gave up eating, indeed, and with the impatience and passion of a lover waited for the evening and his coveted dreams.

The continual concentration of his thoughts on one subject at last so completely mastered his whole being and imagination that the coveted image appeared before him almost every day, always in positions that were the very opposite of reality, for his thoughts were as pure as a child's. Through these dreams, the subject of them became in his imagination more pure and was completely transformed.

The opium inflamed his thoughts more than ever, and if there ever was a man passionately, terribly and ruinously in love to the utmost pitch of madness, he was that luckless man.

Of his dreams, one rejoiced him more than any: he saw himself in his studio. He was in good spirits and sitting happily with the palette in his hand! And she was there. She was his wife. She sat behind him, leaning her lovely elbow on the back of his chair and looking at his work. Her eyes were languid and weary with excess of bliss; everything in his room breathed of paradise; it was so bright, so neat. Good God! She leaned her lovely head on his bosom . . . He had never had a better dream than that. He rose after it fresher, less absent-minded than before. A strange idea came into his mind. 'Perhaps,' he thought, 'she has been drawn into vice by some awful chance, through no will of her own; perhaps her soul is disposed to penitence; perhaps she herself is longing to escape from her awful position. And am I to stand aside indifferently and let her go to ruin when I have only to hold out a hand to save her from drowning?' His thoughts carried him further. 'No one knows me,' he said to himself, 'and no one cares what I do, and I have nothing to do with anyone either. If she shows herself genuinely penitent and changes her mode of life, I will marry her. I ought to marry her, and no doubt I should do much better than many who marry their housekeepers or sometimes the most contemptible creatures. But my action will be disinterested and very likely a good deed. I shall restore to the world the loveliest of its ornaments!'

Making this light-hearted plan, he felt the colour flushing in his cheek; he went up to the looking-glass and was frightened at his hollow cheeks and the paleness of his face. He began carefully dressing; he washed, smoothed his hair, put on a new coat, a smart waistcoat, flung on his cloak, and went out into the street. He breathed the fresh air and had a feeling of freshness in his heart, like a convalescent who has gone out for the first time after a long illness. His heart throbbed when he turned into the street, which he had not passed through again since that fatal meeting.

He was a long time looking for the house. He walked up and down the street twice, uncertain before which to stop. At last one of them seemed to him like it. He ran quickly up the stairs and knocked at the door: the door opened, and who came out to meet him? His ideal, his mysterious divinity, the original of his dream pictures – she who was his life, in whom he lived so terribly, so agonisingly, so blissfully – she,

she herself, stood before him! He trembled; he could hardly stand on his feet for weakness, overcome by the rush of joy. She stood before him as lovely as ever, though her eyes looked sleepy, though a pallor had crept over her face, no longer quite so fresh; but still she was lovely.

'Ah!' she cried on seeing Piskarev and, rubbing her eyes (it was two o'clock in the afternoon); 'Why did you run away from us that day?'

He sat down in a chair, feeling faint, and looked at her.

'And I am only just awake; I was brought home at seven in the morning. I was quite drunk,' she added with a smile.

Oh, better you had been dumb and could not speak at all than uttering such words! She had shown him in a flash the whole panorama of her life. But, in spite of that, struggling with his feelings, he made up his mind to try whether or not his representations would have any effect on her. Pulling himself together, he began in a shaking but ardent voice to depict her awful position. She listened to him with a look of attention and with the feeling of wonder which we display at the sight of something strange and unexpected. She looked with a faint smile towards her friend, who was sitting in a corner, and who left off cleaning a comb and also listened with attention to this new preacher.

'It is true that I am poor,' said Piskarev, at last, after a prolonged and persuasive appeal, 'but we will work, we will do our best, side by side, to improve our position. Yes, nothing is sweeter than to owe everything to one's own work. I will sit at my pictures, you shall sit by me and inspire my work, while you are busy with sewing or some other handicraft, and we shall not need for anything.'

'Indeed!' she interrupted his speech with an expression of some scorn. 'I am not a washerwoman or a seamstress that I should have to work.'

Oh God! In those words the whole of a mean, degraded life was portrayed, a life of emptiness and idleness, the loyal companions of vice!

'Marry me!' her friend who had until then sat silent in the corner put in, with a saucy air. 'When I am your wife I will sit like this!' As she spoke she pursed up her pitiful face and assumed a silly expression, which greatly diverted the beauty.

Oh, that was too much! That was more than he could bear! He rushed away with every thought and feeling in a turmoil. His mind was clouded; stupidly, aimlessly, he wandered about all day, seeing nothing, hearing nothing, feeling nothing. No one could say whether he slept anywhere or not; only the next day, by some blind instinct, he found his way to his room, pale and terrible-looking, with his hair dishevelled and signs of madness in his face. He locked himself in his room and admitted no one, asked for nothing. Four days passed and his door was not once opened; at last a week had passed, and still the door was locked. People went to the door and began calling him, but there was no answer; at last the door was broken open and his lifeless corpse was found with the throat cut. A bloodstained razor lay on the floor. From his arms, flung out convulsively, and his terribly distorted face, it might be concluded that his hand had faltered and that he had suffered in agony before his soul left his sinful body.

So perished the victim of frantic passion, poor Piskarev, the gentle, timid, modest, childishly simple-hearted artist whose spark of talent might with time have glowed into a full and bright flame. No one wept for him; no one was seen beside his dead body except the regulation police superintendent and the indifferent face of the town doctor. His coffin was taken to Ohta quickly, without even the rites of religion; only a soldier-watchman who followed it wept, and that simply because he had had a bottle too much of vodka. Even Lieutenant Pirogov did not come to look at the dead body of the poor luckless artist to whom he had extended his exalted patronage. He had no thought to spare for him; indeed, he was absorbed in a very exciting adventure. But let us turn to him. I do not like corpses, and it is always disagreeable to me when a long funeral procession crosses my path and some veteran dressed in a sort of capuchin takes a pinch of snuff with his left hand because he has a torch in his right. I always feel annoyed at the sight of a magnificent catafalque with a velvet pall; but my annoyance is mingled with sadness when I see a cart dragging the red, uncovered coffin of some poor fellow and only some old beggar woman who has met it at the crossways follows it weeping, because she has nothing else to do.

I believe we left Lieutenant Pirogov at the moment when he parted with Piskarev and went in pursuit of the fair-haired charmer. The latter was a lively, rather attractive little creature. She stopped before every shop and gazed at the sashes, kerchiefs, ear-rings, gloves and other trifles in the shop-windows, was continually twisting and turning and gazing about her in all directions and looking behind her. 'You'll be mine, you darling dove!' Pirogov said confidently as he pursued her, turning up the collar of his coat for fear of meeting someone of his acquaintance. It will be as well, however, to let the reader know what sort of person Lieutenant Pirogov was.

But before we describe Lieutenant Pirogov, it will be as well to say something of the circle to which Lieutenant Pirogov belonged. There are officers who form a kind of middle class in Petersburg. You will always find one of them at every evening party, at every dinner given by a civil councillor or an actual civil councillor who has risen to that grade by forty years of service. The group of pale daughters, as colourless as Petersburg, some of them no longer in their first youth, the tea-table, the piano, the impromptu dance, are all inseparable from the gay epaulette which gleams in the lamplight between the virtuous young lady and the black coat of her brother or of some old friend of the family. It is extremely difficult to arouse and divert these phlegmatic misses. To do so needs a great deal of skill, or rather perhaps the absence of all skill. One has to say what is not too clever or too amusing and to bring in the trivialities that women love. One must give credit for that to the gentlemen we are discussing. They have a special gift for making these colourless beauties laugh and listen. Exclamations, smothered in laughter, of 'Oh, do stop! Aren't you ashamed to be so absurd!' are often their highest reward. They rarely, one may say never, get into higher circles: from those regions they are completely crowded out by the so-called aristocrats. At the same time, they pass for well-bred, highly educated men. They are fond of talking about literature; praise Bulgarin, Pushkin and Gretch, and speak with contempt and witty sarcasm of A. A. Orlov. They never miss a public lecture, though it may be on bookkeeping or even forestry. You will always find one of them at the theatre, whatever the play, unless, indeed, it be one of the farces of the 'Filatka' class, which greatly offend their fastidious taste.

They are ever-present at the theatre and the greatest asset to managers. They are particularly fond of fine verses in a play, and they are greatly given to calling loudly for the actors; many of them, by teaching in government establishments or preparing pupils for them, arrive at keeping a carriage and pair. Then their circle becomes wider and in the end they succeed in marrying a merchant's daughter who can play the piano, with a dowry of a hundred thousand, or something near it, in cash, and a lot of bearded relations. They can never attain to this honour, however, till they have reached the rank of colonel, at least, for Russian merchants, though there may still be a smell of cabbage about them, will never consent to see their daughters married to any but generals, or colonels at the lowest.

Such are the leading characteristics of this class of young men. But Lieutenant Pirogov had a number of talents belonging to him individually. He recited verses from *Dimitry Donsky* and *Woe from Wit* with great effect, and possessed the art of blowing smoke out of a pipe in rings so successfully that he could string a dozen of them together in a chain. He could tell a very good story to the effect that a cannon was one thing and a unicorn was another. It is difficult to enumerate all the qualities with which fate had endowed Pirogov. He was fond of talking about actresses and dancers, but not quite in such a crude way as young lieutenants commonly hold forth on that subject. He was very much pleased with his rank in the service, to which he had only lately been promoted, and although he did occasionally say as he lay on the sofa, 'Oh dear, vanity, all is vanity. What if I am a lieutenant?' yet his vanity was secretly much flattered by his new dignity; he often tried in conversation to allude to it in a roundabout way, and on one occasion when he jostled against a copying clerk in the street who struck him as uncivil he promptly stopped him and in few but vigorous words pointed out to him that there was a lieutenant standing before him and not any other kind of officer. He was the more eloquent in his observations as two very nice-looking ladies were passing at the moment. Pirogov displayed a passion for everything artistic in general and encouraged the artist Piskarev; this may have been partly due to a desire to see his manly countenance portrayed on canvas. But enough of Pirogov's good qualities. Man is such a strange creature that one can never enumerate all his good points, and the more we look into him the more new characteristics we discover and the description of them would be endless.

And so Pirogov continued to pursue the unknown fair one; from time to time he addressed her with questions to which she responded infrequently with abrupt and incoherent sounds.

They passed by the wet Kazan gate into Myeshtchansky Street — a street of tobacconists and little shops, of German artisans and Finnish nymphs. The fair lady ran faster than ever, and scurried in at the gate of a rather dirty-looking house. Pirogov followed her. She ran up a narrow, dark staircase and went in at a door through which Pirogov boldly followed her. He found himself in a big room with black walls and a grimy ceiling. A heap of iron screws, locksmith's tools, shining tin coffee pots and candlesticks lay on the table; the floor was littered with brass and iron filings. Pirogov saw at once that this was a workman's lodging. The unknown charmer darted away through a side door. He hesitated for a minute, but, following the Russian rule, decided to push forward. He went into the other room, which was quite unlike the first and very neatly furnished, showing that it was inhabited by a German. He was struck by an extremely strange sight: before him sat Schiller. Not the Schiller who wrote *William Tell* and the *History of the Thirty Years War*, but the famous Schiller: the ironmonger and tinsmith of Myeshtchansky Street. Beside Schiller stood Hoffmann. Not the writer Hoffmann, but a rather high-class bootmaker who lived in Ofitsersky Street and was a great friend of Schiller's. Schiller was drunk and was sitting on a chair, stamping and saying something with heat. All this would not have surprised Pirogov, but what did surprise him was the extraordinary attitude of the two figures. Schiller was sitting with his head flung up and his rather thick nose in the air, while Hoffmann was holding the nose between his finger and thumb and was brandishing the blade of his cobbler's knife over its very surface. Both individuals were talking in German, and so Lieutenant Pirogov, whose knowledge of German was confined to '*Gut Morgen*' could not make out what was going on. However, what Schiller said amounted to this: 'I don't want it, I have no need of a nose!' he said, waving his hands. 'I use three pounds of snuff a month on my nose alone. And I pay in a nasty Russian shop, for a German shop does not keep Russian snuff. I pay in a nasty Russian shop forty kopecks a pound – that makes one rouble twenty kopecks, twelve times one rouble twenty kopecks – that makes fourteen roubles forty kopecks. Do you hear, friend Hoffmann? Fourteen roubles forty kopecks on my nose alone! And on holidays I take a pinch of rappee, for I don't care to use nasty Russian snuff on a holiday. In the year I use two pounds of rapper at two roubles the pound. Six and fourteen makes twenty roubles forty kopecks on snuff alone. It's a robbery. I ask you, my friend Hoffmann, isn't it?' Hoffmann, who was drunk himself, answered in the affirmative. 'Twenty roubles and forty kopecks. I am a Swabian; we have a king in Germany. I don't want a nose! Cut off my nose! Here is my nose.'

And had it not been for Lieutenant Pirogov's suddenly appearing, Hoffmann would certainly, for no rhyme or reason, have cut off Schiller's nose, for he already had his knife in position, as though he were going to cut a sole.

Schiller seemed very much annoyed that an unknown and uninvited person should so inopportunely interrupt him. Although he was in a state of blissful intoxication from beer and wine, he felt that it was rather improper to be seen in such a state and engaged in such proceedings in the presence of an outsider. Meanwhile Pirogov made a slight bow and, with his characteristic agreeableness, said: 'Excuse me . . . !'

'Shove off!' Schiller responded protractedly.

Lieutenant Pirogov was taken aback at this. Such treatment was absolutely new to him. A smile which had begun faintly to appear on his face vanished at once. With a feeling of wounded dignity he said: 'I am surprised, sir . . . I suppose you have not observed . . . I am an officer . . .'

'And what's an officer? I am a Swabian myself –' at this Schiller banged the table with his fist – 'will be an officer; a year-and-a-half a junker, two years a lieutenant, and tomorrow I shall be an officer at once. But I don't want to serve. This is what I'd do to officers: *phoo!* Schiller held his open hand before him and blew at it.

Lieutenant Pirogov saw that there was nothing for him to do but retire. Such a proceeding, however, was quite out of keeping with his rank, and was disagreeable to him. He stopped several times on the stairs as though trying to rally his forces and to think how to make Schiller feel his impudence. At last he decided that Schiller might be excused because his head was fuddled with wine and beer; besides, he recalled the image of the charming blonde, and he made up his mind to consign it to oblivion.

Early next morning Lieutenant Pirogov appeared at the tinsmith's workshop. In the outer room he was met by the fair-haired charmer, who asked him in a rather austere voice, which went admirably with her little face: 'What do you want?'

'Oh, good morning, my pretty dear! Don't you recognise me? You little rogue, what charming eyes!'

As he said this, Lieutenant Pirogov tried very charmingly to chuck her under the chin; but the lady uttered a frightened exclamation and with the same austerity asked: 'What do you want?'

'To see you, that's all I want,' answered Lieutenant Pirogov, smiling rather agreeably and going nearer; but noticing that the timorous beauty was about to slip through the door, he added: 'I want to order some spurs, my dear. Can you make me some spurs? Though indeed no spur is needed to make me love you – a curb is what one needs, not a spur. What charming little hands!'

Lieutenant Pirogov was particularly agreeable in declarations of this kind.

'I will call my husband at once,' cried the German, and went out, and within a few minutes Pirogov saw Schiller come in with sleepy-looking eyes; he had only just woken up after the drunkenness of the previous day. As he looked at the officer, he remembered as though in a confused dream what had happened the previous day. He could recall nothing exactly as it was, but felt that he had done something stupid, and so received the officer with a very sullen face. 'I can't ask less than fifteen roubles for a pair of spurs,' he brought out, hoping to get rid of Pirogov, for as a respectable German he was shamed to look at anyone who had seen him in an unseemly condition. Schiller liked to drink without spectators, in company with two of three friends, and at such times locked himself in and would not admit even his own workman.

'Why are they so expensive?' asked Pirogov genially.

'German work,' Schiller pronounced coolly, stroking his chin. 'A Russian will undertake to make them for two roubles.'

'Well, to show you that I like you and should be glad to make your acquaintance, I will pay fifteen roubles.'

Schiller remained for a minute pondering; as a respectable

German he felt a little ashamed. Hoping to put him off the order, he declared that he could not undertake it for a fortnight. But Pirogov, without making any objections, readily assented to this.

The German mused and began pondering how he could best do the work so as to make it really worth fifteen roubles.

At this moment the blonde charmer came into the room and began looking for something on the table, which was covered with coffee pots. The lieutenant took advantage of Schiller's absorption, stepped up to her and pressed her arm, which was bare to the shoulder.

This was very distasteful to Schiller. '*Meine Frau!*' he cried.

'*Was wollen Sie doch?*' answered the fair charmer.

'*Gehen Sie* to the kitchen!'

The lady withdrew.

'In a fortnight then?' said Pirogov.

'Yes, in a fortnight,' replied Schiller, still pondering. 'I have a lot of work now.'

'Goodbye for the present. I will look in again.'

'Goodbye,' said Schiller, closing the door after him.

Lieutenant Pirogov made up his mind not to relinquish his pursuit, though the lady had so plainly rebuffed him. He could not conceive that anyone could resist him, especially as his politeness and the brilliant rank of a lieutenant gave him a full claim to attention. It must be mentioned also that with all her attractiveness Schiller's wife was extremely stupid. Stupidity, however, adds a special charm to a pretty wife. I have known several husbands, anyway, who were in raptures over the stupidity of their wives and saw in it evidence of childlike innocence. Beauty works perfect miracles. All spiritual defects in a beauty, far from exciting repulsion, become somehow wonderfully attractive, even vice has an aroma of charm in the beautiful; but when beauty disappears, a woman needs to be twenty times as intelligent as a man merely to inspire respect, to say nothing of love. Schiller's wife, however, for all her stupidity was always faithful to her duties, and consequently it was no easy task for Pirogov to succeed in his bold enterprise. But there is always a pleasure in overcoming difficulties, and the fair lady became more and more attractive in his eyes every day. He took to enquiring pretty frequently about the progress of the spurs, so that at last Schiller was weary of it. He did his utmost to finish the spurs quickly; at last they were done.

'Oh, what splendid workmanship,' cried Lieutenant Pirogov on seeing the spurs. 'Good heavens, how well it's done! Our general hasn't spurs like that.'

A feeling of self-complacency filled Schiller's soul. His eyes began to look fairly good-humoured, and he felt inwardly reconciled to Pirogov. 'The Russian officer is an intelligent man,' he thought to himself.

'So, then, you could make a sheath for a dagger or for anything else?'

'Indeed I can,' said Schiller with a smile.

'Then make me a sheath for a dagger. I will bring it to you. I have a very fine Turkish dagger, but I should like to have another sheath for it.'

This was like a bomb dropped upon Schiller. His brows were suddenly knitted.

'So that's what you are after,' he thought to himself, inwardly swearing at himself for having praised his own work. To refuse it now he felt would be dishonest; besides, the Russian officer had praised his workmanship. Shaking his head a few times, he gave his consent; but the kiss which Pirogov as he went out impudently printed on the lips of the pretty wife reduced the tinsmith to stupefaction.

I think it will not be superfluous to make the reader better acquainted with Schiller himself. Schiller was a regular German in the full significance of the word. From the age of twenty, that happy time when the Russian lives without a thought of the morrow, Schiller had already mapped out his whole life and did not deviate from his plan under any circumstances. He made it a rule to get up at seven, to dine at two, to be punctual in everything, and to get drunk every Sunday. He set before himself as an object to save a capital of fifty thousand in the course of ten years, and all this was as certain and as unalterable as fate, for sooner would a government clerk forget to look in at the porter's lodge of his chief than a German would bring himself to break his word. Never under any circumstances did he increase his expenses, and if the price of potatoes went up much above the ordinary, he did not spend one ha'penny more on them but simply diminished the amount they consumed, and although he was left sometimes feeling rather hungry, he soon got used to it. His exactitude was such that he made it his rule to kiss his wife twice in the twenty-four hours but not more, and that he might not exceed the number, he never put more than one small teaspoonful of pepper in his soup; on Sunday, however, this rule was not so strictly kept, for then Schiller used to drink two bottles of beer and one bottle of caraway-flavoured vodka which, however, he always abused. He did not drink like an Englishman, who locks his doors directly after dinner and gets drunk in solitude. On the contrary, like a German he always drank with inspiration either in the company of Hoffmann the bootmaker or with Kunts the carpenter, who was also a German and a great drunkard. Such was the disposition of the worthy Schiller, who was indeed placed in a very difficult position. Though he was phlegmatic and a German, Pirogov's behaviour excited in him a feeling akin to jealousy. He racked his brains and could not think of how to get rid of this Russian officer. Meanwhile Pirogov, smoking a pipe in the company of his brother officers – since Providence has ordained that wherever there is an officer there is a pipe – alluded significantly and with an agreeable smile on his lips to his little intrigue with the pretty German, with whom he was, according to his account, already on the best of terms, though as a matter of fact he had almost lost all hope of winning her favour.

One day he was walking along Myeshtchansky Street, looking at the house adorned by Schiller's signboard with coffee pots and samovars on it; to his great joy he caught sight of the fair charmer's head thrust out of window watching the passers-by. He stopped, kissed his hand to her and said: '*Gut Morgen*.'

The fair lady bowed to him as to an acquaintance.

'I say, is your husband at home?'

'Yes,' she answered.

'And when is he out?'

'He is not at home on Sundays,' said the foolish little German.

'That's not bad,' Pirogov thought to himself. 'I must take advantage of that.'

And the following Sunday he suddenly and unexpectedly

stood facing the fair German. Schiller really was not at home. The pretty wife was frightened; but Pirogov on this occasion behaved rather warily, he was very respectful in his manner, and, making his bows, displayed all the elegance of his supple figure in his close-fitting uniform. He made polite and agreeable jests, but the silly little German responded with nothing but monosyllables. At last, having made his attack from all sides and seeing that nothing would entertain her, he suggested that they should dance. The German agreed in a trice, for all German girls are passionately fond of dancing. Pirogov rested great hopes upon this: in the first place it gave her pleasure, in the second place it displayed his figure and dexterity; and thirdly he could get so much closer to her in dancing, and put his arm round the pretty German, and lay the foundation for everything else; in short, he reckoned on complete success resulting from it. He began humming a gavotte, knowing that Germans must have something sedate.

The pretty German walked into the middle of the room and lifted her shapely foot. This attitude so enchanted Pirogov that he flew to kiss her. The lady began to scream, and this only enhanced her charm in Pirogov's eyes. He was showering kisses on her when the door suddenly opened and Schiller walked in, together with Hoffmann and Kunts the carpenter. All these worthy persons were as drunk as cobblers.

But . . . I leave the reader to imagine the wrath and indignation of Schiller.

'Ruffian!' he shouted in the utmost indignation. 'How dare you kiss my wife? You are a scoundrel and not a Russian officer. The devil take you! That's right, isn't it so, friend Hoffmann? I am a German and not a Russian swine.' (Hoffmann gave him an affirmative answer.) 'Oh, I don't want to be made a fool of! Take him by the collar, friend Hoffmann; I won't have it,' he went on, brandishing his arms violently, while his whole face was the colour of his red waistcoat. 'I have been living in Petersburg for eight years, I have a mother in Swabia and an uncle in Nuremberg, I am a German and not a horned ox. Away with him altogether, my friend Hoffmann. Hold him by his arms and his legs, comrade Kunts!'

And the Germans seized Pirogov by his arms and his legs.

He tried in vain to get away; these three tradesmen were among the sturdiest people in Petersburg, and they treated him so roughly and disrespectfully that I cannot find words to do justice to the unfortunate incident.

I am sure that next day Schiller was in a perfect fever, that he was trembling like a leaf, expecting from moment to moment the arrival of the police, that he would have given anything in the world for what had happened on the previous day to be a dream. But what has been cannot be changed. No comparison could do justice to Pirogov's anger and indignation. The very thought of such an unbearable insult drove him to fury. He thought Siberia and the lash too slight a punishment for Schiller. He flew home to dress himself and go at once straight to the general to paint to him in the most vivid colours the seditious insolence of the Germans. He meant to lodge a complaint in writing with the general staff; and, if the punishment meted out to the offenders was not satisfactory, to carry the matter to State Council, or even to the Sovereign himself.

But all this ended rather strangely; on the way he went into a café, ate two jam puffs, read something out of *The Northern Bee* and left the café with his wrath somewhat cooled. Then a pleasant fresh evening led him to take a few turns along Nevsky Prospect; by nine o'clock he had recovered his serenity and decided that he had better not disturb the general on Sunday; especially as he would be sure to be away somewhere. And so he went to spend the evening with one of the directors of the control committee, where he met a very agreeable party of government officials and officers of his regiment. There he spent a very pleasant evening, and so distinguished himself in the mazurka that not only the ladies but even their partners were moved to admiration.

'Marvellously is our world arranged,' I thought as I walked

two days later along Nevsky Prospect, and mused over these two incidents. 'How strangely, how unaccountably fate plays with us! Do we ever get what we desire? Do we ever attain what our powers seem especially fitted for? Everything goes by contraries. Fate gives splendid horses to one man and he drives in his carriage without noticing their beauty, while another who is consumed by a passion for horses has to go on foot, and all the satisfaction he gets is clicking with his tongue when trotting horses are led past him. One has an excellent cook, but unluckily so small a mouth that he cannot take more than two tiny bits; another has a mouth as big as the arch of the Staff Headquarters, but also has to be content with a German dinner of potatoes. What strange pranks fate plays with us!'

But strangest of all are the incidents that take place in Nevsky Prospect. Oh, do not trust that Nevsky Prospect! I always wrap myself more closely in my cloak when I pass along it and try not to look at the objects which meet me. Everything is a cheat, everything is a dream, everything is other than it seems! You think that that gentleman who walks along in a splendidly cut coat is very wealthy? Not a bit of it. All his wealth lies in his coat. You think that those two stout men who stand facing the church that is being built are discussing its architecture? Not at all. They are saying how queerly two crows are sitting opposite each other. You think that that enthusiast waving his arms about is describing how his wife was throwing marbles out of the window to an officer who was a complete stranger to him? Not so at all, he is talking of Lafayette. You imagine those ladies . . . but ladies are least of all to be trusted. Do not look into the shop-windows; the trifles exhibited in them are delightful, but they are suggestive of a fearful pile of notes. But God preserve you from peeping under the ladies' hats! However attractively in the evening a fair lady's cloak may flutter in the distance, nothing would induce me to follow her and try to get a closer views. Keep your distance, for God's sake, keep your distance from the lamp-post! And pass by it quickly, as quickly as you can! It is a happy escape if you get off with nothing worse than some of its stinking oil on your foppish coat.

But it is not just the lamp-post – everything breathes deception. It deceives at all hours, Nevsky Prospect does, but most of all when night falls in masses of shadow on it, throwing into relief the white-and-dun-coloured walls of the houses when all the town is transformed into noise and brilliance, when myriads of carriages roll over bridges, postilions shout and jolt up and down on their horses and when the demon himself lights the street lamps to show everything in false colours.

Old-World Landowners

I AM VERY FOND OF the modest manner of life of those solitary owners of remote villages, who in Little Russia are commonly called 'old-fashioned', who are like tumble-down picturesque little houses, delightful in their simplicity and complete unlikeness to the new smooth buildings whose walls have not yet been discoloured by the rain, whose roofs are not yet covered with green lichen and whose porch does not display its red bricks through the peeling stucco. I like sometimes to enter for a moment into that extraordinarily secluded life in which not one desire flits beyond the palisade surrounding the little courtyard, beyond the hurdle of the orchard filled with plum and apple trees, beyond the village huts surrounding it, lying all aslant under the shade of willows, elders and pear trees. The life of their modest owners is so quiet, so quiet, that for a moment one is lost in forgetfulness and imagines that those passions, desires and restless promptings of the evil spirit that trouble the world have no real existence, and that you have only beheld them in some lurid dazzling dream. I can see now the low-pitched little house with the gallery of little blackened wooden posts running right round it, so that in hail or storm they could close the shutters without being wetted by the rain. Behind it a fragrant bird-cherry, rows of dwarf fruit trees, drowned in a sea of red cherries and amethyst plums, covered with lead-coloured bloom; a spreading maple in the shade of which a rug is laid to rest on; before the house a spacious courtyard of short fresh grass with a little pathway trodden from the storehouse to the kitchen and from the kitchen to the master's apartments; a long-necked goose drinking water with young goslings soft as down around her; a palisade hung with strings of dried pears and apples and rugs put out to air; a cartful of melons standing by the storehouse; an unharnessed ox lying lazily beside it – they all have an inexpressible charm for me, perhaps because I no longer see them and because everything from which we are parted is dear to us.

Be that as it may, at the very moment when my chaise was driving up to the steps of that little house, my soul passed

into a wonderfully sweet and serene mood; the horses gal-
loped merrily up to the steps; the coachman very tranquilly
clambered down from the box and filled his pipe as though
he had reached home; even the barking set up by phlegmatic
Rovers, Pontos and Neros was pleasant to my ears. But more
than all I liked the owners of these modest little nooks – the
little old men and women who came out solicitously to meet
me. I can see their faces sometimes even now among fashionable dress-coats in the noise and crowd, and then I sink
into a half-dreaming state, and the past rises up before me.
Their faces always betray such kindness, such hospitality and
single-heartedness that unconsciously one renounces, for a
brief spell at least, all ambitious dreams, and imperceptibly
passes with all one's heart into this humble bucolic life.

To this day I cannot forget two old people of a past age,
now – alas! – no more. To this day I am full of regret, and
it sends a strange pang to my heart when I imagine myself
going some time again to their old now deserted dwelling,
and seeing the heap of ruined huts, the pond choked with
weeds, an overgrown ditch on the spot where the little house
stood – and nothing more. It is sad! I am sad at the thought!
But let me turn to my story.

Afanasy Ivanovitch Tovstogub and his wife Pulherya Ivanovna Tovstogubiha, as the surrounding peasants called her,

were the old people of whom I was beginning to tell you. If I were a painter and wanted to portray Philemon and Baucis on canvas, I could choose no other models. Afanasy Ivanovitch was sixty. Pulherya Ivanovna was fifty-five. Afanasy Ivanovitch was tall, always wore a camlet-covered sheepskin, used to sit bent up, and was invariably almost smiling, whether he was telling a story or simply listening. Pulherya Ivanovna was rather grave and scarcely ever laughed; but in her face and eyes there was so much kindness, so much readiness to regale you with the best of all they had, that you would certainly have found a smile superfluously sweet for her kind face. The faint wrinkles on their faces were drawn so charmingly that an artist would surely have stolen them; it seemed as though one could read in them their whole life, clear and serene – the life led by the old, typically Little Russian, simple-hearted and at the same time wealthy families, always such a contrast to the meaner sort of Little Russians who, struggling up from making tar and petty trading, swarm like locusts in the law courts and public offices, fleece their fellow villagers of their last farthing, inundate Petersburg with pettifogging attorneys, make their pile at last and solemnly add 'v' to surnames ending in 'o'. No, they, like all the ancient, deep-rooted Little Russian families, were utterly different from such paltry contemptible creatures.

One could not look without sympathy at their mutual love. They never addressed each other familiarly, but always with formality. 'Was it you who broke the chair, Afanasy Ivanovitch?' 'Never mind, don't be cross, Pulherya Ivanovna, it was I.' They had had no children, and so all their affection was concentrated on each other. At one time in his youth Afanasy Ivanovitch was in the service and had been lieutenant-major; but that was very long ago, that was all over, Afanasy Ivanovitch himself scarcely ever recalled it. Afanasy Ivanovitch was married at thirty when he was a fine young fellow and wore an embroidered waistcoat; he even eloped rather neatly with Pulherya Ivanovna, whose relations opposed their marriage; but he thought very little about that either now, at any rate he never spoke of it.

All these far-away extraordinary adventures had been followed by a peaceful and secluded life, by the soothing and harmonious dreams that you enjoy when you sit on a wooden balcony overlooking the garden, while a delicious rain keeps up a luxurious sound pattering on the leaves, flowing in gurgling streams and inducing a drowsiness in your limbs, while a rainbow steals from behind the trees and in the form of a half-broken arch gleams in the sky with seven soft colours – or when you are swayed in a carriage that drives between green bushes while the quail of the steppes calls and the fragrant grass mingled with ears of corn and wild flowers thrusts itself in at the carriage doors, flicking you pleasantly on the hands and face.

Afanasy Ivanovitch always listened with a pleasant smile to the guests who visited him; sometimes he talked himself, but more often he asked questions. He was not one of those old people who bore one with everlasting praises of old days or denunciations of the new: on the contrary, as he questioned you, he showed great interest and curiosity about the circumstances of your own life, your failures and successes, in which all kind-hearted old people show an interest, though it is a little like the curiosity of a child who examines the seal on your watch at the same time as he talks to you. Then his face, one may say, was breathing with kindliness.

The rooms of the little house in which our old people lived were small and low-pitched, as they usually are in the houses of old-world folk. In each room there was an immense stove which covered nearly a third of the floor space. These rooms were terribly hot, for both Afanasy Ivanovitch and Pulherya Ivanovna liked warmth. The stoves were all heated from the outer room, which was always filled almost up to the ceiling with straw, commonly used in Little Russia instead of firewood. The crackle and flare of this burning straw made the outer room exceedingly pleasant on a winter's evening when ardent young men, chilled with the pursuit of some sun-kissed peasant girl, ran in, clapping their hands. The walls of the room were adorned with a few pictures in old-fashioned narrow frames. I am convinced that their owners had themselves long ago forgotten what they represented, and if some of them had been taken away they would probably not have noticed it. There were two big portraits painted in oils. One depicted a bishop, the other Peter III; a fly-blown Duchesse de La Vallière looked out from a narrow frame. Round the windows and above the doors there were numbers of little pictures which one grew used to looking upon as spots on the wall and so never examined them. In almost all the rooms the floor was of clay, but cleanly painted and kept with a neatness with which probably no parquet floor in a wealthy house, lazily swept by a drowsy gentlemen in livery, has ever been kept.

Pulherya Ivanovna's room was all crammed with chests and boxes, big and little. Numbers of little bags and sacks of flower seeds, vegetable seeds and melon seeds hung on the walls. Numbers of balls of different-coloured wools and rags of old-fashioned gowns made half a century ago were stored in the little chests and between the little chests in the corners. Pulherya Ivanovna was a notable housewife and stored everything, though sometimes she could not herself have said to what use it could be put afterwards.

But the most remarkable thing in the house was the singing of the doors. As soon as morning came the singing of the doors could be heard all over the house, I cannot say why it was they sang: whether the rusty hinges were to blame for it or whether the mechanic who made them had concealed some secret in them; but it was remarkable that each door had its own voice; the door leading to the bedroom sang in the thinnest falsetto and the door into the dining-room in a husky bass; but the one on the outer room gave out a strange cracked and at the same time moaning sound, so that as one listened to it one heard distinctly: 'Holy Saints! I am freezing!' I know that many people very much dislike this sound; but I am very fond of it, and if here I sometimes happen to hear a door creak, it seems at once to bring me a whiff of the country: the low-pitched little room lit by a candle in an old-fashioned candlestick; supper already on the table; a dark May night peeping in from the garden through the open window at the table laid with knives and forks; the nightingale flooding garden, house and far-away river with its trilling song; the tremor and rustle of branches and, my God! what a long string of memories stretches before me then! . . .

The chairs in the room were massive wooden ones such as were common in old days; they all had high carved backs and were without any kind of varnish or stain; they were not even upholstered, and were rather like the chairs on which bishops sit to this day. Little triangular tables in the corners and square ones before the sofa, and the mirror in its thin gold frame carved with leaves which the flies had covered with black spots; in front of the sofa a rug with birds on it that looked like flowers and flowers that looked like birds: that was almost all the furnishing of the unpretentious little house in which my old people lived. The maids' room was packed full of young girls, and girls who were not young, in striped petticoats; Pulherya Ivanovna sometimes gave them some trifling sewing or set them to prepare the fruit, but for the most part they ran off to the kitchen and slept. Pulherya Ivanovna thought it necessary to keep them in the house and looked strictly after their morals; but to her great surprise many months never passed without the waist of some girl or other growing much larger than usual. This seemed the more surprising as there was scarcely a bachelor in the house with the exception of the houseboy, who used to go about barefoot in a grey tail-coat, and if he were not eating was sure to be asleep. Pulherya Ivanovna usually scolded the erring damsel and punished her severely that it might not happen again.

A terrible number of flies were always buzzing on the window-panes, above whose notes rose the deep bass of a bumble-bee, sometimes accompanied by the shrill plaint of a wasp; then as soon as candles were brought the whole gang went to bed and covered the whole ceiling with a black cloud.

Afanasy Ivanovitch took very little interest in farming his land, though he did drive out sometimes to the mowers and reapers and watched their labours rather attentively; the whole burden of management rested upon Pulherya Ivanovna. Pulherya Ivanovna's housekeeping consisted in continually locking up and unlocking the storeroom, and in salting, drying and preserving countless masses of fruits and vegetables. Her house was quite like a chemical laboratory. There was everlastingly a fire built under an apple tree; and a cauldron or a copper pan of jam, jelly, or fruit cheese made with honey, sugar and I don't remember what else, was scarcely ever taken off the iron tripod on which it stood. Under another tree the coachman was forever distilling in a copper retort vodka with peach leaves, or bird-cherry flowers or centaury or cherry stones, and at the end of the process was utterly unable to control his tongue, jabbered such nonsense that Pulherya Ivanovna could make nothing of it, and had to go away to sleep it off in the kitchen. Such a quantity of all this stuff was boiled, salted and dried that the whole courtyard would probably have been drowned in it at last (for Pulherya Ivanovna always liked to prepare a store for the future in addition to all that was reckoned necessary for use), if the larger half of it had not been eaten up by the serf-girls who, stealing into the storeroom, would overeat themselves so frightfully that they were moaning and complaining of stomach ache all day. Pulherya Ivanovna had little chance of looking after the tilling of the fields or other branches of husbandry. The steward, in conjunction with the village elder, robbed them in a merciless fashion. They had adopted the habit of treating their master's forest-land as though it were their own; they made numbers of sledges and sold them at the nearest fair; moreover, all the thick oaks they sold to the neighbouring Cossacks to be cut down for building mills. Only on one occasion Pulherya Ivanovna had desired to inspect her forests. For this purpose a chaise was brought out with immense leather aprons which, as soon as the coachman shook the reins and the horses, who had served in the militia, set off, filled the air with strange sounds, so that a flute and a tambourine and a drum all seemed suddenly audible; every nail and iron bolt clanked so loudly that even at the mill it could be heard that the mistress was driving out of the yard, though the distance was fully a mile and a half. Pulherya Ivanovna could not help noticing the terrible devastation in the forest and the loss of the oaks, which even in childhood she had known to be a hundred years old.

'Why is it, Nitchipor,' she said, addressing her steward who was on the spot, 'that the oaks have been so thinned? Mind that the hair on your head does not grow as thin.'

'Why is it?' the steward said. 'They have fallen down! They have simply fallen: struck by lightning, gnawed by maggots – they have fallen, lady.' Pulherya Ivanovna was completely satisfied with this answer, and on arriving home merely gave orders that the watch should be doubled in the garden near the Spanish cherry trees and the big winter pears.

These worthy rulers, the steward and the elder, considered it quite superfluous to take all the flour to their master's granaries; they thought that the latter would have quite enough with half, and what is more they took to the granaries the half that had begun to grow mouldy or had got wet and been rejected at the fair. But however much the steward and the elder stole; however gluttonously everyone on the place ate, from the housekeeper to the pigs, who guzzled an immense number of plums and apples and often pushed the tree with their snouts to shake a perfect rain of fruit down from it; however much the sparrows and crows pecked; however many presents all the servants carried to their friends in other villages, even hauling off old linen and yarn from the storerooms, all of which went into the ever-flowing stream, that is, to the pot-house; however much was stolen by visitors, phlegmatic coachmen and flunkeys, yet the blessed earth produced everything in such abundance, and Afanasy Ivanovitch and Pulherya Ivanovna wanted so little, that all this terrible robbery made no perceptible impression on their prosperity.

Both the old people were very fond of good fare, as was the old-fashioned tradition of old-world landowners. As soon as the sun had risen (they always got up early) and as soon as the doors set up their varied concert, they were sitting down to a little table, drinking coffee. When he had finished his coffee Afanasy Ivanovitch would go out into the porch and, shaking his handkerchief, say 'Kish, kish! Get off the steps, geese!' In the yard he usually came across the steward. As a rule he entered into conversation with him, questioned him about the field labours with the greatest minuteness, made observations and gave orders which would have impressed anyone with his extraordinary knowledge of farming; and no novice would have dared to dream that he could steal from such a sharp-eyed master. But the steward was a wily old bird: he knew how he must answer, and, what is more, he knew how to manage the land.

After this Afanasy Ivanovitch would go back indoors, and going up to his wife would say: 'Well, Pulherya Ivanovna, isn't it time perhaps for a snack of something?'

'What would you like to have now, Afanasy Ivanovitch?

Would you like lardy-cakes or poppy-seed pies, or perhaps salted mushrooms?'

'Perhaps mushrooms or pies,' answered Afanasy Ivanovitch; and the table would at once be laid with a cloth, pies and mushrooms.

An hour before dinner Afanasy Ivanovitch would have another snack, would empty an antique silver goblet of vodka, would eat mushrooms, various sorts of dried fish and so on. They sat down to dinner at twelve o'clock. Besides the dishes and sauce-boats, there stood on the table numbers of pots with closely covered lids that no appetising masterpiece of old-fashioned cookery might lose flavour. At dinner the conversation usually turned on subjects closely related to the dinner.

'I fancy this porridge,' Afanasy Ivanovitch would say, 'is a little bit burned. Don't you think so, Pulherya Ivanovna?'

'No, Afanasy Ivanovitch. You put a little more butter to it, then it won't taste burned, or have some of this mushroom sauce; pour that over it!'

'Perhaps,' said Afanasy Ivanovitch, passing his plate: 'Let us try how it would be.'

After dinner Afanasy Ivanovitch went to lie down for an hour, after which Pulherya Ivanovna would bring a sliced watermelon and say: 'Taste what a nice melon, Afanasy Ivanovitch.'

'Don't you be so sure of it, Pulherya Ivanovna, because it is red in the middle,' Afanasy Ivanovitch would say, taking a good slice. 'There are some that are red and are not nice.'

But the melon quickly disappeared. After that Afanasy Ivanovitch would eat a few pears and go for a walk in the garden with Pulherya Ivanovna. On returning home Pulherya Ivanovna would go to look after household affairs, while he sat under an awning turned towards the courtyard and watched the storeroom continually displaying and concealing its interior and the serf-girls pushing one another as they brought in or carried out heaps of trifles of all sorts in wooden boxes, sieves, trays and other receptacles for holding fruit. A little afterwards he sent for Pulherya Ivanovna, or went himself to her and said: 'What shall I have to eat, Pulherya Ivanovna?'

'What would you like?' Pulherya Ivanovna would say. 'Shall I go and tell them to bring you the fruit-dumpling I ordered them to keep on purpose for you?'

'That would be nice,' Afanasy Ivanovitch answered.

'Or perhaps you would like some jelly?'

'That would be good too,' Afanasy Ivanovitch would answer. Then all this was promptly brought him and duly eaten.

Before supper Afanasy Ivanovitch would have another snack of something. At half-past nine they sat down to supper.

After supper they at once went to bed, and a universal stillness reigned in this active and at the same time tranquil home.

The room in which Afanasy Ivanovitch and Pulherya Ivanovna slept was so hot that not many people could have stayed in it for several hours; but Afanasy Ivanovitch, in order to be even hotter, used to sleep on the platform of the stove, though the intense heat made him get up several times in the night and walk about the room. Sometimes Afanasy Ivanovitch would moan as he walked about the room. Then Pulherya Ivanovna would ask: 'What are you groaning for, Afanasy Ivanovitch?'

'Goodness only knows, Pulherya Ivanovna; I feel as though I had a little stomach ache,' Afanasy Ivanovitch would say.

'Hadn't you better eat something, Afanasy Ivanovitch?'

'I don't know whether it would be good, Pulherya Ivanovna! What should I eat, though?'

'Sour milk or some dried pears stewed.'

'Perhaps I might try it, anyway,' Afanasy Ivanovitch would say.

Then a sleepy serf-girl would go off to rummage in the cupboards, and Afanasy Ivanovitch would eat a plateful, after which he commonly said: 'Now it does seem to be better.'

Sometimes, if it was fine weather and rather warm indoors, Afanasy Ivanovitch being in good spirits liked to make fun of Pulherya Ivanovna and talk of something.

'Pulherya Ivanovna,' he would say, 'what if our house were suddenly burned down, where should we go?'

'Heaven forbid!' Pulherya Ivanovna would say, crossing herself.

'But suppose our house were burned down, where should we go then?'

'God knows what you are saying, Afanasy Ivanovitch! How is it possible that our house could be burned down? God will not permit it.'

'Well, but if it were burned down?'

'Oh, then we would move into the kitchen. You should have for the time the little room that the housekeeper has now.'

'But if the kitchen were burned too?'

'What next! God will preserve us from such a calamity as both house and kitchen burned down all at once! Well, then we would move into the storeroom while a new house was being built.'

'And if the storeroom were burned?'

'God knows what you are saying! I don't want to listen to you! It's a sin to say it, and God will punish you for saying such things!'

And Afanasy Ivanovitch, pleased at having made fun of Pulherya Ivanovna, sat smiling in his chair.

But the old couple seemed most of all interesting to me on

the occasions when they had guests. Then everything in their house assumed a different aspect. These good-natured people lived, one may say, for visitors: The best of everything they had was all brought out. They vied with each other in trying to regale you with everything their husbandry produced. But what pleased me most of all was that in their solicitude there was no trace of unctuousness. This hospitality and readiness to please were so gently expressed in their faces, so in keeping with them, that the guests could not help falling in with their wishes, which were the expression of the pure serene simplicity of their kindly guileless souls. This hospitality was something quite different from the way in which a clerk of some government office who has been helped in his career by your efforts entertains you, calling you his benefactor and cringing at your feet. The visitor was on no account to leave on the same day: he absolutely had to stay the night.

'How could you set off on such a long journey at so late an hour!' Pulherya Ivanovna always said. (The guest usually lived two or three miles away.)

'Of course not,' Afanasy Ivanovitch said. 'You never know what may happen: robbers or other evil-minded men may attack you.'

'God preserve us from robbers!' said Pulherya Ivanovna. 'And why talk of such things at night? It's not a question of robbers, but it's dark, it's not fit for driving at all. Besides, your coachman . . . I know your coachman, he is so frail, and such a little man, any horse would be too much for him; and besides he has probably had a drop by now and is asleep somewhere.' And the guest was forced to remain; but the evening spent in the low-pitched hot room, the kindly, warming and soporific talk, the steam rising from the food on the table, always nourishing and cooked in first-class fashion, were compensation for him. I can see as though it were today Afanasy Ivanovitch sitting bent in his chair with his invariable smile, listening to his visitor with attention and even delight! Often the talk touched on politics. The guest, who also very rarely left his village, would often with a significant air and a mysterious expression trot out his conjectures, telling them that the French had a secret agreement with the English to let Bonaparte out again in order to attack Russia, or would simply prophesy war in the near future; and then Afanasy Ivanovitch, pretending not to look at Pulherya Ivanovna, would often say: 'I think I shall go to the war myself; why shouldn't I go to the war?'

'There he goes again!' Pulherya Ivanovna interrupted. 'Don't you believe him,' she said, turning to the guest. 'How could an old man like him go to the war! The first soldier would shoot him! Yes, indeed he would! He'd simply take aim and shoot him.'

'Well,' said Afanasy Ivanovitch, 'and I'll shoot him.'

'Just hear how he talks!' Pulherya Ivanovna caught him up. 'How could he go to the war! And his pistols have been rusty for years and are lying in the cupboard. You should just see them: why, they'd explode with the gunpowder before they'd fire a shot. And he'd blow off his hands and disfigure his face and be wretched for the rest of his days!'

'Well,' said Afanasy Ivanovitch, 'I'd buy myself new weapons; I'll take my sabre or a Cossack lance.'

'That's all nonsense. An idea comes into his head and he begins talking!' Pulherya Ivanovna interrupted with vexation. 'I know he is only joking, but yet I don't like to hear it. That's the way he always talks; sometimes one listens and listens till it frightens one.'

But Afanasy Ivanovitch, pleased at having scared Pulherya Ivanovna a little, laughed sitting bent up in his chair. Pulherya Ivanovna was most attractive to me when she was taking a guest in to lunch. 'This,' she would say, taking a cork out of a bottle, 'is vodka distilled with milfoil and sage – if anyone has a pain in the shoulder blades or loins, it is very good; now this is distilled with centaury – if anyone has a ringing in the ears or a rash on the face, it is very good; and this now is distilled with peach stones – take a glass, isn't it a delicious smell? If anyone getting up in the morning knocks his head against a corner of the cupboard or a table and a bump comes up on his forehead, he has only to drink one glass of it before dinner and it takes it away entirely; it all passes off that very minute, as though it had never been there at all.' Then followed a similar account of the other bottles, which all had some healing properties. After burdening the guest with all these remedies she would lead him up to a number of dishes. 'These are mushrooms with wild thyme! These are with cloves and hazelnuts! A Turkish woman taught me to salt them in the days when we still had Turkish prisoners here. She was such a nice woman, and it was not noticeable at all that she professed the Turkish religion: she went about almost exactly as we do; only she wouldn't eat pork; she said it was forbidden somewhere in their law. And these are mushrooms prepared with blackcurrant leaves and nutmeg! And these are big pumpkins: it's the first time I have pickled them in vinegar; I don't know what they'll be like! I learned the secret from Father Ivan; first of all you must lay some oak leaves in a tub and then sprinkle with pepper and saltpetre and then put in the flower of the hawkweed, take the flowers and strew them in with stalks uppermost. And here are the little pies; these are cheese pies. And those are the ones Afanasy Ivanovitch is very fond of, made with cabbage and buckwheat.'

'Yes,' Afanasy Ivanovitch would add, 'I am very fond of them; they are soft and a little sourish.'

As a rule Pulherya Ivanovna was in the best of spirits when she had guests. Dear old woman! She was entirely given up to her visitors. I liked staying with them, and although I overate fearfully, as indeed all their visitors did, and though that was very bad for me, I was always glad to go and see them. But I wonder whether the very air of Little Russia has not some peculiar property that promotes digestion; for if anyone were to venture to eat in that way here, there is no doubt he would find himself lying in his coffin instead of his bed.

Good old people! But my account of them is approaching a very melancholy incident which transformed for ever the life of that peaceful nook. This incident is the more impressive because it arose from such an insignificant cause. But such is the strange order of things; trifling causes have always given rise to great events, and on the other hand great undertakings frequently end in insignificant results. Some military leader rallies all the forces of his state, carries on a war for several years, his generals cover themselves with glory, and in the end it all results in gaining a bit of land in which there is not room to plant a potato; while sometimes two sausage-makers of two towns quarrel over some nonsense, and in the end the towns are drawn into the quarrel, then villages and then the whole kingdom. But let us abandon these reflections: they are out of keeping here; besides I am not fond of reflections, so long as they get no further than being reflections.

Pulherya Ivanovna had a little grey cat, which almost always lay curled up at her feet. Pulherya Ivanovna sometimes stroked her and with one finger scratched her neck, which the spoiled cat stretched as high as she could. I cannot say that Pulherya Ivanovna was excessively fond of her, she was simply attached to her from being used to seeing her about. Afanasy Ivanovitch, however, often teased her about her affection for it.

'I don't know, Pulherya Ivanovna, what you find in the cat: what use is she? If you had a dog, then it would be a different matter: one can take a dog out shooting, but what use is a cat?'

'Oh, be quiet, Afanasy Ivanovitch,' said Pulherya Ivanovna. 'You are simply fond of talking and nothing else. A dog is not clean, a dog makes a mess, a dog breaks everything, while a cat is a quiet creature: she does no harm to anyone.'

Cats and dogs were all the same to Afanasy Ivanovitch, however; he only said it to tease Pulherya Ivanovna a little.

Beyond their garden they had a big forest which had been completely spared by the enterprising steward, perhaps because the sound of the axe would have reached the ears of

Pulherya Ivanovna. It was wild and neglected, the old tree-trunks were covered with overgrown nut bushes and looked like the feathered legs of trumpeter pigeons. Wild cats lived in this forest. Wild forest cats must not be confounded with the bold rascals who run about on the roofs of houses; in spite of their fierce disposition the latter, being in cities, are far more civilised than the inhabitants of the forest. Unlike the town cats the latter are for the most part shy and gloomy creatures; they are always gaunt and lean, they mew in a coarse uncultured voice. They sometimes scratch their way underground into the very storehouses and steal bacon; they even penetrate into the kitchen, springing suddenly in at the open window when they see that the cook has gone off into the high grass.

In fact they are unacquainted with any noble sentiments; they live by plunder, and murder little sparrows in their nests. These cats had for a long time past sniffed through a hole under the storehouse at Pulherya Ivanovna's gentle little cat and at last they enticed her away, as a company of soldiers entices a silly peasant girl. Pulherya Ivanovna noticed the disappearance of the cat and sent to look for her; but the cat was not found. Three days passed; Pulherya Ivanovna was sorry to lose her, but at last forgot her. One day when she was inspecting her vegetable garden and was returning with fresh green cucumbers plucked by her own hand for Afanasy Ivanovitch, her ear was caught by a most pitiful mew. As though by instinct she called, 'Puss, puss!' and all at once her grey cat, lean and skinny, came out from the high grass; it was evident that she had not tasted food for several days. Pulherya Ivanovna went on calling her, but the cat stood mewing and did not venture to come close; it was clear that she had grown very wild during her absence. Pulherya Ivanovna went on still calling the cat, who timidly followed her right up to the fence. At last, seeing the old familiar places, she even went indoors. Pulherya Ivanovna at once ordered milk and meat to be brought her and, sitting before her, enjoyed the greediness with which her poor little favourite swallowed piece after piece and lapped up the milk. The little grey fugitive grew fatter almost before her eyes and soon did not eat so greedily. Pulherya Ivanovna stretched out her hand to stroke her, but the ungrateful creature had evidently grown too much accustomed to the ways of wild cats, or had adopted the romantic principle that poverty with love is better than a palace, and, indeed, the wild cats were as poor as church mice; anyway, she sprang out of a window and not one of the house-serfs could catch her.

The old lady sank into thought. 'It was my death coming for me!' she said to herself, and nothing could distract her mind. All day she was sad. In vain Afanasy Ivanovitch joked and tried to find out why she was so melancholy all of a sudden. Pulherya Ivanovna made no answer, or answered in a way that could not possibly satisfy Afanasy Ivanovitch. Next day she was perceptibly thinner.

'What is the matter with you, Pulherya Ivanovna? You must be ill.'

'No, I am not ill, Afanasy Ivanovitch! I want to tell you something strange; I know that I shall die this summer: my death has already come to fetch me!'

Afanasy Ivanovitch's lips twitched painfully. He tried, however, to overcome his gloomy feeling and with a smile said: 'God knows what you are saying, Pulherya Ivanovna! You must have drunk some peach vodka instead of the concoction you usually drink.'

'No, Afanasy Ivanovitch, I have not drunk peach vodka,' said Pulherya Ivanovna. And Afanasy Ivanovitch was sorry that he had so teased her; he looked at her and a tear hung on his eyelash.

'I beg you, Afanasy Ivanovitch, to carry out my wishes,' said Pulherya Ivanovna; 'when I die, bury me by the church fence. Put my grey dress on me, the one with the little flowers on a brown ground. Don't put on me my satin dress with the crimson stripes: a dead woman has no need of a dress – what use is it to her? – while it will be of use to you: have a fine dressing-gown made of it, so that when visitors are here you can show yourself and welcome them, looking decent.'

'God knows what you are saying, Pulherya Ivanovna!' said Afanasy Ivanovitch. 'Death may be a long way off, but you are frightening me already with such sayings.'

'No, Afanasy Ivanovitch, I know now when my death will come. Don't grieve for me, though: I am an old woman and have lived long enough, and you are old, too; we shall soon meet in the other world.'

But Afanasy Ivanovitch was sobbing like a child.

'It's a sin to weep, Afanasy Ivanovitch! Do not be sinful and anger God by your sorrow. I am not sorry that I am dying; there is only one thing I am sorry about –' a heavy sigh interrupted her words for a minute – 'I am sorry that I do not know in whose care to leave you, who will look after you when I am dead. You are like a little child. You need somebody who loves you to look after you.'

At these words there was an expression of such deep, such distressed heartfelt pity on her face that I doubt whether anyone could have looked at her at that moment unmoved.

'Mind, Yavdoha,' she said, turning to the housekeeper for whom she had purposely sent, 'that when I die you look after your master, watch over him like the apple of your eye, like your own child. Mind that what he likes is always cooked for him in the kitchen; that you always give him clean underwear and clothes; that when visitors come you dress him in his best, or else maybe he will sometimes come out in his old dressing-gown, because even now he often forgets when it's a holiday and when it's a working day. Don't take your eyes off him, Yavdoha; I will pray for you in the next world and God will reward you. Do not forget, Yavdoha, you are old, you have not long to live – do not take a sin upon your soul. If you do not look after him you will have no happiness in life. I myself will beseech God not to give you a happy end. And you will be unhappy yourself and your children will be unhappy, and all your family will not have the blessing of God in anything.'

Poor old woman! At that minute she was not thinking of the great moment awaiting her, nor of her soul, nor of her own future life: she was thinking only of her poor companion with whom she had spent her life and whom she was leaving helpless and forlorn. With extraordinary efficiency she arranged everything, so that Afanasy Ivanovitch should not notice her absence when she was gone. Her conviction that her end was at hand was so strong, and her state of mind was so attuned to it, that she did in fact take to her bed a few days later and could eat nothing. Afanasy Ivanovitch never left her bedside and was all solicitude.

'Perhaps you would eat a little of something, Pulherya Ivanovna,' he said, looking with anxiety into her eyes. But Pulherya Ivanovna said nothing. At last, after a long silence she seemed trying to say something, her lips stirred – and her breathing ceased.

Afanasy Ivanovitch was absolutely overwhelmed. It seemed to him so uncanny that he did not even weep; he looked at her with dull eyes as though not grasping the significance of the corpse.

The dead woman was laid on the table dressed in the gown she had herself fixed upon, her arms were crossed and a wax candle put in her hand – he looked at all this apathetically. Multitides of people of all kinds filled the courtyard; numbers of guests came to the funeral; long tables were laid out in the courtyard; they were covered with masses of funeral rice, of fruit liqueur and pies. The guests talked and wept, gazed at the dead woman, discussed her qualities and looked at him; but he himself looked queerly at it all. The departed was carried out at last, the people crowded after it and he followed it. The priests were in full vestments, the sun was shining, babies were crying in their mothers' arms, larks were singing and children raced and skipped about the road. At last the coffin was put down above the grave, he was bidden approach and kiss the dead woman for the last time. He went up and kissed her; there were tears in his eyes, but they were somehow apathetic tears. The coffin was lowered, the priest took the spade and first threw in a handful of earth; the deep rich voices of the deacon and the two sacristans sang 'Eternal Memory' under the pure cloudless sky; the labourers took up their spades and soon the earth covered the grave and made it level. At that moment he pressed forward, everyone stepped aside and made way for him, anxious to know what he meant to do. He raised his eyes, looked at them vacantly and said: 'So you have buried her already! What for?' He broke off and said no more.

But when he was home again, when he saw that his room was empty, that even the chair Pulherya Ivanovna used to sit on had been taken away – he sobbed, sobbed violently, inconsolably, and tears flowed from his lustreless eyes like a river.

Five years have passed since then. What grief does not time bear away? What passion survives in the unequal combat with it? I knew a man in the flower of his youth and strength, full of true nobility of character. I knew him in love, tenderly, passionately, madly, fiercely, humbly; and before me, and before my eyes almost, the object of his passion, a tender creature, lovely as an angel, was struck down by merciless death. I have never seen such awful depths of suffering, such frenzied poignant grief, such devouring despair as overwhelmed the luckless lover. I had never imagined that a man could create for himself such a hell with no shadow, no shape, no semblance of hope . . . People tried not to leave him alone; all weapons with which he might have killed himself were hidden from him. A fortnight later he suddenly mastered himself, and began laughing and jesting; he was given his freedom, and the first use he made of it was to buy a pistol. One day his family were terrified by the sudden sound of a shot; they ran into the room and saw him stretched on the floor with a shattered skull. A doctor, who happened to be there at the time and whose skill was famous, saw signs of life in him, found that the wound was not absolutely fatal and, to the amazement of everyone, the young man recovered. The watch kept on him was stricter than ever. Even at dinner a knife was not laid for him and everything was removed with which he could have hurt himself; but in a short time he found another opportunity and threw himself under the wheels of a passing carriage. An arm and a leg were broken; but again he recovered. A year after that I saw him in a roomful of people: he was sitting at a table saying gaily 'petit ouvert', as he covered a card, and behind him, with her elbows on the back of his chair, was standing his young wife, turning over his counters.

At the end of the five years after Pulherya Ivanovna's death I was in those parts and drove to Afanasy Ivanovitch's little farm to visit my old neighbour, in whose house I used at one time to spend the day pleasantly and always to overeat myself with the choicest masterpieces of its hospitable mistress.

As I approached the courtyard the house seemed to me twice as old as it had been: the peasants' huts were lying completely on one side, as no doubt their owners were too; the palisade and the hurdle round the yard were completely broken down, and I myself saw the cook pull sticks out of it to heat the stove, though she need have only taken two steps further to reach the faggot-stack. Sadly I drove up to the steps; the same old Neros and Trustys, by now blind or lame, barked, wagging their fluffy tails covered with burdocks. An old man came out to greet me. Yes, it was he! I knew him at once; but he stooped twice as much as before. He knew me and greeted me with the old familiar smile. I followed him indoors. It seemed as though everything was as before. But I noticed a strange disorder in everything, an unmistakable absence of something. In fact I experienced the strange feelings which come upon us when for the first time we enter the house of a widower whom we have known in old days inseparable from the wife who has shared his life. The feeling is the same when we see a man crippled whom we have always known in health. In everything the absence of careful Pulherya Ivanovna was visible: at table a knife was laid without a handle; the dishes were not cooked with the same skill.

I did not want to ask about the farm, I was afraid even to look at the farm buildings. When we sat down to dinner, a maid tied a napkin round Afanasy Ivanovitch, and it was well she did so, as without it he would have spilled sauce all over his dressing-gown. I tried to entertain him and told him various items of news; he listened with the same smile, but from time to time his eyes were completely vacant, and his thoughts did not stray, but vanished. Often he lifted a spoonful of *kasha* and instead of putting it to his mouth put it to his nose; instead of sticking his fork into a piece of chicken, he prodded the decanter, and then the maid, taking his hand, brought it back to the chicken. We sometimes waited several minutes for the next course.

Afanasy Ivanovitch himself noticed it and said: 'Why is it they are so long bringing the food?' But I saw through the crack of the door that the boy who carried away our plates was asleep and nodding on a bench, not thinking of his duties at all.

'This is the dish,' said Afanasy Ivanovitch, when we were handed curd-cakes with sour cream; 'this is the dish,' he went on, and I noticed that his voice began quivering and a tear was ready to drop from his leaden eyes, but he did his utmost to restrain it: 'This is the dish which my . . . my . . .

dear . . . my dear . . .' And all at once he burst into tears; his hand fell on the plate, the plate turned upside down, slipped and was smashed, and the sauce was spilled all over him. He sat vacantly, vacantly held the spoon; and tears like a stream, like a ceaselessly flowing fountain, flowed and flowed on the napkin that covered him.

'My God!' I thought, looking at him. 'Five years of all-destroying time – an old man already apathetic, an old man whose life one would have thought had never once been stirred by a strong feeling, whose whole life seemed to consist in sitting on a high chair, in eating dried fish and pears, in telling good-natured stories – and such long, such burning grief! What is stronger in us – passion or habit? Or are all the violent impulses, all the whirl of our desires and boiling passions, only the consequence of our ardent age, and is it only through youth that they seem deep and shattering?'

Be that as it may, at that moment all our passions seemed like child's play beside this effect of long, slow, almost insensible habit. Several times he struggled to utter his wife's name, but, halfway through the word, his quiet and ordinary face worked convulsively and his childish weeping cut me to the very heart. No, those were not the tears of which old men are usually so lavish, as they complain of their pitiful position and their troubles; they were not the tears which they drop over a glass of punch either. No! They were tears which brimmed over uninvited from the accumulated rankling pain of a heart already turning cold.

He did not live long after that. I heard lately of his death. It is strange, though, that the circumstances of his end had some resemblance to those of Pulherya Ivanovna's death. One day Afanasy Ivanovitch ventured to take a little walk in the garden. As he was pacing slowly along a path with his usual absent-mindedness, without a thought of any kind in his head, he had a strange adventure. He suddenly heard someone behind him pronounce in a fairly distinct voice: 'Afanasy Ivanovitch!' He turned round but there was absolutely nobody there; he looked in all directions, he peered into the bushes – no one anywhere. It was a still day and the sun was shining. He pondered for a minute; his face seemed to brighten and he brought out at last: 'It's Pulherya Ivanovna calling me!'

It has happened to you doubtless some time or other to hear a voice calling you by name, which simple folk explain as a soul grieving for a human being and calling him, and after that, they say, death follows inevitably. I must own I was always frightened by that mysterious call. I remember that in child-hood I often heard it. Sometimes suddenly someone behind me distinctly uttered my name. Usually on such occasions it was a very bright and sunny day; not one leaf in the garden was stirring; the stillness was deathlike; even the grasshopper left off screaming for the moment; there was not a soul in the garden. But I confess that if the wildest and most tempestuous night had lashed me with all the fury of the elements, alone in the middle of an impenetrable forest, I should not have been so terrified as by that awful stillness in the midst of a cloudless day. I usually ran out of the garden in a great panic, hardly able to breathe, and was only reassured when I met some person, the sight of whom dispelled the terrible spiritual loneliness.

Afanasy Ivanovitch surrendered completely to his inner conviction that Pulherya Ivanovna was calling him; he submitted with the readiness of an obedient child, wasted away, coughed, melted like a candle and at last flickered out, as it does when there is nothing left to sustain its feeble flame. 'Lay me beside Pulherya Ivanovna' was all he said before his end.

His desire was carried out and he was buried near the church beside Pulherya Ivanovna's grave. The guests were fewer at the funeral, but there were just as many beggars and peasants. The little house was now completely emptied. The enterprising steward and the elder hauled away to their huts all that were left of the old-fashioned goods and furniture, which the housekeeper had not been able to carry off. Soon there arrived, I cannot say from where, a distant kinsman, the heir to the estate, who had been a lieutenant, I don't know in what regiment, and was a terrible reformer. He saw at once the great slackness and disorganisation in the management of the land; he made up his mind to change all that radically, to improve things and bring everything into order. He bought six splendid English sickles, pinned a special number on each hut, and managed so well that within six months his estate was put under the supervision of a board of trustees.

The sage trustees (consisting of an ex-assessor and a lieutenant in a faded uniform) had within a very short time left no fowls and eggs. The huts, which were almost lying on the earth, fell down completely; the peasants gave themselves up to drunkenness and most of them ran away. The real owner, who got on, however, pretty comfortably with his trustees and used to drink punch with them, very rarely visited his estate and never stayed long. To this day he drives about to all the fairs in Little Russia, carefully enquiring the prices of all sorts of produce sold wholesale, such as flour, hemp, honey and so on; but he only buys small trifles such as flints, a nail to clean out his pipe, in fact nothing which exceeds at the utmost a rouble in price.

The Carriage

THE LITTLE TOWN OF B. has grown much more lively
since a cavalry regiment began to be stationed in it.
Till then it was fearfully dull. When one drove through it
and glanced at the low-pitched, clay-plastered houses which
looked into the street with an incredibly sour expression . . .
well, it is impossible to put into words what things were like
there; it is as dejecting as though one had lost money at cards,
or just said something stupid and inappropriate – in short, it
is depressing. The plaster on the houses has peeled off with
the rain, and the walls instead of being white are piebald; the
roofs are for the most part thatched with reeds, as is usual in
our Southern towns. The gardens have long ago, by order of
the police-master, been cut down to improve the look of the

place. There is never a soul to be met in the streets; at most a cock crosses the road, soft as a pillow from the dust that lies on it eight inches thick and at the slightest drop of rain is transformed into mud, and then the streets of the town of B. are filled with those corpulent animals which the local police-master calls Frenchmen; thrusting out their solemn snouts from their baths, they set up such a grunting that the traveller can do nothing but urge on his horses. It is not easy, however, to meet a traveller in the town of B. On rare, very rare occasions, some country gentleman, owning eleven souls of serfs and dressed in a full nankeen coat, jolts over the road in something between a chaise and a cart, and peeps out from behind piled-up sacks of flour, as he lashes his solemn mare behind whom runs a colt. Even the marketplace has a rather melancholy air: the tailor's shop stands out very foolishly with one corner to the street instead of the whole shopfront; facing it, a stone building with two windows has been in the course of construction for fifteen years; a little further, standing all by itself, there is one of those paling fences so fashionable, painted grey to match the mud, and erected as a model for other buildings by the police-master in the days of his youth, before he had formed the habit of sleeping immediately after dinner and drinking at night a concoction flavoured with dry gooseberries.

In other parts the fences are all of a hurdle. In the middle of the square, there are very tiny shops; in them one may always see a bunch of bread-rings, a peasant woman in a red kerchief, a hundredweight of soap, a few pounds of bitter almonds, small shot for sportsmen, some cotton-shoddy material, and two shopmen who spend all their time playing a sort of quoits near the door.

But as soon as the cavalry regiment was stationed at the little town of B. everything was changed: the streets were full of life and colour, in fact they assumed quite a different aspect; the low-pitched little houses often saw a graceful, well-built officer with a plume on his head passing by on his way to discuss promotion or the best kind of tobacco with a comrade, or sometimes to play cards for the stake of a chaise, which might have been described as the regimental chaise for, without ever leaving the regiment, it had already gone the round of all the officers; one day the major rolled up in it, the next day it was to be seen in the lieutenant's stable, and a week later, lo and behold, the major's orderly was greasing its wheels with lard again. The wooden fence between the houses was always studded with soldiers' caps hanging in the sun; a grey military overcoat was always conspicuous on some gate; on the side streets soldiers were to be seen with moustaches as stiff as boot-brushes. These moustaches were on view everywhere; if workwomen gathered in the market with their tin mugs, one could always get a glimpse of a moustache behind their shoulders. At the ravenstone, a soldier with a moustache was properly lathering the beard of some village oaf, who only groaned, bulging his eyes upward. The officers brought life into the local society which had until then consisted of a judge, who lived in the same house with a deacon's wife, and a police-master, who was a very sagacious person, but slept absolutely the whole day from dinner-time until evening and from evening until dinner-time. Society gained even more in numbers and interest when the headquarters of the general of the brigade were transferred to the town. Neighbouring landowners, whose existence no one would previously have suspected, began visiting the district town more frequently to see the officers and sometimes to play a game of 'bank', of which there was an extremely hazy notion in their brains, busy with thoughts of crops and hares and their wives' commissions.

I am very sorry that I cannot recall what circumstance it was that led the general of the brigade to give a big dinner; preparations for it were made on a vast scale; the clatter of the cooks' knives in the general's kitchen could be heard almost as far as the town-gate. The whole market was completely cleared out for the dinner, so that the judge and his deaconess had nothing to eat but buckwheat cakes and cornflour-jelly. The little courtyard of the general's quarters was packed with chaises and carriages. The company consisted of gentlemen – officers and a few neighbouring landowners. Of the latter, the most noteworthy was Pifagor Pifagorovitch Tchertokutsky, one of the leading aristocrats of the district of B., who made more noise than anyone at the elections and drove to them in a very smart carriage. He had once served in a cavalry regiment and had been one of its most important and conspicuous officers; anyway, he had been seen at numerous balls and assemblies, wherever his regiment had been stationed; the young ladies of the Tambov and Simbirsk provinces, however, could tell us most about that. It is very possible that he would have gained a desirable reputation in other provinces, too, if he had not resigned his commission owing to one of those incidents which are usually described as 'an unpleasantness'; either he had given someone a box on the ear in old days, or was given it, which I don't remember for certain; anyway, the point is that he was asked to resign his commission. He lost nothing of his importance through this, however. He wore a high-waisted dress-coat of military cut, spurs on his boots, and a moustache under his nose, since, but for that, the nobility of his province might have supposed that he had served in the infantry, which he always spoke of contemptuously. He visited all the much-frequented fairs, to which those who make up the heart of Russia, that is, the mammas and the daughters, and stout landowners, flock to enjoy themselves, driving in chaises with hoods, gigs, waggonettes and carriages such as have never been seen in the wildest dreams. He had a good nose for where a cavalry regiment was stationed, and always went to meet the officers, very nimbly leaping out of his light carriage in view of them and very quickly making their acquaintance.

At the last election he had given the nobility of the provinces an excellent dinner, at which he had declared that, if only he were elected Marshal, he 'would put the gentry on the best possible footing'. Altogether he lived like a gentleman, as the expression goes in the provinces; he married a rather pretty wife, getting with her a dowry of two hundred souls and some thousands in cash. This last was at once spent on a team of six really first-rate horses, gilt locks on the doors, a tame monkey and a French butler for the household. The two hundred souls, together with two hundred of his own, were mortgaged to the bank for the sake of some commercial operations.

In short, he was a proper sort of landowner, a very decent sort of landowner . . .

Apart from this gentleman, there were a few other land-owners at the general's dinner, but there is no need to describe them. The other guests were the officers of the same regiment, besides two staff-officers, a colonel and a rather stout major. The general himself was a thick-set, corpulent person, though an excellent commanding officer, so his subordinates said of him. He spoke in a rather thick, consequential bass. The dinner was remarkable; sturgeon of various sorts, as well as sterlet, bustards, asparagus, quails, partridges and mushrooms, testified to the fact that the cook had not had a drop of anything strong between his lips since the previous day, and that four soldiers had been at work with knives in their hands all night, helping him with the fricassee and the jelly. A multitude of bottles, tall ones with Lafite and short ones with Madeira; a lovely summer day, windows wide open, plates of ice on the table, the crumpled shirt-fronts of the owners of extremely roomy dress-coats, a crossfire of conversation drowned by the general's voice and washed down by champagne – all was in keeping. After dinner they all got up from the table with an agreeable heaviness in their stomachs, and, after lighting pipes, some with long and some with short mouth-pieces, went out on to the steps with cups of coffee in their hands. The general, the colonel and even the major had their uniforms unbuttoned, so that their splendid silk braces were ever so slightly exposed, while other officers, being duly respectful, remained all buttoned-up with the exception of the lower three.

'You can look at her now,' said the general; 'if you please, my dear boy,' he went on, addressing his adjutant, a rather sprightly young man of agreeable appearance, 'tell them to bring the bay mare round! Here you shall see for yourself.' At this point the general took a pull at his pipe and blew out the smoke. 'She is not quite well-groomed: this wretched, accursed little town, they don't have a decent stables here. She is a very–' puff-puff – 'decent mare!'

'And have you' – puff-puff – 'had her long, your Excellency?' said Tchertokutsky.

'Well . . .' puff-puff-puff . . . 'not so long; it's only two years since I had her from the stud-stables.'

'And did you get her broken in, or have you been breaking her in here, your Excellency?'

Puff-puff-pu—ff pu—ff. 'Here.' Saying this, the general completely disappeared in smoke.

Meanwhile a soldier skipped out of the stables, the thud of hoofs was audible, and at last another soldier with huge black moustaches, wearing a white smock, appeared, leading by the bridle a trembling and frightened mare, who, suddenly flinging up her head, almost lifted the soldier, together with his moustaches, into the air.

'There, there, Agrafena Ivanovna!' he said, leading her up to the steps.

The mare's name was Agrafena Ivanovna. Strong and wild as a beauty of the South, she stamped her hoof upon the wooden steps, then suddenly stopped.

The general, laying down his pipe, began with a satisfied air to look at Agrafena Ivanovna. The colonel himself went down the steps and took Agrafena Ivanovna by the nose, the major patted Agrafena Ivanovna on the leg, the others made a clicking sound with their tongues.

Tchertokutsky went down and approached her from behind; the soldier, drawn up to attention and holding the bridle, looked straight into the visitor's eyes as though he wanted to jump into them.

'Very, very fine,' said Tchertokutsky, 'a horse with excellent points! And allow me to ask your Excellency, how does she go?'

'Her action is very good, only . . . that fool of a doctor's assistant, the devil knows, gave her pills of some sort and for the last two days she has done nothing but sneeze.'

'Very fine horse, very; and have you a suitable carriage, your Excellency?'

'A carriage? . . . But she is a saddle-horse, you know.'

'I know that, but I asked your Excellency to find out whether you have a suitable carriage for your other horses.'

'Well, I am not very well-off for carriages, I must own; I have long been wanting to get an up-to-date one. I have written to my brother, who is in Petersburg just now, but I don't know whether he'll send me one or not.'

'I think, your Excellency, there are no better carriages than the Viennese.'

'You are quite right there,' puff-puff-puff.

'I have an excellent carriage, your Excellency, of real Vienna make.'

'What is it like? Is it the one you came here in?'

'Oh no, that's just for rough work, for my excursions, but the other . . . It is a wonder! Light as a feather, and when you are in it, it is simply, saving your Excellency's presence, as though your nurse were rocking you in your cradle!'

'So it is comfortable?'

'Very comfortable indeed: cushions, springs and all looking like a picture.'

'That's nice.'

'And so roomy! As a matter of fact, your Excellency, I have never seen one like it. When I was in the service I used to put a dozen bottles of rum and twenty pounds of tobacco

265

in the boxes, and besides that, I used to have about six uniforms and under-linen and two pipes, the very long ones, your Excellency, while you could put a whole ox in the pockets.'

'That's nice.'

'It cost four thousand, your Excellency.'

'At that price it ought to be good; and did you buy it yourself?'

'No, your Excellency, it came to me by chance; it was bought by my friend, the companion of my childhood, a rare man with whom you would have got on perfectly, your Excellency; we were on such terms that what was his was mine, it was all the same, I won it from him at cards. Would you care, your Excellency, to do me the honour to dine with me tomorrow, and you could have a look at the carriage at the same time?'

'I really don't know what to say . . . for me to come alone like that . . . would you allow me to bring my fellow officers?'

'I beg the other officers to come too. Gentlemen! I shall think it a great pleasure to see you in my house.'

The colonel, the major and the other officers thanked him with a polite bow.

'What I think, your Excellency, is that if one buys a thing it must be good, if it is not good there is no use in having it. When you do me the honour to visit me tomorrow, I will show you a few other things I have bought in the useful line.'

The general looked at him and blew smoke out of his mouth. Tchertokutsky was highly delighted at having invited the officers: he was inwardly ordering pasties and sauces while he looked very good-humouredly at the gentlemen in question, who for their part, too, seemed to feel twice as amiably disposed to him, as could be discerned from their eyes and the small movements they made in the way of half-bows. Tchertokutsky put himself forward with a more free-and-easy air, and there was a melting tone in his voice as though it were weighed down with pleasure.

'There, your Excellency, you will make the acquaintance of my wife.'

'I shall be delighted,' said the general, stroking his moustache.

After that Tchertokutsky wanted to set off home at once that he might be beforehand in preparing everything for the reception of his guests and the dinner to be offered them; he took up his hat, but, strangely enough, it happened that he stayed on for some time. Meanwhile card tables were set in the room. Soon the whole company was divided into parties of four for whist and sat down in the different corners of the general's rooms. Candles were brought; for a long time Tchertokutsky was uncertain whether to sit down to whist or not, but as the officers began to press him to do so, he felt that it would be a breach of the rules of civility to refuse and he sat down for a little while. By his side there appeared from somewhere a glass of punch which, without noticing it, he drank off instantly. After winning two rubbers Tchertokutsky again found a glass of punch at hand and again without observing it emptied the glass, though he did say first, 'It's time for me to be getting home, gentlemen, it really is time,' but, again, he sat down to the second game.

Meanwhile conversation assumed an entirely personal character in the different corners of the room. The whist players were rather silent, but those who were not playing sat on sofas at one side and kept up a conversation of their own. In one corner the staff-captain, with a cushion thrust under his back and a pipe between his teeth, was recounting in a free and flowing style his amatory adventures, which completely absorbed the attention of a circle gathered round him. One extremely fat landowner with short hands rather like overgrown potatoes was listening with an extraordinarily mawkish air, and only from time to time exerted himself to get his short arm behind his broad back and pull out his snuffbox. In another corner a rather heated discussion sprang up concerning squadron drill, and Tchertokutsky, who about that time twice threw down a knave instead of a queen, suddenly intervened in this conversation, which was not addressed to him, and shouted from his corner 'In what year?' or 'Which regiment?' without observing that the question had nothing to do with the matter under discussion.

At last, a few minutes before supper, they left off playing, though the games went on verbally and it seemed as though the heads of all were full of whist. Tchertokutsky remembered perfectly that he had won a great deal, but he picked up nothing, and getting up from the tables stood for a long time in the attitude of a man who has found he has no pocket-handkerchief. Meanwhile supper was served. It need hardly be said that there was no lack of wines and that Tchertokutsky was almost obliged to fill up his glass at times, since there were bottles standing on the right and on the left of him.

A very long conversation dragged on at table, but it was rather oddly conducted. One colonel who had served in the campaign of 1812 described a battle such as had certainly never taken place, and then, I am quite unable to say for what reason, took the stopper out of the decanter and stuck it in the pudding. In short, by the time the party began to break up it was three o'clock, and the coachmen were obliged to carry some of the gentlemen in their arms as though they had been parcels of purchases, and in spite of all his aristocratic breeding Tchertokutsky bowed so low and with such a violent lurch of his head, as he got into his carriage, that he brought two burrs home with him on his moustache.

At home everyone was sound asleep. The coachman had some difficulty in finding a footman, who conducted his master across the drawing-room and handed him over to a maid-servant, in whose charge Tchertokutsky made his way to his bedroom and got into bed beside his young and pretty wife, who was lying in the most enchanting way in snow-white sleeping attire. The jolt made by her husband falling upon the bed awakened her. Stretching, lifting her eyelashes and three times rapidly blinking her eyes, she opened them with a half-angry smile, but seeing that he absolutely declined on this occasion to show any interest in her, she turned over on the other side in vexation, and laying her fresh little cheek on her arm soon afterwards fell asleep.

It was at an hour which would not in the country be described as early that the young mistress of the house woke up beside her snoring spouse. Remembering that it had been nearly four o'clock in the morning when he came home, she did not like to wake him, and so, putting on her bedroom slippers which her husband had ordered for her from Petersburg, with a white dressing-gown draped about her like a flowing stream, she washed in water as fresh as herself and proceeded to attire herself for the day. Glancing at herself a couple of times in the mirror, she saw that she was looking very nice that morning. This apparently insignificant circumstance led her to spend two hours extra before the looking-glass. At last she was very charmingly dressed and went out to take an airing in the garden. As luck would have it, the weather was as lovely as it can only be on a summer day in the South. The sun, which was approaching the zenith, was blazing hot; but it was cool walking in the thick, dark avenue, and the flowers were three times as fragrant in the warmth of the sun. The pretty young wife quite forgot that it was now twelve o'clock and her husband was still asleep. Already she could hear the after-dinner snores of two coachmen and one postilion sleeping in the stable beyond the garden, but she still sat on in a shady avenue from which there was an open view of the highroad, and was absent-mindedly watching it, stretching empty and deserted into the distance, when all at once a cloud of dust appearing in that distance attracted her attention. Gazing intently, she soon discerned several carriages. The foremost was a light open carriage with two seats. In it was sitting a general with thick epaulettes that gleamed in the sun, and beside him a colonel. It was followed by another carriage with seats for four in which were the major, the general's adjutant and two officers sitting opposite. Then came the regimental chaise, familiar to everyone, at the moment in the possession of the fat major. The chaise was followed by a *bon-voyage*, in which there were four officers seated and a fifth on their knees, then came three officers on excellent, dark bay dappled horses.

'Then they may be coming to us,' thought the lady. 'Oh my goodness, they really are! They have turned at the bridge!' She uttered a shriek, clasped her hands and ran right over the flower-beds straight to her husband's bedroom; he was sleeping like the dead.

'Get up! Get up! Make haste and get up!' she shouted, tugging at his arm.

'What?' murmured Tchertokutsky, not opening his eyes.

'Get up, poppet! Do you hear, visitors!'

'Visitors? What visitors?' Saying this, he uttered a slight grunt such as a calf gives when it is looking for its mother's udder, 'Mmm . . .' he muttered. 'Stoop your neck, precious! I'll give you a kiss.'

'Darling, get up, for goodness' sake, make haste! The general and the officers! Oh dear, you've got a burr on your moustache!'

'The general! So he is coming already, then? But why the devil did nobody wake me? And the dinner, what about the dinner? Is everything ready that's wanted?'

'What dinner?'

'Why, didn't I order it?'

'You came back at four o'clock in the morning and you did not say one word to me, however much I questioned you. I didn't wake you, poppet, because I felt sorry for you, you had had no sleep . . .'

The last words she uttered in an extremely supplicating and languishing voice.

Tchertokutsky lay for a minute in bed with his eyes starting out of his head, as though struck by a thunderbolt. At last he jumped out of bed with nothing but his shirt on, forgetting that this was quite unseemly.

'Oh, I am an ass!' he said, slapping himself on the forehead. 'I invited them to dinner! What's to be done? Are they far off?'

'I don't know . . . I expect they will be here any minute.'

'My love . . . hide yourself . . . Hey, who's there? You wretched girl, come in; what are you afraid of, silly? The officers will be here in a minute: you say that our master is not at home, say that he won't be home at all, that he went out early in the morning . . . Do you hear? And tell all the servants the same; make haste!'

Saying this, he hurriedly snatched up his dressing-gown and ran to hide in the carriage-house. He saw that even there he might be discovered. 'Ah, this will be better' flashed through his mind, and in one minute he flung down the steps of the carriage standing near, leaped in, closed the door after him, for greater security covering himself with the apron and the leather, and lay perfectly still, curled up in his dressing-gown.

Meanwhile the carriages drove up to the front steps. The general stepped out and shook himself; after him the colonel, smoothing the plume of his hat with his hands, then the fat major, holding his sabre under his arm, jumped out of the chaise, the slim sub-lieutenants slipped down from the *bonvoyage* with the lieutenant, who had been sitting on the others' knees and, last of all, the officers who had been elegantly riding on horseback alighted from their saddles.

'The master is not at home,' said a footman, coming out on to the steps.

'Not at home? He'll be back to dinner, I suppose?'

'No. His Honour has gone out for the whole day. He won't be back until tomorrow about this time perhaps.'

'Well, upon my soul,' said the general. 'What is the meaning of this?'

'I must own it is queer,' said the colonel, laughing.

'No, really . . . how can he behave like this?' the general went on with displeasure. 'Whew! . . . The devil! . . . Why, if he can't receive people, what does he ask them for?'

'I can't understand how anyone could do it, your Excellency,' a young officer observed.

'What, what?' said the general, who had the habit of always uttering this interrogative monosyllable when he was talking to an officer.

'I said, your Excellency, that it is not the way to behave!'

'Naturally . . . why, if anything has happened, he might let us know at any rate, or else not have asked us.'

'Well, your Excellency, there is no help for it, we shall have to go back,' said the colonel.

'Of course, there is nothing else for it. We can look at the carriage, though, without him; it is not likely that he has taken it with him. Hey, you there! Come here, my man!'

'What is your pleasure?'

'Are you the stable-boy?'

'Yes, your Excellency.'

'Show us the new carriage your master got lately.'

'This way, sir; come to the carriage-house.'

The general went to the carriage-house together with the officers.

'Shall I push it out a little? It is rather dark in here.'

'That's enough, that's enough, that's right!'

The general and the officers went round the carriage and carefully examined the wheels and the springs.

'Well, there is nothing special about it,' said the general. 'It is a most ordinary carriage.'

'A very ugly one,' said the colonel; 'there is nothing good about it at all.'

'I fancy, your Excellency, it is not worth four thousand,' said the young officer.

'What?'

'I say, your Excellency, that I fancy it is not worth four thousand.'

'Four thousand, indeed! Why, it is not worth two, there is nothing in it at all. Perhaps there is something special about the inside . . . Unbutton the leather, my dear fellow, please.'

And what met the officers' eyes was Tchertokutsky, sitting in his dressing-gown curled up in an extraordinary way. 'Ah, you are here!' said the astonished general.

Saying this, he slammed the carriage door at once, covered Tchertokutsky with the apron again and drove away with the officers.

The Nose

I.

An extraordinarily strange incident took place in Petersburg on the 25th of March. The barber, Ivan Yakovlevitch, who lives in the Voznesensky Prospect (his surname is lost, and nothing more appears even on his signboard, where a gentleman is depicted with his cheeks covered with soapsuds, together with the inscription ALSO LETS BLOOD) – the barber Ivan Yakovlevitch woke up rather early and was aware of a smell of hot bread. Raising himself in bed he saw his spouse, a rather portly lady who was very fond of drinking coffee, engaged in taking out of the oven some freshly baked loaves.

'I won't have coffee today, Praskovya Osipovna,' said Ivan Yakovlevitch; 'instead I should like some hot bread with onion.' (The fact is that Ivan Yakovlevitch would have liked both, but he knew that it was utterly impossible to ask for two things at once, for Praskovya Osipovna greatly disliked such caprices.)

'Let the fool have bread, so much the better for me,' thought his spouse to herself, 'there will be an extra cup of coffee left,' and she flung one loaf on the table.

For the sake of propriety Ivan Yakovlevitch put a tail-coat over his shirt, and sitting down to the table, sprinkled with salt and prepared two onions, took a knife in his hand and, making a solemn face, set to work to cut the bread. After dividing the loaf in two halves he looked into the middle of it – and to his amazement saw there something that looked white. Ivan Yakovlevitch scooped at it carefully with his knife and felt it with his finger: 'It's solid,' he said to himself. 'Whatever can it be?'

He thrust in his finger and drew it out – it was a nose! . . . Ivan Yakovlevitch's hand dropped with astonishment, he rubbed his eyes and felt it: it actually was a nose, and, what's more, it looked to him somehow familiar. A look of horror came into Ivan Yakovlevitch's face. But that horror was nothing to the indignation with which his wife was overcome.

'Where have you cut that nose off, you brute?' she cried wrathfully. 'You scoundrel, you drunkard, I'll go to the police myself to tell of you! You bandit! Here I have heard from three men that when you are shaving them you pull at their noses till you almost tug them off.'

But Ivan Yakovlevitch was more dead than alive: he perceived that the nose was no other than that of Kovalyov, the collegiate assessor, whom he shaved every Wednesday and every Sunday.

'Stay, Praskovya Osipovna! I'll wrap it up in a rag and put it in a corner. Let it stay there for a bit; I'll take it out later on.'

'I won't hear of it! As though I would allow a cut-off nose to lie about in my room. You dried-up biscuit! To be sure, he can do nothing but sharpen his razors on the strop, but soon he won't be fit to do his duties at all, the gad-about, the rake! As though I were going to answer to the police for you . . . Oh, you sloven, you stupid blockhead. Away with it, away with it! Take it where you like! Don't let me get even a whiff of it again!'

Ivan Yakovlevitch stood as though utterly crushed. He thought and thought, and did not know what to think.

'The devil only knows how it happened,' he said at last, scratching behind his ear. 'Did I come home drunk last night or not? I can't say for certain now. But from all the signs and tokens it must be a thing quite unheard of, for bread is a thing that is baked, while a nose is something quite different. I can't make head or tail of it.'

Ivan Yakovlevitch sank into silence. The thought that the police might make a search there for the nose and throw the blame of it on him reduced him to complete prostration. Already the red collar, beautifully embroidered with silver, the sabre, hovered before his eyes, and he trembled all over. At last he got his breeches and his boots, pulled on these wretched objects, and, accompanied by the stern upbraidings of Praskovya Osipovna, wrapped the nose in a rag and went out into the street.

He wanted to thrust it out of sight somewhere, under a gate, or somehow accidentally to drop it and then turn off into a side street, but as ill-luck would have it he kept coming upon someone he knew, who would at once begin by asking 'Where are you going?' or 'Whom are you going to shave so early?' so that Ivan Yakovlevitch could never find a good moment. Another time he really did drop it, but a sentry pointed to it with this halberd from a long way off, saying as he did so, 'Pick it up, you have dropped something!' and Ivan Yakovlevitch was obliged to pick up the nose and put it in his pocket. He was overcome by despair as the number of people in the street was continually increasing as the shops and stalls began to open.

He made up his mind to go to St Isaac's Bridge in the hope of being able to fling it into the Neva . . . But I am rather in fault for not having hitherto said anything about Ivan Yakovlevitch, a worthy man in many respects.

Ivan Yakovlevitch, like every self-respecting Russian workman, was a terrible drunkard, and though every day he shaved other people's chins, his own went forever unshaven. Ivan Yakovlevitch's tail-coat (he never wore any other shape) was piebald, that is, it was black dappled all over with brown and yellow and grey; the collar was shiny, and instead of three buttons there were only hanging threads. Ivan Yakovlevitch was a great cynic, and when Kovalyov, the collegiate assessor, said to him while he was being shaved, 'Your hands always stink, Ivan Yak,' the latter would reply with the question: 'What should make them stink?' 'I can't tell, my good man, but they do stink,' the collegiate assessor would say, and, taking a pinch of snuff, Ivan Yakovlevitch lathered him for it on his cheeks and under his nose and behind his ears and under his beard – in fact wherever he chose.

The worthy citizen found himself by now on St Isaac's Bridge. First of all he looked about him, then bent over the parapet as though to look under the bridge to see whether there were a great number of fish racing by, and stealthily flung in the rag with the nose. He felt as though with it a heavy weight had rolled off his back. Ivan Yakovlevitch even grinned. Instead of going to shave the chins of government clerks, he repaired to an establishment bearing the inscription TEA AND REFRESHMENTS and asked for a glass of punch, when he suddenly observed at the end of the bridge a police inspector of respectable appearance with full whiskers, a three-cornered hat and sword. He turned cold, and meanwhile the inspector beckoned to him and said: 'Come this way, my good man.'

Ivan Yakovlevitch, knowing the etiquette, took off his hat some way off and, as he approached, said, 'I wish your honour good health.'

'No, no, old fellow, I am not "your honour". Tell me what you were about, standing on the bridge.'

'Upon my soul, sir, I was on my way to shave my customers, and I was only looking to see whether the current was running fast.'

'That's a lie, that's a lie! You won't get off with that. Kindly answer!'

'I am ready to shave you, gracious sir, two or even three times a week with no conditions whatever,' answered Ivan Yakovlevitch.

'No, my friend, that is nonsense; I have three barbers to

shave me and they think it is a great honour, too. But be so kind as to tell me what you were doing there?'

Ivan Yakovlevitch turned pale . . . but the incident is completely veiled in obscurity, and absolutely nothing is known of what happened next.

2.

Kovalyov the collegiate assessor woke up early next morning and made the sound *brrrr* with his lips as he always did when he woke up, though he could not himself have explained the reason for his doing so. Kovalyov stretched and asked for a little looking-glass that was standing on the table. He wanted to look at a pimple which had come out upon his nose on the previous evening, but to his great astonishment there was a completely flat space where his nose should have been. Kovalyov in a fright asked for some water and a towel to rub his eyes: there really was no nose. He began feeling around with his hand to see whether he was still asleep: it appeared that he was not asleep. The collegiate assessor, Kovalyov, jumped out of bed, he shook himself – there was still no nose . . . He ordered his clothes to be given him at once and flew off straight to the head police-master.

But meanwhile we must say a word about Kovalyov in order that the reader may have some idea of what kind of collegiate assessor he was. Collegiate assessors who receive that title through learned diplomas cannot be compared with those who are created collegiate assessors in the Caucasus. They are two quite different species. The learned collegiate assessors . . . But Russia is such a wonderful country that, if you say a word about one collegiate assessor, all the collegiate assessors from Roga to Kamchatka would certainly take it to themselves, and it is the same, of course, with all grades and titles. Kovalyov was a collegiate assessor from the Caucasus. He had only been of that rank for the last two years, and so could not forget it for a moment, and to give himself greater weight and dignity he did not call himself simply collegiate assessor but always spoke of himself as a major. 'Listen, my dear,' he would usually say when he met in the street a woman selling shirt-fronts, 'you go to my house; I live in Sadovoy Street; just ask, "Does Major Kovalyov live here?" Anyone will show you.' If he met some prepossessing little baggage he would give her besides a secret instruction, adding: 'You ask for Major Kovalyov's flat, my love.' For this reason we will for the future speak of him as the major.

Major Kovalyov was in the habit of walking every day up and down Nevsky Prospect. The collar on his shirt-front was always extremely clean and well starched. His whiskers were such as one may see nowadays on provincial and district surveyors, on architects and army doctors, also on those employed on special commissions, and in general on all such men as have full ruddy cheeks and are very good hands at a game of boston: these whiskers start from the middle of the cheek and go straight up to the nose. Major Kovalyov used to wear a number of cornelian seals, some with crests on them and others on which were carved Wednesday, Thursday, Monday and so on. Major Kovalyov had come to Petersburg on business, that is, to look for a post befitting his rank: if he were successful, the post of a vice-governor, and failing that the situation of an executive clerk in some prominent department. Major Kovalyov was not averse to matrimony, but only on the condition he could find a bride with a fortune of two hundred thousand. And so the reader may judge for himself what was the major's position when he saw, instead of a nice-looking, well-proportioned nose, an extremely stupid level space.

As ill-luck would have it, not a cab was to be seen in the street, and he was obliged to walk, wrapping himself in his cloak and hiding his face in his handkerchief, as though his nose were bleeding. 'But perhaps it was my imagination: it's impossible I could have been so silly as to lose my nose,' he thought, and went into a confectioner's on purpose to look at himself in the looking-glass. Fortunately there was no one in the shop: some boys were sweeping the floor and putting all the chairs straight; others with sleepy faces were bringing in hot turnovers on trays: yesterday's papers covered with coffee stains were lying about on the tables and chairs. 'Well, thank God, there is nobody here,' he thought, 'now I can look.' He went timidly up to the mirror and looked. 'What the devil's the meaning of it? How nasty!' he commented, spitting. 'If only there had been something instead of a nose, but there is nothing! . . .'

Biting his lips, he went out of the confectioner's with annoyance, and resolved, contrary to his usual practice, not to look or smile at anyone. All at once he stood as though rooted to the spot before the door of a house. Something inexplicable took place before his eyes: a carriage was stopping at the entrance; the carriage door flew open; a gentleman in uniform, bending down, sprang out and ran up the steps. What was the horror and at the same time amazement of Kovalyov when he recognised that this was his own nose! At this extraordinary spectacle it seemed to him that everything was heaving before his eyes; he felt that he could scarcely stand; but he made up his mind, come what may, to await the gentleman's return to the carriage, and he stood trembling all over as though in fever. Two minutes later the nose actually did come out. He was in a gold-laced uniform with a big stand-up collar; he had on chamois-leather breeches, at his side was a sword. From his plumed hat it might be gathered that he was of the rank of a civil councillor. Everything showed that he was going somewhere to pay a visit. He looked to both sides, called to the coachman to open the carriage door, got in and drove off.

Poor Kovalyov almost went out of his mind; he did not know what to think of such a strange occurrence. How was it possible for a nose – which had only yesterday been on his face and could neither drive nor walk – to be in uniform! He ran after the carriage, which luckily did not go far, but stopped before Kazan Cathedral.

He hurried into the cathedral, made his way through a row of old beggar women with their faces wrapped up and two chinks in place of their eyes at whom he used to laugh so merrily, and went into the church. There were not many worshippers inside the church, and they were all huddled around the door. Kovalyov was so agitated that he was utterly unable to pray, and he looked in every corner of the church trying to catch a glimpse of this gentleman. At last he saw him standing off to one side. The nose was completely covering up his face with a large stiff collar and was praying with an expression of the greatest devoutness.

'How am I to approach him?' thought Kovalyov. 'One can see by everything – from his uniform, from his hat – that he is a civil councillor. The devil only knows how to do it!'

He began by coughing at his side; but the nose never changed his devout attitude and continued to bow very low.

'Sir,' said Kovalyov, inwardly forcing himself to speak confidently. 'Sir . . .'

'What do you want?' answered the nose, turning around.

'It seems . . . strange to me, sir . . . You ought to know your proper place, and all at once I find you, where? . . . In church. You will admit . . .'

'Excuse me, I cannot understand what you are talking about . . . Explain.'

'How am I to explain to him?' thought Kovalyov, and plucking up his courage he began: 'Of course I . . . I am a major, by the way. For me to go about without a nose you must admit is improper. An old woman selling peeled oranges on Voskresensky Bridge may sit there without a nose; but having prospects of obtaining . . . and being besides acquainted with a great many ladies in the families of Tchehtarev, the civil councillor and others . . . You can judge for yourself . . . I don't know, sir –' at this point Major Kovalyov shrugged his shoulders – 'excuse me . . . if you look at the matter in accordance with the principles of duty and honour . . . you can understand of yourself . . .'

'I don't understand a word,' said the nose. 'Explain it more satisfactorily.'

'Sir,' said Kovalyov, with a sense of his own dignity, 'I don't know how to understand your words. The matter appears to me perfectly obvious . . . either you wish . . . Why, you are my own nose!'

The nose looked at the major and his eyebrows slightly quivered.

'You are mistaken, sir, I am an independent individual. Moreover, there can be no sort of close relations between us. I see, sir, from the buttons of your uniform, you must be serving in a different department.' Saying this, the nose turned away and continued to pray.

Kovalyov was utterly confused, not knowing what to do or even what to think. Meanwhile they heard the agreeable rustle of a lady's dress: an elderly lady was approaching, all decked out in lace, and with her a slim lady in a white dress which looked very charming on her slender figure, in a straw-coloured hat as light as a pastry puff. Behind them stood, opening his snuffbox, a tall footman with big whiskers and quite a dozen collars.

Kovalyov came nearer, pulled out the cambric collar of

his shirt-front, arranged the seals on his gold watch-chain, and, smiling from side to side, turned his attention to the ethereal lady who, like a spring flower, faintly swayed forward and put her white hand with its half-transparent fingers to her brow. The smile of Kovalyov's face broadened when he saw under her hat the round, dazzlingly white chin and part of her cheek flushed with the hues of the first spring rose; but all at once he skipped away as though he had been scalded. He recollected that he had absolutely nothing on his face in place of a nose, and tears oozed from his eyes. He turned away to tell the gentleman in uniform straight out that he was only pretending to be a civil councillor, that he was a rogue and a scoundrel, and that he was nothing else than his own nose ... But the nose was no longer there; he had managed to gallop off, probably again to call on someone.

This reduced Kovalyov to despair. He went back and stood for a minute or two under the colonnade, carefully looking in all directions to see whether the nose was anywhere about. He remembered very well that there was a plume in his hat and gold lace on his uniform; but he had not noticed his greatcoat nor the colour of his carriage, nor his horses, nor even whether he had a footman behind him and if so in what livery. Moreover, such numbers of carriages were driving backwards and forwards and at such a speed that it was difficult even to distinguish them; and if he had distinguished one of them he would have had no means of stopping it. It was a lovely, sunny day. There were masses of people on Nevsky; ladies were scattered like a perfect cataract of flowers all over the pavement from Politseysky to Anitchkin Bridge. Here he saw coming towards him an upper-court councillor of his acquaintance whom he used to call 'Lieutenant-Colonel', particularly if he were speaking to other people. There he saw Yaryzhkin, a head clerk in the senate, a great friend of his, who always lost points when he went eight at boston. And here was another major who had received the rank of assessor in the Caucasus, beckoning to him . . .

'Ah, deuce take it,' said Kovalyov. 'Hi, cab! Drive straight to the police-master's.'

Kovlayov got into a cab and shouted to the driver: 'Drive like a house on fire!'

'Is the police-master at home?' he cried, going into the entry.

'No,' answered the porter, 'he has only just gone out.'

'Well, I declare!'

'Yes,' added the porter, 'and he has not been gone so long; if you had come but a tiny minute earlier you might have found him.'

Kovalyov, still keeping the handkerchief over his face, got into the cab and shouted in a voice of despair: 'Drive on.'

'Where?' asked the cabman.

'Drive straight on!'

'How straight on? Here's the turning, is it to the right or to the left?'

This question pulled Kovalyov up and forced him to think again. In his position he ought first of all to address himself to the department of law and order, not because it had any direct connection with the police but because the intervention of the latter might be far more rapid than any help he could get in other departments. To see satisfaction from the higher officials of the department in which the nose had announced himself as serving would have been injudicious, since from the nose's own answers he had been able to perceive that nothing was sacred to that man and that he might tell lies in this case too, just as he had lied in declaring that he had never seen him before. And so Kovalyov was on the point of telling the cabman to drive to the Department of Law and Order, when again the idea occurred to him that this rogue and scoundrel who had at their first meeting behaved in such a shameless way might seize the opportunity and slip out of the town – and then all his searches would be in vain, or might be prolonged, which God forbid, for a whole month. At last it seemed that Heaven itself directed him. He decided to go straight to a newspaper office and without loss of time to publish a circumstantial description of the nose, so that anyone meeting it might at once present it to him or at least let him know where it was. And so, deciding upon this course, he told the cabman to drive to the newspaper office, and all the way never ceased pommelling him with his fist on the back, saying, as he did so, 'Quicker, you rascal; make haste, you knave!'

'Ugh, sir!' said the cabman, shaking his head and flicking with the reins at the horse, whose coat was as long as a lap-dog's. At last the cab stopped and Kovalyov ran panting into a little reception-room where a grey-headed clerk in spectacles, wearing an old tail-coat, was sitting at a table, and with a pen between his teeth was counting over some coppers he had before him.

'Who receives enquiries here?' cried Kovaylov. 'Ah, good day!'

'I wish you good day,' said the grey-headed clerk, raising his eyes for a moment and then dropping them again on the money lying in heaps on the table.

'I want to insert an advertisement . . .'

'Allow me to ask you to wait a minute,' the clerk pronounced, with one hand noting a figure on the paper and with the finger of his left hand moving two beads on the reckoning board. A flunkey with braid on his livery and a rather clean appearance, which betrayed that he had at some time served in an aristocratic family, was standing at the table with a written paper in his hand and thought fit to display his social abilities: 'Would you believe it, sir, that the little cur is not worth eighty kopecks; in fact I wouldn't give eight for it, but the countess is fond of it – my goodness, she is fond of it – and here she will give a hundred roubles to anyone who finds it! To speak politely, as you and I are speaking now, people's tastes are quite incompatible. When a man's a sportsman, then he'll keep a setter or a poodle; he won't mind giving five hundred or a thousand so long as it is a good dog.'

The worthy clerk listened to this with a significant air, and at the same time was reckoning the number of letters in the advertisement. Along the sides of the room stood a number of old women, shop-boys and house-porters who had brought advertisements. In one it was announced that a coachman of sober habits was looking for a situation; in the next a second-hand carriage brought from Paris in 1814 was offered for sale; next a maid-servant, aged nineteen, experienced in laundry work and also competent to do other work, was looking for a situation; a strong droshky with only one spring broken was for sale; a spirited, young, dappled grey horse, only seventeen years old, for sale; a new consignment of turnip and radish seed from London; a summer villa with all conveniences, stabling for two horses and a piece of land that might well be planted with fine birches and pine trees; there was also an appeal to those wishing to purchase old boot-soles, inviting such to come for the same every day between eight o'clock in the morning and three o'clock in the afternoon. The room in which all this company was assembled was a small one and the air in it was extremely thick, but the collegiate assessor Kovalyov was incapable of noticing the smell both because he kept his handkerchief over his face and because his nose was goodness knows where.

'Dear sir, allow me to ask you . . . my case is very urgent,' he said at last impatiently.

'In a minute, in a minute! . . . Two roubles, forty-three kopecks! . . . This minute! One rouble and sixty-four kopecks!' said the grey-headed gentleman, flinging the old women and house-porters the various documents they had brought. 'What can I do for you?' he said at last, turning to Kovalyov.

'I want to ask . . .' said Kovalyov. 'Some robbery or trickery has occurred; I cannot make it out at all. I only want you to advertise that anyone who brings me the scoundrel will receive a handsome reward.'

'Allow me to ask what is your surname?'

'No, why put my surname? I cannot give it to you! I have a large circle of acquaintances: Madame Tchehtarev, wife of a civil councillor, Pelageya Grigoryevna Podtatchin, widow of an officer . . . they will find out. God forbid! You can simply put "a collegiate assessor", or better still, "a person of major's rank".'

'Is the runaway your house-serf then?'

'A house-serf indeed! That would not be so great a piece of knavery! It's . . . my nose has run away from me . . . my own nose.'

'Hm, what a strange surname! And is it a very large sum that Mr Nosov has robbed you of?'

'Nosov! . . . you are on the wrong tack. It is my nose, my own nose that has disappeared, I don't know where. The devil wanted to have a joke at my expense.'

'But in what way did it disappear? There is something I can't quite understand.'

'And indeed, I can't tell you how it happened – the point is that now it is driving about the town, calling itself a civil councillor. And so I beg you to announce that anyone who catches him must bring him at once to me as quickly as possible. Only think, really, how can I get on without such a conspicuous part of my person. It's not like a little toe, the loss of which I could hide in my boot and no one could say whether it was there or not. I go on Thursdays to Madame Tchehtarev's; Pelageya Grigoryevna Podtatchin, an officer's widow, and her very pretty daughter are great friends of mine; and you can judge for yourself what a fix I am in now . . . I can't possibly show myself now . . .'

The clerk pondered, a fact which was manifest from the way he compressed his lips.

'No, I can't put an advertisement like that in the paper,' he said at last, after a long silence.

'What? Why not?'

'Well. The newspaper might lose its reputation. If everyone is going to write that his nose has run away, why . . . As it is, they say we print lots of absurd things and false reports.'

'But what is there absurd about this? I don't see anything absurd in it.'

'You fancy there is nothing absurd in it? But last week, now, this was what happened. A government clerk came to me just as you have; he brought an advertisement, it came to two roubles seventy-three kopecks, and all the advertisement amounted to was that a poodle with a black coat had strayed. You wouldn't think that there was anything in that, would you? But it turned out to be a lampoon on someone: the poodle was the cashier of some department, I don't remember which.'

'But I am not asking you to advertise about poodles but about my own nose; that is almost the same as about myself.'

'No, such an advertisement I cannot insert.'

'But since my nose really is lost!'

'If it is lost, that is a matter for the doctor. They say there are people who can fit you with a nose of any shape you like. But I observe you must be a gentleman of merry disposition and are fond of having your joke.'

'I swear as God is holy! If you like, since it has come to that, I will show you.'

'I don't want to trouble you,' said the clerk, taking a pinch of snuff. 'However, if it is no trouble,' he added, moved by curiosity, 'it might be desirable to have a look.'

The collegiate assessor took the handkerchief from his face.

'It really is extremely strange,' said the clerk. 'The place is perfectly flat, like a freshly fried pancake. Yes, it's incredibly smooth.'

'Will you dispute it now? You see for yourself I must advertise. I shall be particularly grateful to you and very glad this incident has given me the pleasure of your acquaintance.'

The major, as may be seen, made up on this occasion to resort to a little flattery.

'To print such an advertisement is, of course, not such a

very great matter,' said the clerk. 'But I do not foresee any advantage to you from it. If you do want to, put it in the hands of someone with a skilful pen, describe it as a rare freak of nature, and publish the little article in the *Northern Bee* –' at this point he once more took a pinch of snuff – 'for the benefit of youth –' at this moment he wiped his nose – 'or anyway as a matter of general interest.'

The collegiate assessor felt quite hopeless. He dropped his eyes and looked at the bottom of the paper where there was an announcement of an entertainment; his face was ready to break into a smile as he saw the name of a pretty actress, and his hand went to his pocket to feel whether he had a five-rouble note there, for an officer of his rank ought, in Kovalyov's opinion, to have a seat in the stalls; but the thought of his nose spoiled it all.

Even the clerk seemed touched by Kovalyov's difficult position. Desirous of relieving his distress in some way, he thought it befitting to express his sympathy in a few words: 'I am really very much grieved that such an incident should have occurred to you. Wouldn't you like a pinch of snuff? It relieves headache and dissipates depression; even in intestinal trouble it is of use.' Saying this, the clerk offered Kovalyov his snuffbox, rather neatly opening the lid with a portrait of a lady in a hat on it.

This unpremeditated action drove Kovalyov out of all patience.

'I can't understand how you can think to make a joke of it,' he said angrily. 'Don't you see that I am without just what I need for sniffing! The devil take your snuff! I can't bear the sight of it now, not merely your miserable Berezina snuff but even if you were to offer me rappee itself!' Saying this, he walked out of the newspaper office, deeply mortified, and went in the direction of the local police superindendent, a fanatic lover of sugar. At his home, the whole of his front room, which was also the dining-room, was filled with sugar loaves, delivered to him in friendship by sugar traders. At that point, the cook was removing the superintendent's reg-ulation boots; his sword and other military accoutrements were already calmly hanging in the corners, and his terrible three-cornered hat had already been grabbed by his three-year old son; and he, after a military life of combat, was ready to taste the pleasure of peace.

Kovalyov walked in at the very moment when he was stretching and clearing his throat and saying: 'Ah, I should enjoy a couple of hours' nap!' So it might be foreseen that the collegiate assessor's visit was not very opportune, and I do not know whether he would have been received too warmly even had he brought several pounds of tea or cloth.

The police superintendent was a great patron of all arts and manufactures; but the paper note he preferred to everything. 'That is a thing,' he used to say, 'there is nothing better than that thing; it does not ask for food, it takes up little space, there is always room for it in the pocket, and if you drop it, it does not break.'

The police superintendent received Kovalyov rather coldly and said that after dinner was not the time to make an enquiry, that nature itself had ordained that man should rest a little after eating (the collegiate assessor could see from this that the sayings of the ancient sages were not unfamiliar to the local superintendent) that a respectable man does not have his nose pulled off and that there are many majors in the world who do not even own underclothes that are in proper condition, as they drag themselves around to all kinds of obscene places.

This was adding insult to injury. It must be said that Kovalyov was very easily offended. He could forgive anything whatever said about himself, but could never forgive insult to his rank or his calling. He was even of the opinion that any reference to officers of the higher ranks might be allowed to pass in stage plays, but that no attack ought to be made on those of a lower grade. The reception given him by the local superintendent so disconcerted him that he tossed his head and said with an air of dignity and a slight gesticulation of surprise: 'I must observe that after observations so insulting on your part I can add nothing more . . .' and went out.

He went home hardly conscious of the ground under his feet. By now it was dusk. His lodgings seemed to him melancholy, or rather utterly disgusting, after all these unsuccessful efforts. Going into his entry-hall he saw his valet, Ivan, lying on his dirty leather sofa; he was spitting on the ceiling and rather successfully aiming at the same spot. The nonchalance of his servant enraged him; he hit him on the forehead with his hat, saying: 'You pig, you are always doing something stupid.' Ivan leaped up and rushed headlong to help him off with his cloak.

Going into his room, weary and dejected, the major threw himself into an easy chair, and, at last, after several sighs, said: 'My God, my God! Why has this misfortune befallen me? if I had lost an arm or a leg – anyway it would have been better; but without a nose a man is goodness knows what: neither fish nor fowl nor human being, good for nothing but to fling out of the window! And if only it had been cut off in battle or in a duel, or if I had been the cause of it myself, but, as it is, it is lost for no cause of reason, it is lost for nothing, absolutely nothing! But no, it cannot be,' he added after a moment's thought. 'It's incredible that a nose should be lost. It must be a dream or an illusion. Perhaps by some mistake I drank instead of water the vodka I use to rub my chin after shaving. Ivan, the fool, did not remove it and very likely I took it.' To convince himself that he was not drunk, the major pinched himself so painfully that he shrieked. The pain completely convinced him that he was living and acting in real life. He slowly approached the looking-glass and at first screwed up his eyes with the idea that maybe his nose would appear in its proper place; but at the same minute sprang back, saying: 'What a caricature!'

It really was incomprehensible; if a button had been lost or a silver spoon or a watch or anything similar – but to have lost this, and in one's own flat too! . . . Thinking over all the circumstances, Major Kovalyov reached the supposition that what might be nearest the truth was that the person responsible for this could be no other than Madam Podtatchin, who wanted him to marry her daughter. He himself liked flirting with her, but avoided a definite engagement. When the mother had informed him directly that she wished for the marriage, he had slyly put her off with his compliments, saying that he was still too young, that he must serve for four years so as to be exactly forty-two. And that Madame Podtatchin had therefore made up her mind, probably out of revenge, to ruin him, and had hired for the purpose some peasant witches, because it was impossible to suppose that the nose had been cut off in any way; no one had come into his room; the barber Ivan Yakovlevitch had shaved him on Wednesday, and all Wednesday, and even all Thursday, his nose had been all right – that he remembered and was quite certain about; besides, he would have felt pain, and there could have been no doubt that the wound could not have healed so soon and been as flat as a pancake. He formed various plans in his mind: either to summon Madame Podtatchin formally before the court or to go to her himself and tax her with it. These reflections were interrupted by a light which gleamed through all the cracks of the door and let him know that a candle had been lit in the entry by Ivan. Soon Ivan himself appeared, holding it before him and lighting up the whole room. Kovalyov's first movement was to snatch up his handkerchief and cover the place where yesterday his nose had been, that his really stupid servant might not gape at the sight of anything so peculiar in his master.

Ivan had hardly time to retreat to his lair when there was the sound of an unfamiliar voice in the entry, pronouncing the words: 'Does the collegiate assessor Kovalyov live here?'

'Come in, Major Kovalyov is here,' said Kovalyov, jumping up hurriedly and opening the door.

There walked in a police officer of handsome appearance,

with whiskers neither too fair nor too dark, and rather fat cheeks, the very one who at the beginning of our story was standing at the end of St Isaac's Bridge.

'You, if you please, have lost your nose, sir?'

'That is so.'

'It is now found.'

'What are you saying?' cried Major Kovalyov. He could not speak for joy. He gazed open-eyed at the police officer standing before him, on whose full lips and cheeks the flickering light of the candle was brightly reflected. 'How?'

'By a strange chance: he was caught almost on the road. He had already taken his seat in the diligence and was intending to go to Riga, and had already taken a passport in the name of a government clerk. And the strange thing is that I myself took him for a gentleman at first, but fortunately I had my spectacles with me and I soon saw that it was a nose. You know I am short-sighted. And if you stand before me I only see that you have a face, but I don't notice your nose or your beard or anything. My mother-in-law, that is my wife's mother, doesn't see anything either.'

Kovalyov was beside himself with joy. 'Where? Where? I'll run at once.'

'Don't disturb yourself. Knowing that you were in need of it, I brought it along with me. And the strange thing is that the man who has had the most to do with the affair is a rascal of a barber in Voznesensky Street, who is now in custody. I have long suspected him of drunkenness and thieving, and only the day before yesterday he carried off a strip of buttons from one shop. Your nose is exactly as it was.' With this the police officer put his hand in his pocket and drew out the nose, which was wrapped in paper.

'That's it!' Kovalyov cried. 'That's certainly it. You must have a cup of tea with me this evening.'

'I should look upon it as a great pleasure, but I can't possibly manage it: I have to go from here to the penitentiary . . . How the prices of all provisions are going up! . . . At home I have my mother-in-law, that is my wife's mother, and my children, the eldest particularly gives signs of great promise, he is a very intelligent child; but we have absolutely no means for his education . . .'

Kovalyov understood him perfectly and grabbed a red banknote from the table and put it in the hands of the officer, who shuffled about and then walked out, and at almost the same minute, Kovalyov heard his voice on the street, where he was knocking the teeth from a stupid *muzhik* who had driven his cart right on to the boulevard.

For some time after the policeman's departure the collegiate assessor remained in a state of bewilderment, and it was only a few minutes later that he was capable of feeling and understanding again: he was reduced to such stupefaction by this unexpected good fortune. He took the recovered nose carefully in his two hands, holding them together like a cup, and once more examined it attentively.

'Yes, that's it, it's certainly it,' said Major Kovalyov. 'There's the pimple that came out on the left side yesterday.' The major almost laughed aloud with joy.

But nothing in this world is of long duration, and so his joy was not so great the next moment; and the moment after, it was still less, and in the end he passed imperceptibly into his ordinary frame of mind, just as a circle on the water caused by a falling stone gradually passes away into the unbroken smoothness of the surface. Kovalyov began to think, and reflected that the business was not finished yet; the nose was found, but it had to be put on, fixed in its proper place.

'And what if it won't stick?' Asking himself this question, the major turned pale.

With a feeling of irrepressible terror he rushed to the table and moved the looking-glass forward that he might not put the nose on crooked. His hands trembled. Cautiously and circumspectly he replaced it in its former position. Oh, horror, the nose would not stick on! . . . He put it to his lips, slightly warmed it with his breath, and again applied it to the flat space between his two cheeks; but nothing would make the nose keep on.

'Come, come, stick on, you fool!' he said to it; but the nose seemed made of wood and fell on the table with a strange sound as thought it were a cork. The major's face worked convulsively.

'Is it possible that it won't grow on again?' he kept saying in distress. But, however often he applied it to the proper place, the attempt was as unsuccessful as before.

He called Ivan and sent him for a doctor who tenanted the best flat on the first storey of the same house. The doctor was a handsome man, he had magnificent pitch-black whiskers, a fresh and healthy wife, ate fresh apples in the morning and kept his mouth extraordinarily clean, rinsing it out for nearly three-quarters of an hour every morning and cleaning his teeth with five different sorts of brushes. The doctor appeared immediately. Asking how long ago the trouble had occurred, he took Major Kovalyov by the chin and with his thumb gave him a flip on the spot where the nose had been, making the major jerk back his head so abruptly that he knocked the back of it against the wall. The doctor said that that did not matter, and, advising him to move a little away from the wall, he told him to bend his head round first to the right, and feeling the place where the nose had been, said, 'Hm!' Then he told him to turn his head round to the left side and again said, 'Hm!' And in conclusion he gave him again a flip with his thumb, so that Major Kovalyov threw up his head like a horse when his teeth are being looked at. After making this experiment the doctor shook his head and said: 'No, it's impossible. You had better stay as you are, for it may be made much worse. Of course, it might be stuck on; I could stick it on for you at once, if you like; but I assure you it would be worse for you.'

'That's a nice thing to say! How can I stay without a nose?' said Kovalyov. 'Things can't possibly be worse than now. It's simply beyond everything. Where can I show myself with such a caricature of a face? I have a good circle of acquaintances. Today, for instance, I ought to be at two evening parties. I know a great many people; Madame Tchehtarev, the wife of a civil councillor, Madame Podtatchin, an officer's widow . . . though after the way she has behaved, I'll have nothing more to do with her except through the police. Do me a favour,' Kovalyov went on in a supplicating voice; 'is there no means of sticking it on? Even if it were not neatly done, so long as it would keep on; I could even hold it up with my hand at critical moments. I don't dance, in any case, so there wouldn't be any rash movements could upset it. As for remuneration for your services, you may be assured that as far as my means allow . . .'

'Believe me,' said the doctor, in a voice neither loud nor low but persuasive and magnetic, 'that I never work from mercenary motives; that is opposed to my principles and my science. It is true that I accept a fee for my visits, but that is simply to avoid wounding my patients by refusing it. Of course I could replace your nose; but I assure you on my honour, since you do not believe my word, that it will be much worse for you. You had better wait for the action of nature itself. Wash it frequently with cold water, and I assure you that even without a nose you will be just as healthy as with one. And I advise you to put the nose in a bottle, in spirits or, better still, put two tablespoonfuls of sour vodka on it and heated vinegar – and then you might get quite a sum of money for it. I'd even take it myself, if you don't ask too much for it.'

'No, no, I wouldn't sell it for anything,' Major Kovaylov cried in despair. 'I'd rather it were lost than that!'

'Excuse me!' said the doctor, bowing himself out, 'I was trying to be of use to you . . . Well, there is nothing for it! Anyway, you see that I have done my best.' Saying this, the doctor walked out of the room with a majestic air. Kovalyov did not notice his face, and, almost lost to consciousness, saw nothing but the cuffs of his clean and snow-white shirt peeping out from the sleeves of his black tail-coat.

Next day he decided, before lodging a complaint with

the police, to write to Madame Podtatchin to see whether she would consent to return him what was needful without a struggle. The letter was as follows:

DEAR MADAM ALEXANDRA GRIGORYEVNA —

I cannot understand this strange conduct on your part. You may rest assured that you will gain nothing by what you have done, and you will not get a step nearer forcing me to marry your daughter. Believe me, that business in regard to my nose is no secret, no more than it is that you and no other are the person chiefly responsible. The sudden parting of the same from its natural position, its flight and masquerading, at one time in the form of a government clerk and finally in its own shape, is nothing else than the consequence of the sorceries practised by you or by those who are versed in the same honourable arts as you are. For my part I consider it my duty to warn you, if the above mentioned nose is not in its proper place today, I shall be obliged to resort to the assistance and protection of the law.

I have, however, with complete respect to you, the honour to be

Your respectful servant,

PLATON KOVALYOV

DEAR SIR, PLATON KUZMITCH! – Your letter greatly astonished me. I must frankly confess that I did not expect it, especially in regard to your unjust reproaches. I assure you I have never received the government clerk of whom you speak in my house, neither in masquerade nor in his own attire. It is true that Filipp Ivanovitch Potantchikov has been to see me, and although, indeed, he is asking me for my daughter's hand and is a well-conducted, sober man of great learning, I have never encouraged his hopes. You make some reference to your nose also. If you wish me to understand by that that you imagined that I meant to make a long nose at you, that is, to give you a formal refusal, I am surprised that you should speak of such a thing when, as you know perfectly well, I was quite of the opposite way of thinking, and if you are courting my daughter with a view to lawful matrimony I am ready to satisfy you immediately, seeing that has always been the object of my keenest desires, in the hope of which I remain always ready to be of service to you.

ALEXANDRA PODTATCHIN

'No,' said Kovalyov to himself after reading the letter, 'she really is not to blame. It's impossible. The letter is written as it could not be written by anyone guilty of a crime.' The collegiate assessor was an expert on this subject, as he had been sent several times to the Caucasus to conduct investigations. 'In what way, by what fate, has this happened? Only the devil could make it out!' he said at last, letting his hands fall to his sides.

Meanwhile, the rumours of this strange occurrence were spreading all over the town, and of course not without especial additions. Just at that time the minds of all were particularly interested in the marvellous: experiments in the influences of magnetism had been attracting public attention only recently. Moreover, the story of the dancing chairs in Konyushenny Street was still fresh, and so there is nothing to be surprised at in the fact that people were soon beginning to say that the nose of a collegiate assessor called Kovalyov was walking along Nevsky Prospect at exactly three in the afternoon. Numbers of inquisitive people flocked there every day. Somebody said that the nose was in Yunker's shop – and near Yunker's there was such a crowd and such a crush that the police were actually obliged to intervene. One speculator, a man of dignified appearance with whiskers, who used to sell all sorts of cakes and tarts at the doors of the theatres, made purposely some very strong wooden benches, which he offered to the curious to stand on, for eighty kopecks each. One very worthy colonel left home earlier on account of it, and with a great deal of trouble made his way through the crowd; but to his great indignation, instead of the nose, he saw in the shop-windows the usual woollen vest and a lithograph depicting a girl pulling up her stocking while a foppish young man, with a waistcoat with revers and a small beard, peeps at her from behind a tree; a picture which had been hanging in the same place for more than ten years. As he walked away he said with vexation: 'How can people be led astray by such stupid and incredible stories!' Then rumour would have it that it was not on Nevsky Prospect but in the Tavritchesky Park that Major Kovaylov's nose took its walks abroad; that it had been there for ever so long; that, even when Hozrev-Mirza used to live there, he was greatly surprised at this strange freak of nature. Several students from the Academy of Surgery made their way to the park. One worthy lady of high rank wrote a letter to the superintendent of the park asking him to show her children this rare phenomenon with, if possible, an explanation that should be edifying and instructive for the young.

All the gentlemen who invariably attend social gatherings and like to amuse the ladies were extremely thankful for all these events, for their stock of anecdotes was completely exhausted. A small group of worthy and well-intentioned persons were greatly displeased. One gentleman said with indignation that he could not understand how in the present enlightened age people could spread abroad these absurd inventions, and that he was surprised that the government took no notice of it. This gentleman, as may be seen, belonged to the number of those who would like the government to meddle in everything, even in their daily quarrels with their wives. After this . . . but here again the whole adventure is lost in fog, and what happened afterwards is absolutely unknown.

3.

What is utterly nonsensical happens in the world. Sometimes there is not the slightest resemblance to truth about it: all at once, that very nose which had been driving about the place in the form of a civil councillor and had made such a store in the town, turned up again as though nothing had happened, in its proper place, that is, precisely between the two cheeks of Major Kovalyov. This took place on the seventh of April. Waking up and casually glancing into the looking-glass, he sees – his nose! He grabs it with his hands – it was actually his nose! 'Aha!' said Kovalyov, and in his joy he almost danced a jig barefoot about his room; but the entrance of Ivan checked him. He ordered the latter to bring him water at once, and as he washed he glanced once more into the looking-glass – the nose! As he wiped himself with the towel he glanced again into the looking-glass – the nose!

'Look, Ivan, I fancy I have a pimple on my nose,' he said, while he thought: 'How dreadful if Ivan says, "No, indeed, sir, there's no pimple and, indeed, there is no nose either!"'

But Ivan said: 'There is nothing, there is no pimple: your nose is quite clear!'

'Good, dash it all!' the major said to himself, and he snapped his fingers.

At that moment Ivan Yakovlevitch the barber peeped in at the door, but as timidly as a cat who has just been beaten for stealing the bacon.

'Tell me first: are your hands clean?' Kovalyov shouted to him while he was still some way off.

'Yes.'

'You are lying!'

'Upon my word, they are clean, sir.'

'Well, mind now.'

Kovalyov sat down, Ivan Yakovlevitch covered him up with a towel, and in one instant with the aid of his brushes had smothered the whole of his beard and part of his cheek in cream, like that which is served at merchants' name-day parties.

'My eye!' Ivan Yakovlevitch said to himself, glancing at the nose and then turning his customer's head on the other side and looking at it sideways. 'There it is, sure enough. What can it mean?' He went on pondering, and for a long while he gazed at the nose. At last, lightly, with a cautiousness which may well be imagined, he raised two fingers to take it by the tip. Such was Ivan Yakovlevitch's system.

'Now, now, now, mind!' cried Kovalyov. Ivan Yakovlevitch let his hands drop, and was flustered and confused as he had never been confused before. At last he began circumspectly tickling him with the razor under his beard, and, although it was difficult and not at all handy for him to shave without holding on to the olfactory portion of the face, yet he did at last somehow, pressing his rough thumb into his cheek and lower jaw, overcome all difficulties, and finish shaving him.

When it was all over, Kovlayov at once made haste to dress, took a cab and drove to the confectioner's shop. Before he was inside the door he shouted, 'Waiter, a cup of chocolate!' and at the same instant peeped at himself in the looking-glass. The nose was there. He turned round gaily and, with a satirical air, slightly screwing up his eyes, looked at two military men, one of whom had a nose hardly bigger than a waistcoat button. After that he set off for the office of the department, in which he was urging his claims to post as vice-governor or, failing that, the post of an executive clerk. After crossing the waiting-room he glanced at the mirror; the nose was there. Then he drove to see another collegiate assessor or major, who was much given to making fun of people, and to whom he often said in reply to various sharp observations: 'There you are, I know you, you are as sharp as a pin!' On the way he thought: 'If even the major does not split with laughter when he sees me, then it is a sure sign that everything is in its place.' But the sarcastic collegiate assessor said nothing. 'Good, good, dash it all!' Kovalyov thought to himself. On the way he met Madame Podtachin with her daughter; he was profuse in his bows to them and was greeted with exclamations of delight – so there could be nothing amiss with him, he thought. He conversed with them for a long time and, taking out his snuffbox, purposely put a pinch to each nostril while he said to himself: 'So much for you, you petticoats, you hens! But I am not going to marry your daughter all the same. Just simply *par amour* – I dare say!'

And from that time forth Major Kovalyov promenaded about, as though nothing had happened, on Nevsky Prospect, and at the theatres and everywhere. And the nose, too, as though nothing had happened, sat on his face without even a sign of coming off at the sides. And after this Major Kovalyov was always seen in a good humour, smiling, resolutely pursuing all the pretty ladies, and even on one occasion stopping before a shop in Gostiny Dvor and buying the ribbon of some order, I cannot say with what object, since he was not himself a cavalier of any order.

So this is the strange event that occurred in the Northern capital of our spacious empire! Only now, on thinking it all over, we perceive that there is a great deal that is improbable in it. Apart from the fact that it certainly is strange for a nose supernaturally to leave its place and to appear in various places in the guise of a civil councillor – how was it that Kovalyov did not grasp that he could not advertise about his nose in a newspaper office? I do not mean to say that I should think it too expensive to advertise: that is nonsense, and I am by no means a mercenary person: but it is unseemly, awkward, not nice! And again: how did the nose come into the loaf, and how about Ivan Yakovlevitch himself? . . . No, that I cannot understand, I am absolutely unable to understand it! But what is stranger, what is more incomprehensible than anything, is that authors can choose such subjects. I confess that is quite beyond my grasp, it really is . . . No, no! I cannot understand it at all. In the first place, it is absolutely without profit to the fatherland; in the second place . . . but in the second, too, there is no profit. I really do not know what to say of it . . .

And yet, with all that, though of course one may admit

the first point, the second and the third ... may even ...
but there, are there not inconsequences everywhere? – and
yet, when you think it over, there really is something in it.
Whatever anyone may say, such things do happen – not often,
but they do happen.